1773

MOLLY LAKE

in

The Treasure of
Le Nain Rouge

1773

MOLLY LAKE

in

The Treasure of
Le Nain Rouge

Samuel Endicott

GRIFFIN PRESS

Griffin Press
Cover and interior design, by David Moratto
www.davidmoratto.com

For Elaine

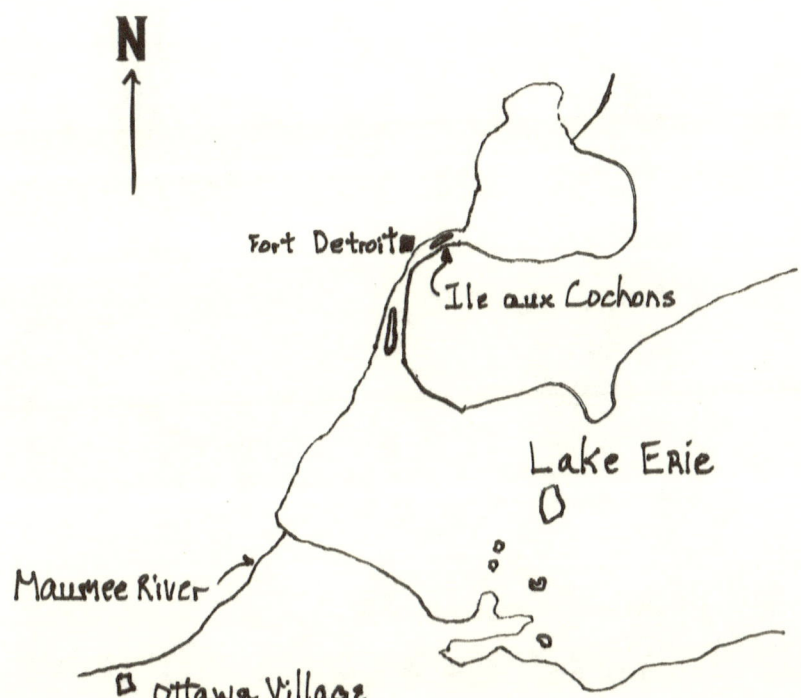

CONTENTS

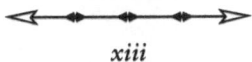

Molly's Remarks

"THE YEAR 1773 began with us colonists in North America feeling that France, our long-time enemy, would never again threaten our existence. Unfortunately, King George III saw this resulting era of peaceful prosperity as his opportunity to recoup his treasury's deficits. Parliament's concern over England's war debt, amassed from defeating the powerful French in battles over many parts of the globe, led her members to vote to raise existing taxes and impose new ones on their North American colonies. Despite the inevitable complaints, Parliament insisted that the overseas colonists must pay their fair share. This conviction initiated an ever-widening divide between Mother England and the American colonists. Jealousy of the New World's wealth consumed the English aristocracy like a cancer.

Cooler heads in England understood that Parliament had ignored the American region far too long and that it might well be too late to impose their fiscal will or to do anything to quell growing tax protests. But not King George III! Mean-spirited and stubborn, he vowed to teach us upstart tax protesters a lesson about who was in charge.

Another result of the French and Indian War was that our respect for the British soldier had eroded. Having proved inept against the Huron in the wilderness, the redcoats additionally angered us by failing to defend our settlers during Pontiac's Rebellion. Lowering further their dismal reputation, the redcoats gave every appearance of favoring their new allies, the Indians, against us—their colonists. The unpopular Proclamation of 1763 restricted us to east of the Appalachian Mountains, stoking our indignation. Ten years earlier, King George had ordered his redcoats to enforce penalties for colonists who penetrated the Appalachian Mountain chain that runs from the Maine area of Massachusetts to Georgia.

By 1773, Jean-Luc and I had been supporting those advocating independence for over eight years. Jean-Luc had even joined the Sons of Liberty in late '65. And he and I, as well as our fellow colonists, had grown increasingly disgusted with the English Army's forced quartering of soldiers in our homes, their searches of our residences and businesses, and, dare I say, the royal governor's corruption.

Our story begins in Quebec Ville in the year 1697, when the infamous red sprite, *Le Nain Rouge,* made his first recorded appearance. Yes, the same red goblin who to this day continues his haunting of Great Lakes' localities."

PROLOGUE

JANUARY 1, 1697, SATURDAY EVENING,
QUEBEC VILLE

ANTOINE LAUMET DE LA MOTHE, *Sieur* de Cadillac, and his wife, Marie-Therese, hurriedly walked through ankle-deep snow to arrive at the door of some dear Quebecois friends. The night air was frigid, and they could feel the cold winds penetrating their garments. But they were also anticipating a warm fire and the warmer friendship of their fellow settlers. Thankfully, the distance from their home to the social gathering was short. Pushing against a strong headwind, made stronger from the channeling effect of the narrow, house-lined streets, they arrived at a dwelling on Rue Hébert that radiated an inviting golden glow from its windows. Cadillac knocked three times while his wife held her cowl tight against her head. As they waited, they marched in place to keep warm.

Sieur Raoul Bandemain opened the door and excitedly shook hands with his guests, and said, "Welcome. We are in the parlor. Was the walk over difficult?"

"We are used to the weather, Raoul. Here, allow me to present this bottle of wine." Cadillac handed his bottle to his host, and then scraped the snow from his boots on the irons that Bandemain had set out for that purpose. Then, he followed his wife into the parlor. Madame Celine Bandemain crossed the room and handed her guests full goblets of wine and kissed *Madame* de Cadillac's cold cheeks.

Cadillac said to the gathering, "It is good to see you, my friends. I—have had a miserable day. Today, I bartered for three hours with a native trapper."

"How grueling!" said Sieur Claude Le Mans, who was known to his social circle as 'Little Claude' He added, "I so dislike listening to their pleas for generosity and their whining when our goods are not given to them." A second-generation aristocrat of New France, he was plump, wealthy, and anything but little.

Cadillac nodded and smiled at Little Claude; he then walked to the mantle and set down his goblet. He said, "After you left today, a particularly difficult savage who claimed to be an Ottawa—but honestly, can any of you tell an Ottawa from a Wabanaki? He said he had paddled here from a place called 'the strait.' He argued on and on over my offer of cloth for his mangy fur stack."

Madame Bandemain asked, "Do you think this strait might lead to the great western ocean, Antoine?"

"An important matter, isn't it, Celine? Do any of us doubt there is a waterway leading to the great western ocean? This strait may be part of it. I know this; the distance this fellow had travelled compelled his bargaining strategy." Cadillac inched closer to the crackling fire and turned to warm his backside. He looked out the window at the falling snow and allowed it to distract him momentarily. While he pondered Celine's query, his friends respectfully waited for him to resume. After several moments, he turned back and said, "We really should begin establishing trading centers further west. The natives will not continue coming here for our goods and products should the English provide them a more convenient option."

"Where do you suggest we establish these trading posts, Antoine?" asked Bandemain. Their friends inched closer to the fireplace to hear Cadillac's answer.

"I feel we should build a series of posts. We must continue westward until we have reached (at least) the land the natives call 'Meicigama.' It means 'great water' and it might lead to the great western ocean." He paused to take a sip of wine. "Those inland seas probably have a water route that leads to the Pacific. Of course, we cannot be defenseless on the western frontier. And if there is a waterway to the great ocean in the west, we must begin building forts to control it for France. Only French cannon manned by Frenchmen will discourage the Englishmen from making mischief."

The other six laughed at his jest. But, soon afterward, they changed their discussions to the amiable topics of plans for the spring months, trading opportunities, and new foods they had discovered. Madame Bandemain moved smoothly about the room, ensuring that her guests' glasses never were in want. As she listened to them laughing at one *bon mot* after another, she felt satisfied by how much they enjoyed one another's company. The New Year's Day revelers' voices rose in volume in correlation to the amount of wine consumed, so that only Madame Bandemain (the only partier without a pleasant buzz) heard a gentle knock on the door.

"Dear, someone is at the door. Would you answer it?" asked Madame Bandemain of her spouse.

Bandemain crossed the room and opened the oaken door; he was greeted with a blast of wind and snow flurries that blew with a howl into the hallway. He turned his face away from the flurries but quickly returned his attention to the unknown before him. On his front step stood a shivering but attractive maiden with raven hair and an alluring olive-skinned complexion; she wore a heavy gray cape and fur boots (the kind Bandemain had observed being worn by *voyageurs*). He thought he knew all the residents of Quebec, but her face wasn't familiar.

"May I come in, *monsieur*?" she asked.

"What is it you want?"

"Monsieur, I am passing through Quebec and am chilled to the bone. When I saw your chimney smoke and the light shining through your window, I thought I might warm myself and find relief from the winds. In exchange for allowing me to stand by your fire, I could entertain your company with some palm reading."

Certain that his (male) friends would enjoy the company of this mysterious and beautiful woman, Bandemain stood aside and said, "Though we are entertaining friends, I feel compelled to provide you succor this wintry evening. As for your other offer, it will be only at their invitation. Do you understand?" he said in mock sternness. "What is your name, my dear?"

Smiling demurely, the maiden said, "My name is Anna." She stepped inside and untied her cape. As Bandemain supposed, the cape covered an ample bosom with an enticing amount of cleavage revealed by her low-collared blouse. After this revelation, he felt certain that his male guests would enjoy her reading their palms. Perhaps not so much Madame Bandemain and the other spouses.

Bandemain walked ahead of Anna into the parlor and addressed his guests. He said, "This traveler has asked for temporary shelter from the cold. Her name is Anna, and she is a palm reader. If you would like, she will amuse you with her prognostications. Any takers?" Bandemain noticed Little Claude perking up. Turning to Anna, Bandemain suggested, "Why don't you begin with Sieur Le Mans?"

When the partiers realized that the entertainment would be provided at no cost, they murmured their agreement and expressed their willingness to have their palms read. Cadillac studied the dark beauty as she considered Little Claude's palm. Anna began with his three main lines. Cadillac watched her massage his friend's palm slowly while studying the lines and creases. She moved her fingers over his love line at the top, his head line in the middle, and his life line near his wrist. In melodramatic fashion she gasped.

"What is the matter?" asked Little Claude, his brow furrowed.

"I am sorry, monsieur. I see your head line has a break."

"Is that bad? Will something terrible happen to me?"

"Monsieur, I do not foretell the future. Your palm is the story of your *past*." She returned her eyes to his hand and studiously read the lines. She said, "You have suffered a great loss—and recently."

Little Claude said anxiously, "Yes, yes. Go on. Tell me more." Anna looked at him with compassion but waited for Little Claude's (inevitable) revelation. He said slowly, "I lost my wife six months ago."

Gently closing his hand, she said, "It pains me to have revived this memory. I shall move to the next gentleman and hopefully find happier memories. Will you forgive me?" she asked. Little Claude graciously nodded but was disappointed in her decision to attend to another.

Sieur de Thierry spoke up and said, "My dear, tell me about my life."

Anna smiled and said, "Of course, monsieur." She studied his palm a moment and focused on his head line, which she noted was curved and sloping. "You are creative, are you not?"

Thierry broke into a wide grin. "I like to think so. I am adept at problem solving—or so I have been told." The wives giggled. Thierry cast a dark glance at the wives.

Defending his friend, especially with the wives having such fun at his expense, Cadillac said, "Quite so. We do turn to Paul when we need assistance with planning our excursions."

Anna regarded Cadillac a moment and then slowly nodded. Experienced at working a room, she recognized an ally. She returned her gaze to Thierry and whispered several interpretations that only he could hear.

Satisfied that Anna had demonstrated admirable social dexterity, Cadillac walked over and asked, "You have an engaging way, young lady. Will you read my palm?"

The dark beauty softly rubbed the back of Thierry's hand, and unhurriedly turned toward Cadillac. Thierry felt disappointed but deferred to his old friend.

Anna then took Cadillac's hand and massaged the flesh softly and slowly. She moved her finger along his head line, paused, and looked directly into his eyes. "Your head line and life line are separated," she said.

"Is that good—or bad?" asked Cadillac with a roll of his eyes and his voice revealing skepticism.

Ignoring his incredulity, Anna looked closer at Cadillac's palm and read it carefully. Apparently, she was finding his hand more interesting than the others'. She knitted her brow and said with caution, "You have a taste for adventure. No?"

"I suppose I do. *Living* in New France is an adventure."

Anna stopped moving her finger and looked deeply into Cadillac's eyes. "You are to be the founder of a great city."

Little Claude said in protest, "But you do not tell the future. You said so yourself!" He was still resentful that Anna had moved on after such a short session with him.

Anna kept her gaze on Cadillac to study his reaction. She said in a low, suggestive voice, "A rule may be broken when it is necessary. Do you not agree?"

"Oh, of course." Remaining unconvinced of Anna's powers, Cadillac turned to Little Claude and said, "You may have another turn. She is almost finished with me." Turning his gaze back to the beautiful palm reader, he asked, "Do you see anything else?" Skeptical by nature, he resisted using sarcasm with the visitor.

"Yes," she said with apparent foreboding. "I do."

"Why? Is it bad?" asked Cadillac suddenly alarmed.

Appearing anxious, Anna turned to Bandemain and nervously said, "I should go. You have been most kind to allow me to escape the icy winds."

Cadillac said, "Raoul, I want to know what Anna sees in my future."

Madame de Cadillac walked over to her husband and placed her hand on his forearm and said, "Antoine, do not tempt fate. To know the future would be terrifying."

Cadillac took another sip of wine and winked at his wife. He turned back to Anna and directed, "Continue, if you please."

Anna returned her attention to his palm. Madame de Cadillac inched closer. "Monsieur, I see trouble in your later years." Cadillac's brow knitted. Anna glanced at Madame de Cadillac with a supplicating expression. Her plea was answered with a decidedly displeased countenance.

Now in a snit, Marie-Therese said, "Are you satisfied, Antoine? Now this witch has placed a curse on you." She turned and walked back in a huff to her friends.

"Pray continue, Anna," said Cadillac, his voice and manner masking his alarm.

Anna reluctantly pressed forward with her final prediction. "I sense that you may yet avoid this dark period, but to do so you must listen carefully and heed my words."

Cadillac leaned forward and asked, "What?"

"You will encounter *Le Nain Rouge*. When? I cannot say."

Cadillac laughed derisively and said, "You had me vexed for a moment." He turned to his friends and said, "A red gnome doesn't sound threatening."

"He is no *physical* threat, monsieur, to be sure, but please, you must do as I say, and you may yet escape your fate."

Not used to being spoken to like this, the Sieur de Cadillac's expression betrayed his irritation. He said, "Speak plainly, Anna, I am losing patience."

"When you come upon Le Nain Rouge," said Anna, who spoke with a desperate edge in her voice, "whatever he says or does—neither mistreat him nor hurt his feelings. He is capable of bringing ruin upon your house and woe upon the citizens of your future city, should you ignore my supplication. Please, monsieur, listen and obey."

Cadillac coughed nervously and asked, "Mistreat? Why would I mistreat this abject creature? I—" he hesitated, "I would pity him." He turned to his friends. "Have any of you seen this red creature?"

The wives were huddled near the mantle whispering, and their husbands laughed with nervous bravado that comes only from being surrounded by allies. Cadillac turned his attention from his friends back to the soothsayer, and asserted, "Anna, I want to know more —much more." But Anna no longer stood in front of him. "Where did she go, Raoul?" Hearing the door open and the winter winds howling, an exasperated Cadillac said, "Do not allow her to leave yet, Raoul."

Bandemain nodded and jogged to his foyer but arrived too late.

Anna had pulled the door shut behind her a moment earlier. Without delay, Bandemain threw open the portal. Because it had been but a split second, he expected to see the young lady still on his stoop. He was greeted instead by a dark, empty street. Speechless, he looked up and down the cobblestone street for the palm reader.

From the hearth area, Cadillac asked impatiently, "Have you enticed her to return, Raoul?"

Bandemain did not answer. He stood speechless in his doorway, with the snow and chilly winds blowing into his home, Bandemain and Cadillac rushed outside without their coats, looking for Anna. They returned within moments, unsuccessful. Anna had disappeared into the frigid darkness.

The uneasy social gathering broke up soon afterward. After departing their friend's cozy house and walking the short distance to the river overlook, Cadillac and Madame de Cadillac stopped to gaze upon the mighty river flowing beneath their vantage point. In an attempt to lessen the tension created by the fortune teller's forecast, Cadillac put his arm around his wife's shoulder and called her attention to a shooting star streaking across the sky. In silence, they watched the tiny light flicker out. Thinking that the phenomenon was a good luck omen, Marie-Therese began to feel better. She smiled at her husband and rested her head on his shoulder. Marie-Therese recalled the memories of the journey across the Atlantic Ocean and their shared efforts in making new lives in Canada. Perhaps because of the late hour or because of the frigid winds blowing across the escarpment, her husband nodded in the direction of their home, one street over. Rather than taking the direct route, they continued to walk along the romantic cobblestone overlook for several minutes in silence. Before leaving France, the couple used to enjoy walking at night and discussing their future in the new world. Upon hearing a sound behind him, Cadillac whirled around, fearing that a forest beast or, worse, a savage was approaching.

"*En garde*, Frenchman!" said a three-foot-tall dwarf standing in the path. The little man wore a red tunic that matched his ruddy complexion.

He held a pointed stick as long as he was tall, and he brandished it theatrically.

Startled, Marie-Therese shrieked, and her husband instinctively reached for his rapier. In the moonlight, he couldn't quite make out who or what stood before them. Just then, the clouds that obscured the moonlight parted, and he observed his adversary's stature and wooden sword. To a soldier, the unexpected confrontation took on a comical tone. Cadillac released his fingers from the hilt of his rapier. "You speak my language, and yet I do not recognize you. Where are you from?" asked Cadillac.

"Draw your weapon!" demanded the red-cheeked little man. Not waiting for a response, he lunged with his stick and tried to poke Cadillac.

The small man's histrionic attack developed slowly enough that it allowed Cadillac to easily sidestep the thrust. Turning to Marie-Therese, he said, "This is ridiculous. I do not wish to hurt this man."

Madame de Cadillac said, "Make him leave us, Antoine."

"Put your stick down, little fellow," said Cadillac, "I will not harm you."

The red dwarf grinned, showing pointed teeth, and said, "I do not think I will. I observed you gawking at my river. I warn you—never travel on *my* river."

"Your river? But why? Travel by water is preferable. What is so valuable about the river that you claim it as yours? You do realize it has already been claimed for the King of France, do you not?"

"It leads to my treasure. And since I am the guardian of said treasure, I must take action to prevent its loss." The little fellow tried a second time to jab Cadillac in a clumsy lunge that Cadillac easily sidestepped.

Once more, Madame de Cadillac tugged on her husband's overcoat and said, "He frightens me. Make him go away, Antoine."

"In a moment, Marie-Therese." He whispered into her ear, "I want to learn more about the treasure." Cadillac turned back to the red dwarf and asked, "Where is the treasure? What is the treasure? Is it gold?"

The little fellow answered, "The treasure does not exist—*yet*."

Marie-Therese, cringing behind her husband, said, "I do not like this, Antoine."

Cadillac turned to pat his wife's hand just as the little fellow attacked a third time. This assault succeeded, and he poked Cadillac's thigh.

"Ow!" cried the Frenchman, rubbing his smarting thigh. He watched his diminutive adversary bobbing and weaving in the moonlight as if fencing with another invisible swordsman. Cadillac said, "Now you have made me angry."

Le Nain Rouge slowly brought his stick up to his forehead, melodramatically saluting his opponent. He asked innocently, "Did I not say, 'En garde,' monsieur?" His pointed teeth and ruddy complexion grew more ominous by the minute. And he repeatedly poked at the tall Frenchman with the stick sword; the spirit's attacks were no longer laughable.

Cadillac said, "I am no longer in the mood for your foolishness. Return whence you came." He drew his sword and went on the offense. Without any difficulty, he deflected the red dwarf's thrusts several more times. A skilled swordsman, Cadillac spotted an easy opening in the enfant terrible's defense. Cadillac used his steel to slap away the stick, deftly sidestepped to his opponent's flank, and tapped the dwarf on his buttocks. When the little fellow cried out loudly (more so than the gentle strike from Cadillac warranted), Cadillac asked, "How do you like it now that the shoe is on the other foot? Now, will you depart in peace?"

In Quebec's moonlight, the offended troll said, "I do not like you. I want you to stay off my river and not go near my treasure. There will soon be an army of dragons to guard my precious wealth." Then, he slowly vanished. Both Cadillacs rubbed their astonished eyes. Spooked, Cadillac turned in one direction, and then another, trying to locate his adversary. Mindful of his training to quickly draw your sword but to be doubly slow in returning it to its scabbard, he remained in a wary posture for several moments. He put his hand to his forehead and said, "I must have had too much wine this evening. Did the troll disappear or did he back into the shadows?"

Madame de Cadillac said, "I do not know! I just want to go home."

They took several tentative steps away from the overlook when Cadillac stopped abruptly. He asked warily, "Marie-Therese, did we just encounter the creature the palmist warned about?"

Marie-Therese did not answer but tugged his sleeve and jerked her head in the direction of their house. Cadillac looked over his shoulder repeatedly as they trudged home through the snow.

PART I

Unexpected Visitors

CHAPTER ONE

"RICI, COME BACK to bed. I want to make love once more." Propped on one elbow, the Duchesse Demarais rolled onto her back and smiled at her nude lover fussing with his hair in the looking glass.

Albaric, *Comte* de Belfort, did not have much time to get ready for his installation ceremony as King Louis XV's twelfth paladin. Belfort began to dress, though he paused to regard the duchess's figure under the sheets. Though sorely tempted by her offer of renewing their afternoon lust, he said, "I cannot be late for this ceremony. Tardiness will get me on the wrong side of the king."

With a sigh, the Duchesse Demarais threw the sheets off and quickly slipped into a sheer nightgown. "I understand, Rici. Here, let me assist you," she said. She picked up her tall, handsome paramour's garments. As he sat on the bed, she handed them to him one after another to facilitate his rush to make his ceremony on time. As he buttoned his blouse, she sat beside him and ran her fingers through his hair, but he did not act as though he noticed. "You are stressed about being late for your ceremony." Probing his feelings for her, she asked. "Are you worried about seeing my husband there?"

"No, he never entered my mind," said Belfort matter-of-factly. Had Belfort looked at his lover's face, he would have seen her disappointment. He continued, "It is the king I do not wish to face should a late arrival delay the proceedings."

Discouraged by his answer, the duchesse Demarais said, "We are alike."

Belfort stopped preening and regarded her. Not wishing to get into an argument, he changed the subject. "I suspect that the king is going to send me overseas," he said, returning his gaze to the looking glass. He didn't wish to see her reaction. He gave himself the once-over in the full-length mirror. "I will see you when I return," he said and opened the door.

The *Duchesse* Demarais said with a hint of desperation in her voice, "I will leave my husband for you, Rici."

Belfort smiled and said softly, "I have not asked you to do that." He kissed her forehead. "*Au revoir, mon cher.*" Noting her wounded expression, he knew that he needed to make an exit before the tears began. After closing the door, had his mind not been fixed on his impending appointment, he might have heard her pitiful sobs. He dashed across the gardens encircling Versailles and through a ground-level side door held open by a guard wearing a white overcoat trimmed in French blue. He panted, trying to catch his breath, as he knocked on a heavy door leading to basement.

An old paladin with white hair and a trim build opened the door and regarded the inductee with skepticism. The Comte de Belfort did not recognize the old man. From the color of the old man's epaulets, Belfort concluded that the old man had at one time been assigned to the Champagne region. Belfort, a Franche-Comté citizen himself, regarded his region as more hospitable than the French regions bordering Prussia. Belfort realized that the old man was not to be trifled with. The solemn old man physically epitomized the saying "once a paladin, always a paladin." Holding his palms upward in a gesture that said "what can one do?" Belfort smiled at the senior paladin and could only accept his glare without protest. Belfort composed himself, slowed his breathing, and asked, "What do you want me to do? Where am I to go?"

"Silence!" whispered the elderly gentlemen. "You are not yet one of us." He then took a pillowcase and placed it over Belfort's head. "Place your right hand on my shoulder. When I begin walking, do not lose your grip." He led Belfort down a hallway and through another door and into a dimly lit meeting room illuminated by a few dozen candles. The old paladin slowly removed Belfort's pillowcase.

Belfort blinked several times. As his eyes adjusted to the low light, Belfort realized he was standing before King Louis XV and thirty of the most senior and influential aristocrats in France. The silence in the room was deafening and rather intimidating. Suddenly, the men comprising the chorus to his right began to sing a rousing French Army ballad praising heroism and *honour*. Startled, Belfort felt at sea — should I salute, come to attention, or something else, he wondered.

The old guard gently but firmly placed his hand on Belfort's shoulder and pressed downward to indicate that Belfort should kneel before these august individuals. When the song concluded, the chorus began another song with a slower cadence. The music sounded almost mournful. However, the lyrics were in Latin, and Belfort did not understand a single word.

In turn, six paladins sitting behind desks lit by a single candle explained the meaning of the paladins' motto — *Missi Dominici,* which meant emissaries of the master. They explained the significance of the four pillars of their order and administered an ominous warning against failing in one's duty. The last to step forward was King Louis. He was old and sickly (in truth, he had not long to live). He slowly drew his sword from its scabbard and feebly placed the blade on the initiate's right shoulder. "Do you swear to render sound judgment and swift justice in the Bourbon King's stead wherever duty takes you?" Belfort did not know whether to speak or not. King Louis asked in added emphasis (and perhaps as a prompt), "Do you?"

Gathering himself, Belfort said firmly, "I do."

The King then asked, "Do you swear fealty to the King and to all in this room? Do you?"

"I do." Belfort began to feel more comfortable now, having the gist of how the ceremony would unfold.

King Louis asked, "Do you swear to be candid in all your dealings with the Bourbon King and with your fellow paladins, and with the subjects of this realm? Do you?"

"I do."

"Are you committed to France, her monarchy, her aristocracy, and her citizens? Are you?"

"I am, I am, I am, I am," answered Belfort.

Because the ceremony required only one response, several attendees snickered in the background. King Louis looked up and slowly shook his head at the offenders. He slowly raised the blade and tapped Belfort's left shoulder and then gently placed it upon Belfort's pate. He asked, "As the Bourbon King's emissary, will you demonstrate courage in your decisions, proficiency in your legal instructions, and sound judgment in governmental affairs assigned to you? Will you?"

Embarrassed, Belfort answered but once this instance, "I will."

The Bourbon monarch raised the sword and weakly tapped Belfort's right shoulder. He barely managed to return his sword to its scabbard. The chorus began a medley to the glory of God, the angels on earth (which Belfort flippantly assumed meant the aristocracy), and the monarch's paladins. When the song ended, the chorus and all observers took one step forward. The men in the room were so close, even the ones in the rear could have reached out and touched him.

King Louis said, "You are now to be called Sir Albaric." The ceremony attendees murmured their approval. "Arise, Sir Albaric." The king turned to address the assemblage and said, "Lords of the Realm, we present to you France's twelfth paladin—Sir Albaric, Comte de Belfort."

The assembly crowded around the neophyte, and there followed much back slapping, hearty handshaking, and good-natured joshing.

The first aristocrat to embrace him was the *Duc* Demarais (which didn't faze Belfort in the least).

After five minutes of celebratory compliments, the smarmy Duc d'Aiguillon motioned to Belfort for him to come across the room for a *tête-à-tête*. Newly appointed to the vital position of Minister of Foreign Affairs (formerly the Minister of the Marine), the duc d'Aiguillon said with a creepy smile, "Congratulations, Sir Albaric." He paused to look around for eavesdroppers before continuing. "Well, Rici, you have navigated the king's corridors well. And though it is unusual to give a newly appointed paladin his first assignment so soon, the king and I have discussed this, and—" The Duc spied the king approaching and said ingratiatingly. "Sire, I was just saying to the Comte de Belfort that we have discussed his first assignment."

King Louis nodded and turned to Belfort. He said, "Sir Albaric, while the others *fairent la fête*, let us adjourn to my private quarters. One cannot be too careful with delicate matters. *N'est ce pas?*" King Louis turned to go but stopped and said, "We will not keep you long. We are certain that you would like to enjoy some cake and champagne, too."

Belfort said, "Of course, sire." He dutifully followed the king and the duc through a side door that led to an exterior stone staircase that accessed the king's antechamber two floors above ground level. As Belfort climbed the steps behind these powerful men, his ego swelled at the idea that his first assignment was a "delicate" matter. Upon entering his antechamber, the king motioned for Belfort and d'Aiguillon to be seated.

"When necessary, we will send a paladin overseas, though we have a preference to keep our golden boys close to home," said the king. "It is better that their first assignment be within the border of France. We feel that they should cut their teeth domestically. Isn't that correct, Duc?"

The duc d'Aiguillon nodded and bowed slightly. "That is correct, sire." Turning to Belfort, d'Aiguillon continued, "However, Sir Albaric, the other paladins are heavily in demand at the moment. And with growing unrest within the realm, His Majesty and I remain concerned about the rioting that has broken out in Provence. And this may well be a good time when we would be wise to make an exception." The king made a circular motion with his forefinger, indicating that the duc needed to get to the point. Embarrassed, d'Aiguillon shut up.

The king said, "Remember, no assignment is unimportant when you are representing the throne, and failure is not tolerated. It has been eight years since we inserted someone of your rank into North America. On two occasions, our paladins' efforts bore little fruit and the mission ended unsatisfactorily."

Belfort observed the duc's growing unease and reasoned that it was because, even though he was a new paladin, he had vaulted past d'Aiguillon in prestige and power, if not in rank. In the corridors of power, the courtiers were aware that the sickly king and his oily minister were unpopular with the peasants, but most aristocrats chalked it up to the whims of the common people, which was of no great concern.

Belfort proffered, "Perhaps, sire, I may be of greater assistance to His Majesty if I remained in France to represent the Crown in the negotiations with the people of Provence."

"Of course, Sir Albaric, that would please us greatly, but, alas, France's influence in the new world has slipped. And for the time being, we care more about North American affairs than about our popularity with the peasant population. World affairs beckon for men of your talent. We will speak no more of your remaining in France." The king glanced down and smoothed out his ermine robe, but the implication was clear—any suggestions from the newbie were not welcomed. King Louis sat up and said, "Your first stop is to assess the British colonials' progress toward organizing for independence." King Louis believed it critical for France to separate the English colonies and leave King George III without the means to pay his war debts.

The duc d'Aiguillon interjected, "From the previous paladin, the Comte de Charnay, we know that a resistance movement has begun. But he was discovered and had to depart New York *tout de suite*."

King Louis coughed once, signaling his desire to speak. D'Aiguillon fell silent.

The king subsequently said, "The second half of your assignment is to proceed to *Les Îles Malouines* [Falkland Islands, off Argentina] and assess the political and military situation there. I want to know whether the Spanish are maintaining adequate defenses. France sold the islands to Spain several years ago, and we do not want an English takeover. The English already occupy the adjacent island. Judge whether the Spanish defenses are adequate, craft the most accurate diagram possible, and provide me with your recommendations."

Belfort asked, "If Your Majesty does not want the English to control the islands, why were they sold to the Spanish?"

"We needed to replenish the treasury. The [Seven Years] war practically bankrupted us, and the last four harvests have been wildly inconsistent. Another reason was to keep the one of the two islands out of the hands of the English. Our daring explorer *sui generis,* the Comte de Bougainville, was quite unhappy. He had discovered and claimed the islands for France in '64, and he designed and constructed their fortifications." The monarch coughed softly before continuing. "But we must do what we must. Today, the Spanish are resentful that the English have built a settlement on the adjacent isle. We do not wish the English to obtain both islands." The king tried to smile, but his ague was giving him problems today. "We did not wish to make Bougainville quite so unhappy, but we compensated him for his troubles."

"Yes, sire." Turning to the Duc d'Aiguillon, Belfort asked, "Do we have contacts in New York and in *Les Îles Malouines*—people who can assist in concealing me from the English authorities, if necessary?"

The duc said, "I will consult with the Minister of the Marine in office 8 years ago and provide you with a name."

King Louis waved his hand feebly and said, "That won't be necessary. Let us remember that we were king eight years ago and possess a memory." The monarch again coughed softly and said, "We sent Rene d'Alquier to Quebec to salvage the Canadian situation. Six years later, we directed Geoffrey, Comte de Charnay, to sail to Manhattan for the purpose of establishing contact with a former militia soldier of New France who resided there. He was to convert him into a spy. Now, during your training, you learned of their assignments and why they ended unsuccessfully. Today, we still wish to remain close to our contact in Manhattan. The fellow's name is St. Alembert. When you contact him, he will cooperate and facilitate your mission to assess New York's political winds."

"Perhaps I should speak with the Comte de Charnay before departing. It could prove helpful," said Belfort.

The king nodded in agreement and said, "That can be arranged; he is in the Bastille. We imprisoned him for failing in his mission. Remember that failure as a paladin is unacceptable and never will be tolerated. He *chose* not to do what we had tasked him to."

Belfort, who knew Charnay by his war hero reputation, turned to the king and asked, "How did the Comte de Charnay fail, exactly?"

The king looked out the window and his mood turned melancholy. He said softly, "In '59 we sent a paladin to Quebec—Rene d'Alquier. A war dispatch from General Montcalm said that d'Alquier had been shot by an English colonial. Montcalm's letter mentioned a girl. The details are murky, but we will neither allow harm to come to our paladins nor allow an attack to go unavenged. The Comte de Charnay disobeyed our instructions. The Comte de Charnay discovered that his contact, a Canadian named St. Alembert, had married this girl. Charnay judged it counterproductive to assassinate her—as he put it at the time. We wanted d'Alquier avenged, and it did not happen. The Comte de Charnay had the opportunity to kill her, but he let that opportunity pass. It pained us to send him to the Bastille. You can see that, can you not? D'Alquier and Charnay are not the only paladins I have ever lost, but each loss is nigh unbearable."

The Duc d'Aiguillon, silent during the king's explanation, spoke up. "Perhaps, sire, this imprisoned fellow could yet provide valuable services to his king. Perhaps this prisoner could be of assistance to Sir Albaric in New York. The Comte de Charnay had established a working relationship with St. Alembert. He could still prove of value to Your Majesty."

The king thought a moment and uttered, "We had great expectations for Sir Geoffrey, but his noncompliance upset us. Regrettably, we felt compelled to make an example of him."

Belfort said, "Truly a grand tragedy, is it not? Monsieur le duc, is this the same Comte de Charnay who heroically defended Marshall de Saxe's center at the Battle of Fontenoy? As a child, my father told me the tale many times. He is a hero of France. How could I ever order this person about?"

The king said, "We see that you are a young man with empathy. We like that in our paladins. Remember, he remains in prisoner status under you. Interview him, and if, in your judgment, he can assist your mission, he may accompany you to New York. By bringing you success, he may earn the chance to redeem himself."

Two hours later, Belfort entered the Bastille and was escorted by a guard to the administrative office. There, he signed in and then was led through clammy hallways. As Belfort walked through the prison, foul odors assaulted his nose. The stench was so bad that he was tempted to walk out, yet he pretended not to notice. As Belfort passed through the casemate arches, each pair of guards snapped to attention and presented a rifle salute. After learning of the visit from someone carrying the royal seal, a bowlegged sergeant from the second floor scurried up to him, out of breath. The man asked, "How may I be of help, your honor?"

Belfort said matter-of-factly, "I am to see the prisoner Charnay." Belfort pushed past the fat sergeant of the guard and strode down the dank hall, his highly polished boots glistening in the candlelight. The sergeant hustled to catch up. Belfort splashed through the puddles in the prison hallways, oblivious to the stares from the emaciated prisoners who were awake. When Belfort and the sergeant arrived at the desired cell, the sergeant fumbled with his oversized key ring (much to Belfort's annoyance). With apparent impatience, Belfort motioned for the sergeant to unlock the cell.

The sergeant hesitated because he knew from experience that *this* prisoner could be belligerent. He said, "We are but two people. I have seen five struggle to subdue him.

Belfort said sternly, "Open it—*now*!"

"But, sire, this prisoner is dangerous." Clearly afraid, the sergeant fumbled with the keys. Exasperated, Belfort snatched them from him and turned the key until it clicked. The cell door creaked wide enough for Belfort to brush past the guard and enter the dark and reeking cell.

Belfort shook a prisoner sleeping on the floor and asked, "Are you Charnay?" The emaciated fellow shook his head. He walked to the next sleeping prisoner and asked, "Are you Charnay?"

The bearded prisoner in soiled prison garb blinked several times and sat up. He rubbed his eyes and brushed straw from his prison uniform and hair. "Who are *you*?" he asked reproachfully.

The sergeant kicked the prisoner in his flank, and said in a stern voice, "Hold your tongue."

Belfort's eyes widened when he recognized the aristocrat even in the low light. Belfort backhanded the sergeant's face, and the blow sent him tumbling backward into the filthy straw. The sergeant sat on his backside in silence rubbing his jaw, and the other prisoners crawled away from the commotion and huddled in a frightened mass against the stone walls. Belfort said in a stern voice, "Never kick this man again." Belfort knelt by the prisoner.

The inmate said, "I am Geoffrey, Comte de Charnay."

"My name is Sir Albaric, Comte de Belfort. I am going to the Americas and want to ask you some questions."

The prisoner rubbed his hair and said, "Comte de Belfort, you say?" The new paladin nodded. Then Charnay yawned and said, "Then you must be Jacques's boy?"

Belfort said gently, "I am. And you look like hell, Sir Geoffrey."

The man before him looked twenty years older than his true age of forty-six years. Sir Geoffrey retorted, "We have nothing to discuss. Go away."

Belfort said, "Your attitude is perfectly understandable. I would not want to answer questions either. But you will want to answer these particular queries. You see, I am here to interview you about this St. Alembert fellow who lives in Manhattan." Lowering his voice, he said, "I am the twelfth paladin, and my initial assignment is New York.

And you did work with him on your last assignment, did you not?"
Charnay did not answer; Belfort pressed on. "His name is Jean-Luc St.
Alembert. How would you describe him? What manner of man is he?"
When Belfort noted that the prisoner's expression had morphed into
one of interest. Belfort continued, "I am going to Manhattan and will
be meeting with him. I thought since you already know him and have
a working relationship, it would be useful for us to have a chat."

"Jean-Luc is a good man—loyal to France to a point, and loathes the
English. Does that satisfy you?" Charnay rolled over and shut his eyes.

"To a point, you say. What point is that?"

"He considers himself a New Yorker now. He married an English
woman." Charnay rolled over and pulled his thin, grimy blanket over
his shoulders.

Belfort scowled. Again, he tapped the prisoner's shoulder and said,
"I have more questions, Sir Geoffrey. Turn back around—please."

It had been more than eight years since Charnay had been addressed
by his paladin title. Charnay opened his eyes and rolled over. He asked,
"I do not know you. You must be new. What happened to Roger? I cannot remember his name." Charnay snapped his fingers repeatedly trying to recall the paladin's name. He was a fellow from Normandy?"

"Sir Roger, Comte de Branville, was killed on assignment in Prussia. And since I am *your* replacement, there is now a new opening—if
you get my meaning. You are here because you failed in your assignment in New York. What happened?"

Charnay's eyes flashed anger (though his ire wasn't for Belfort).

The sergeant inched away and looked out the door for others to
help should the prisoner start a ruckus.

Charnay said, "I used judgment. That is what a paladin is called to
do—or so I thought." His words expressed his bitterness over the in-
justice done to him. "His Majesty is already surrounded by enough
sycophants. It is true; I did not assassinate St. Alembert's wife as instructed. We would have lost him as a field contact. I was sure that he
would have returned to Quebec. He cannot organize the Manhattan
tax resisters from Montréal, can he?"

Belfort said, "Not afraid of candor, I see."

"Any paladin worth his salt must be candid with his king. I made the error of thinking that I could sway His Majesty to my viewpoint." Lowering his voice to a whisper, he added, "Nothing good would have resulted if I had killed the man's wife. The ultimate prize is to separate the colonies from Mother England. That was my focus. To reward my frank assessment, the king sent me here to rot."

"Did you not anticipate His Majesty's reaction to your decision?"

"Of course, I anticipated it," Charnay hissed sarcastically. His voice returned to a normal level and he said, "I simply did not anticipate the irrationality of insisting that this woman's death overrode all else. St. Alembert would not have remained in New York nor in a position to help had I assassinated his wife. I still hold that view."

"I could obtain your release."

Charnay looked suspicious. "Why would you do that?"

"Would you be interested in accompanying me to Manhattan?"

Intensely interested, but not wishing to show it, Charnay mused on the proposition for several pregnant moments. He asked, "If we are successful, then what?"

"Then, I would argue your case before His Majesty."

"For reinstatement?"

"Yes, but, first things first. Let us complete this assignment satisfactorily."

"But there is a *chance* for reinstatement?"

"We will discuss that with His Majesty upon our return. His Majesty is aware that I came here to speak with you. That is a positive sign for you, I think. It has to be in the back of His Majesty's mind. Besides, I was not told to assassinate anyone, so that concern will not hamper our success."

"You were not told, but does he expect me to kill that woman during this trip? It was a bad idea in '65 and is probably still a bad idea. Assassinating women is not something at which I excel," said Charnay as his voice trailed away.

"And yet, you accepted the assignment."

"I was new to the paladin system, new to Versailles, and inexperienced in the ways of the palace corridors. I thought I could handle it. I had shot and killed men in battle, so I believed it would not be an issue for my conscience."

"It would go a long way to restoring you into His Majesty's good graces?" said Belfort.

"Did His Majesty happen to mention that it was St. Alembert's wife who arranged for my escape from the English authorities? The memory of her dropping a load of flour on the Englishmen who were looking to capture me still brings a smile to my face."

Belfort absorbed this new piece of information but did not respond. Motioning for the sergeant of the guard to return, he said, "The prisoner is leaving with me. Let us return to your office and do the appropriate paperwork, shall we?"

DURHAM, ENGLAND NOVEMBER 16, 1772, 10 A.M.

Captain Wesley Archer walked down the hallway of the Durham Militia's headquarters, studying the numbers painted above the door to locate his friend's office. He removed his black three-cornered hat, which had confined his strawberry blond hair that he had pulled and tied behind his head. He stopped before a full-length looking glass to inspect his white blouse and white pants for blemishes. Relieved at seeing none, he inspected his teeth for food stuck between them, and then pulled taut his scarlet jacket. Finally, he straightened his gorget and, with his fingers, combed his silver epaulets to untangle them. He wanted to make a good impression, thinking it might influence his assignment. Confident in his appearance, he renewed his search. A few doors later, he found the office he needed. He knocked twice.

"Come in," said Captain Wilson, the assignments officer for the regiment stationed in Durham County. Expecting his visitor, Wilson said, "Have a seat, Wes. We'll discuss your assignment in a moment."

Captain Archer sat down and gazed out the window at the River Wear. "Nice view you have, Richard."

Captain Wilson stacked the papers he had been working on and said, "You must have made someone angry, Wes."

"Why is *that*?" asked Captain Archer, surprised.

"I have your orders. You are being sent to a detachment of the 37th Foot as the executive officer."

"Bollocks! Isn't that outfit in Canada, Richard?"

Captain Wilson said, "Practically, my sad news is that the 37th Foot is posted in the lake region at a place called Fort Detroit—on the, uh, frontier." Captain Archer groaned, closed his eyes, and sank in his chair. "Cheer up, Wes. It's only two years. And, I will do all in my power to make your follow-on assignment in Philadelphia. I hear the Philadelphia ladies are beautiful—and there's a great deal of money in that town, so there must be wealthy widows and daughters of rich colonials all over. At the Fort Detroit environs, I am afraid the only women are Indian squaws. It will be good duty, Wes, since the Indians are peaceful around there. This assignment is important for your promotion chances."

"You haven't said one thing about Detroit that cheers me up."

"Look, Wes, I was only teasing about you making someone angry. The requirement came from London, and the commander selected you. The 'needs of the service,' old boy, you know how it is. You need to be in Portsmouth to catch your ship in four weeks. The particulars are in your orders."

"Richard, is there any way out of a frontier assignment—out of *this* assignment?"

"I am afraid not. As you know, Wes, lackluster performance in any assignment can sink your career. Execute your duties well and you will earn that slot in the Philadelphia garrison. Two years of hell followed by two years of heaven—you can do two years standing on your head."

Captain Archer stood and turned for the door. He stopped and said, "Richard, say something positive about Fort Detroit. Anything."

"There is one thing. When we captured the fort in '60, we suspected that the enemy had buried their garrison's pay chests to prevent their capture." Captain Wilson grinned and added, "Rumor has it that there is a pot of gold in that area waiting to be discovered. Perhaps you could be the one to locate the French Army's gold and return to England a wealthy treasure hunter."

Captain Archer scowled and said, "May I have my copies of the orders, please?" After perusing them carefully, he folded the pieces of paper and muttered, "I had better pack. I haven't time to waste."

As he was pulling Wilson's office door shut, Archer heard his assignments officer say, "Good luck, Wes." Archer smiled grimly, nodded, and closed the door behind him. Alone in the hall, he looked at the ceiling and closed his eyes, hoping against hope that this was all a bad dream. After opening his eyes and seeing that he was still standing outside Wilson's office, he said, "Bloody hell!" He slapped his tricorner hat against his thigh, closed his eyes again, and asked sarcastically under his breath, "Why me?"

CHIPPEWA COUNTRY (MICHIGAN), DECEMBER 12, 1772

The five Ottawas halted their ponies and dismounted just outside the Chippewa village. They walked their mounts in to show respect for their hosts and the tribe's sachem. Now, nine years after Pontiac's Rebellion had been quashed, the delegation had come to visit their former enemies and to discuss issues of mutual importance. The region's tribes were slowly discarding ancient enmities and were reluctantly discussing a unified strategy to combat encroachment of the European settlers. Certainly, the Ottawas recognized the necessity to work on their unnatural armistice after centuries of hostilities.

The most striking of the braves, Opechwan, had been newly elected sachem of the Ottawas at age thirty-one, and was paying a diplomatic call on his older, more tenured counterpart, Ahmik of the Chippewas.

Opechwan walked with his head up, his shoulders back, and his eyes on the sachem's lodge. Neither the young chief, nor his associates, felt particularly welcome and did not wish to fool themselves about the Chippewas tolerating Ottawas among their lodges. Those who observed them enter their village watched with dour expressions. By coming in person, Opechwan gambled with his life that the fragile armistice between the tribes had value to the Chippewas and that they, too, would want to preserve it. He desired peace and wanted to secure its benefits for his tribe.

The Chippewa villagers stopped what they were doing to observe the delegation. Among these villagers were ten young Chippewa maidens who were receiving instruction in weaving. One of the maidens was the chief's comely daughter, Kateri. She looked on appreciatively as the tall Ottawa chief passed nearby. She was thunderstruck by his dignity and handsome features. The older woman teaching the girls scolded Kateri for not paying attention, but Kateri somehow knew, she just knew, that this stranger was the man she was waiting for. When she observed her father receive the young sachem, she excused herself from the instruction. Many considered Kateri a striking beauty. She had never wanted for Chippewa braves, who all vied for her attention. Kateri moved quickly across the open area, and then waited patiently a short space from her family's lodge intending to come face to face with this man.

Kateri grew restless as her father's meeting with his visitor dragged on. She walked past several men standing outside and brashly entered the wigwam. She found her father and the visitor sitting on mats, speaking quietly. Knowing that she had interrupted part of the peace discussions, she said with feigned innocence, "Forgive me, Father. I did not know you were with someone."

Kateri's father, Chief Ahmik, said, "Actually, my child, we are done and were about to go outside."

Kateri knelt near her bedding and pretended to look for something.

Speaking to his daughter, Ahmik said, "Chief Opechwan is from the Ottawa tribe three moons to the south. I knew his older brother,

Pontiac, and Chief Opechwan wants to continue the unifying work his brother began."

Kateri's smiled demurely, and her eyes met Opechwan's briefly. It would have been inappropriate for her to gawk at her father's guest, but their eyes met long enough *for her purposes*. She said, "Welcome Chief Opechwan. Our village is honored to host the sachem of the Ottawas." She coyly flipped her hair back to reveal her smooth neck and a glimpse of her shoulder. Though the object of her crush did not alter his expression, she succeeded in getting him to notice her.

Opechwan said, "Thank you."

Kateri said, "Will you be staying a few *days?*" Her emphasis on the last word caught her father's attention.

Ahmik glanced at his visitor and then said, "Yes. His tribe's delegation will rest a day before their return."

Opechwan said, "I should not be gone for long periods, I am looking forward to spending time with my Chippewa brethren."

Kateri stood and said, "I should go. You and father have business to conduct." She walked to the doorway of the wigwam. Then she hesitated and touched Opechwan lightly on the arm. "Perhaps we will have another opportunity to talk."

Completely smitten, Opechwan turned his head to keep this Chippewa beauty in his view and said, "I—I hope so."

Kateri ducked outside. Inside the wigwam, there was an awkward silence. In a lame attempt to decrease the father's disapproval, Opechwan said, "You have a beautiful—I mean, a nice daughter, Chief Ahmik."

"Yes, she is a good *Chippewa* girl."

Opechwan understood the implication, but neither his intention nor his expression changed. He reminded himself that he came here on official business and ought not to allow his visit's purpose to be thwarted by hot blooded thoughts for a woman he had only just laid eyes on. He chided himself and thought it better that he should put her out of his mind.

However, Kateri intended to be pursued by this man—until she caught him. Planning to keep herself foremost in his thoughts, she invented opportunities to bump into her father and Opechwan the following day, for she knew when Ahmik would escort the Ottawa delegation around the village.

The latest "accidental meeting" occurred back at Ahmik's lodge. The Chippewa chieftain said, "Tonight we will celebrate our accord with a feast and tribal council. I will come just before sundown to your camp and escort you to our council lodge."

Opechwan said, "We are grateful for Chief Ahmik's hospitality and look forward to tonight's festivities."

Ahmik held his hand up as a peace gesture and then turned and went inside his lodge. Opechwan turned to leave and spotted Kateri standing ten feet away. He blurted out, "I did not see you standing there."

Kateri playfully motioned for Opechwan to follow. Opechwan glanced at his four friends. Realizing that their chief and this beautiful girl wanted to spend time alone, the four Ottawas tactfully retired to their campsite. Kateri led Opechwan outside the village's boundary the distance an arrow can fly before falling to earth. She took him to a clearing near a brook. Though the afternoon air was chilly, as evidenced by ice forming by the banks. Opechwan's breath was visible in the cold air, and he became self-conscious of his shivering. Choosing a safe topic, he said, "Your village has shown us many courtesies."

Kateri nodded and looked into this visitor's eyes. She smiled demurely, but knew she had to get down to business. She asked, "Does the chief of the Ottawa have a wife?"

Opechwan's demeanor turned melancholy. He said, "I did have a wife. She died three summers ago after a lengthy illness."

Kateri said, "I am sorry." But she felt elated that this man was available.

Opechwan asked, "And you? How can the daughter of Ahmik be so beautiful *and* unattached? There must be many men wanting to be your husband."

Kateri said, "There was a man who caught my eye, but I discovered his true nature before the courtship became marriage."

The cold wind blew some dead leaves across their path, and though Opechwan and Kateri were wearing warm fur clothing, they recognized the benefit of standing next to one another for additional warmth. Opechwan asked, "What did he do?"

Kateri said, "As the summer warmth turned to cooler days, my tribe celebrated the annual Feast of the Virgins. The man my father (and my tribe) expected me to marry was in attendance. As I and my friends assembled near the festival fire, this man came before the tribe and falsely accused my best friend of being *ineligible* to participate." Opechwan's eyes widened at this serious, open accusation. "My girl-friend did not shrink from this slur on her honor. I stood a short distance away and could feel my stomach knotting. She angrily challenged him to produce evidence. He could only glare at her and said nothing further. He lost face before the entire village." Opechwan shook his head sadly at the breach of etiquette. Kateri looked away wistfully and said, "I ended the relationship that evening. I could never give myself to such a man."

Opechwan said softly, "I understand. Is this man still in your village?"

"Yes. He accepted his punishment for his smear and remained in the tribe. After all, he is our best hunter and bravest warrior."

"But your heart could not forgive?"

"I learned later that he was pursuing both my friend and me at the same time. When she learned he had been seeing me she ended it with him. His pride hurt, he retaliated by trying to shame her publicly. His heart is not pure, and I needed no further evidence that he is not the person for me." Kateri looked into the brook and watched the sun sparkling on the ripples. For several moments, she was silent. "My father, as chief, forgave him as is required by our custom, but my father understood that my engagement must also end. Today, this person is away on a hunting trip, and when he returns, he will give away much of his venison to the tribe's widows. He will be trying for a long time to get the villagers to forgive his rash behavior."

With the path to love unencumbered, Opechwan and Kateri spoke in the hushed tones of two completely smitten lovers. As they flirted and snuggled against the cold winds, both wanted this special moment to last for all time. He placed his arm around her shoulder and she placed her head on his chest. With each passing minute, their connection deepened.

That evening, Opechwan lay in his bedding with his hands behind his head. He watched his fire's smoke drift upwards and out the wigwam's vent. All he could think about was this Chippewa woman who had captured his heart. His mind spun with thoughts of their moments together. He made up his mind to ask Chief Ahmik for the hand of his daughter and the sachem's blessing of the union the following day. Following his key decision, his mind relaxed. Opechwan rolled over and went to sleep shortly thereafter.

Two days after Opechwan left the Chippewa village, four Chippewa braves entered the village, returning from a successful deer hunt. These young men were lifelong companions: Abooksigun, Kiwidinok, Ominotago, and Migisi. Migisi walked at the head of the group. They proceeded proudly on the beaten path through the Chippewa village. Each led a horse-drawn travois, and on each two-pole litter lay tied a gutted deer carcass.

The village maidens, attending their weaving instruction, regarded them appreciatively as the braves passed en route to the sachem's dwelling to announce their return. Per tribal custom, the sachem would distribute the venison bounty to the villagers. After being welcomed home by the sachem, Migisi and the others spent the evening dressing out the carcasses, flirting with the maidens assisting, and preparing their venison for smoking.

The next morning, Migisi emerged from his wigwam rested, but hungry. He walked to a nearby stream for water. As he had been gone for fourteen nights, the essentials were depleted in his lodge. He looked with annoyance at his empty leather water pail. He snatched it off the center pole, put on his fur wrap and went outside. He walked the short distance to the stream. As he knelt, a village maiden named Aiyana came up beside him. The Chippewa villagers knew that she was smitten with Migisi and had done everything in her power to catch his eye since his breakup with Kateri.

She said, "Did Chief Ahmik tell you the news?"

Migisi asked, petulantly, "What are you talking about, Yani?" Migisi and Aiyana's families had always lived beside one another. Like the rest of her friends in the village, he still called her by her childhood nickname.

Aiyana said, "The chief of the Ottawas came to our village on a diplomatic mission."

Migisi grimaced and said, "The Ottawa are not welcome. We fight the Ottawa when they encroach."

"Chief Ahmik rebuffed them not. Our visitors stayed among our lodges for three nights. The Ottawa chief is strong and tall. He pleased Kateri's eye. Our chief appeared to enjoy this unexpected visit."

"Yani, why do you tell this to me?"

"Because, now Kateri is engaged." She paused, "To the chief of the Ottawa."

Migisi's eyes narrowed as the announcement's implications sank in. His hands clenched. Then, he realized that Aiyana was caressing his back with her fingertips. He stood, took Aiyana by the hand, and motioned toward his wigwam.

Inside the lodge, she asked softly, "You desire Yani, yes?"

Migisi pulled Yani to him and began removing her clothing. As he kissed her with passion, he imagined she was Kateri. Though Aiyana knew his heart was with Kateri, Migisi was with her, and that was all that mattered at the moment.

CHAPTER TWO

THE DARK CLOUDS in the Manhattan sky cast an ominous pall over the street. Widow McTavish and her next-door neighbor, Mrs. Sherman, stood chatting on the dirt street. The tidy homes behind them (like most of the other houses) had smoke wafting from the flues. The air felt chilly, and with neither woman inclined to pass news in the bleakness, the conditions assured that the morning gathering would be brief. Widow McTavish glanced at the clouds and said, "A storm might roll in this afternoon."

"Wouldn't be surprised," said Mrs. Sherman, looking skyward. Then she looked about to see whether her neighbor on her other side was coming to join them. Initially motivated to sweep their steps, the two ladies were taking a lengthy breather to chat. The blustery wind made the morning feel chillier than usual. Mrs. Sherman, ever the worrier, kept her eye on the whitecaps frothing on the waters visible in the distance. Her husband worked at the pier as a joiner repairing ships, and weather such as this caused her concern for his well-being. Wanting to change the subject, she said, "I hope Mrs. St. Alembert is not ill. She has usually started to her husband's office by now."

Holding her bonnet in place while waiting for the wind to die down, Widow McTavish said, "There she is now."

Holding her front door to prevent the wind from damaging the hinges, Molly Lake St. Alembert smiled and waved to her neighbors. The blustery gusts quickly reddened Molly's cheeks, and she placed a hand on top of her head to hold her bonnet in place. She quickly pulled its drawstrings tightly around her chin and tied a strong knot.

"That should hold it," laughed Mrs. Sherman.

Molly smiled and asked, "Are you ready for spring?"

Mrs. Sherman said, "Oh my, yes."

Molly noticed a slight frown on her neighbor's face and asked, "Is anything wrong?"

"Just this morning, my husband began talking about this harebrained idea of moving to the frontier to get rich trapping beavers." Widow McTavish started to say something, but Mrs. Sherman continued, "Have you ever heard of anything so senseless? No one actually makes a living trapping beaver anymore, do they?"

If only Mrs. Sherman would allow the elderly Widow McTavish a word in edgewise! The elderly neighbor's husband had been a successful trapper for a time but had been killed by the Huron. Molly knew that, and she and the older lady exchanged knowing glances.

"I used to know someone in the fur trade. He has done very well," said Molly matter-of-factly. "Although I have not seen him in years, my parents relay news of his success from time to time. It must still be possible to get rich trapping."

What Molly didn't reveal was that this fur trader once had been in love with her and, in a pique of jealousy, was going to shoot her future (and now current) husband. He would have pulled the trigger, too, had Molly not shielded Jean-Luc. This broken-hearted trapper had been her shipmate during the war with France. Now, Rhisiart Nance had made a fortune being the middle-man between the lake Indians and the merchants of London.

Molly said, "Well, I really must get the day started. It was wonderful seeing you this morning. Good-bye."

Turning at the corner, Molly entered Wall Street and walked past the busy shops and taverns. An odd sense though came over her. Looking about, Molly stopped and observed the bustling scene of men and women hurrying about. Seeing nothing out of the ordinary, she resumed walking. Ten minutes later, Molly entered the family's shipping business.

Her husband, Jean-Luc St. Alembert, looked up and smiled. "Quite chilly this morning, no?"

Molly untied her bonnet and said, "I really hadn't noticed." Jean-Luc returned to his ledger (not fully appreciating his potential violation of rules 2, 5, and 6 in Molly's personal marital code). These paraphrased rules state that Molly is never wrong (2), Molly can always trust her feelings (5), and when Molly is upset, Jean-Luc must remain calm (6). Molly said, with a hint of irritation in her voice, "I had the feeling I was being followed." Jean-Luc placed his quill pen on the desktop and gave his wife his full attention. Molly noted her husband's marital training kicking in, even if sub-consciously. She continued, "What was particularly odd is that I stopped numerous times attempting to locate the person—but never was able to."

"Perhaps you were mistaken," suggested Jean-Luc.

"Perhaps," said Molly as she hung her cape and bonnet on a coat rack. "Do you realize that the last time I felt this way was eight years ago? Something is up. I feel it in my bones."

"I will go out to the street and see if I can detect anyone suspicious."

Molly felt better seeing her Jean-Luc in the hunt. She watched him open the door, go outside, and look up and down the street. She had seen him in dangerous situations and knew her husband could handle himself.

After looking up and down the street, Jean-Luc came back inside and said, "Let us hope you are wrong. I could not see anyone standing out as unusual."

Jean-Luc returned to his desk, and Molly sat at hers (which faced her husband's). "How can I help this morning?" she asked.

Jean-Luc said, "I have been trying to rearrange the cargo load plans for our deliveries to Boston. Any thoughts?"

"Well, yes, I—" but before Molly could finish her thought, a man dressed in frontier clothing rapped loudly on the door. Slightly annoyed that the visitor had banged imprudently, Jean-Luc walked over and opened it. Though a touch irritated, he nevertheless asked politely, "How may I help you?"

"Are you the son of Monsieur Rafael St. Alembert?" he asked.

"I am," Jean-Luc said hesitantly. "Why do you ask?"

"Might I come inside? It is cold enough to freeze the balls off a brass monkey." With deliberate slowness, Jean-Luc stood aside, and the stranger shuffled inside. The visitor stood there blowing on his hands but did not remove his beaver hat or overcoat. That shortcoming made Molly regard him with something short of enthusiasm. When giving him the once over, she noted a teardrop tattoo under his left eye.

Jean-Luc said sternly, "Need I remind you there is a lady present."

He said with a hint of sarcasm, "You did jus' now, Cap'n." Lowering his gaze, he turned to Molly and said, "Beggin' your pardon, miss. I been in the forest amongst savages for too many years and, at times, forget my manners." The frontiersman looked around uneasily and shifted his weight time and again. After several awkward, moments, he broke the silence and said, "I just arrived from Montréal with this here letter. Your pa asked me to deliver it, since I was a-coming in this direction." He again blew on his fingers to warm them.

Jean-Luc masked his surprise and concern, and then asked, "May I see it, please?"

After studying the messenger's face, Molly remembered seeing him on the street. It might have been this fellow who was following me, she thought.

Jean-Luc said a second time, "The letter, if you please."

The visitor looked like his mind was elsewhere and had been caught off guard for a moment. He then blurted out, "Oh, of course, what was me thinking?" He quickly reached into his coat and handed Jean-Luc the letter, and stepped back. He promptly returned to warming on his hands.

Jean-Luc unfolded the correspondence and scanned it. As Jean-Luc read, the letter bearer ogled Molly with a smirk. When his leering came to Molly's attention, she glared at him with a withering look that forced his gaze elsewhere. The man's previous apology now seemed contrived, and his behavior made her anxious for him to leave.

When Jean-Luc's expression turned dark, Molly asked with concern, "What does it say, dear?"

"Father is sick, and indicates it is serious. He wants me to return and see to his final arrangements."

"Oh, no," said Molly. "Dear, we have much to do before we can set sail for Montréal. Please thank this man properly and send him on his way."

Jean-Luc gave the man a reasonable payment for his trouble (or so it became apparent by his expression). Jean-Luc then opened the door for the letter bearer. The visitor crammed the money into his pocket, tipped his hat, and departed.

Outside, the frontiersman sneered as he walked toward the wharf tavern. Amused by the thought that he had been paid twice for the same task, he ambled smugly, as though the chilly winds no longer bothered him. Feeling thirsty, he ducked into the tavern.

After Jean-Luc closed the door, he turned to Molly and said, "We must prepare for an immediate departure."

Molly said, "If Rafael is sick, he will want to see his grandchildren. We should take Nancy, Peter, and Rafe with us."

Jean-Luc said, distractedly, "Yes, of course."

Only a few minutes, later, there was a second rap on the door. Molly said sympathetically, "I'll get it." She walked quietly over and turned the doorknob. Standing before her were two men. Molly recognized one of the visitors and said inhospitably, "I never thought we would see you again!"

CHAPTER THREE

MONDAY, FEBRUARY 15, 1773, 8:30 A.M.

MOLLY'S FRENCH NEMESIS, Geoffrey, Comte de Charnay, stood in the doorway. Shocked and angry, she fought for self-control. Her initial reaction quickly gave way to a questioning look. He had at his side another individual. The second man looked years younger, and Molly assumed that he was a subordinate. Trying to disguise her emotions at encountering Charnay, she said, "You have taken a huge risk. If the sheriff sees you, he will arrest you on the spot."

Charnay replied in flawless English, "Mrs. St. Alembert, we are here to speak with your husband. Is he here?"

As Molly pondered the consequences of slamming the door in his face, Jean-Luc asked from the back of the office, "Who is at the door, dear?"

Realizing that "Schout Jack" Freeman, who was the sheriff, or Clay, who was one of the sheriff's several deputies, could walk around the corner at any moment, Molly took Charnay's elbow and said, "Hurry! Get in here."

During his last visit to New York City, Charnay had been briefly arrested by "Schout Jack" (as everyone called him) and brutalized by the deputy during an intense interrogation. Molly had enabled Charnay to escape from his cell and then concocted a ruse that enabled Charnay to sneak aboard a French merchant ship, which whisked him to safety. After Charnay and the stranger hustled inside, Molly looked up and down the street for the sheriff.

Jean-Luc hurried toward the door but stopped in his tracks upon seeing Charnay. "I was glad to hear that you had escaped, your Excellency. Events have made New York even more dangerous than they were eight years ago."

Charnay removed his hat and replied in French, "We will get to that, Jean-Luc, but first a formality." He turned to his travelling partner and said, "Albaric, Comte de Belfort, may I present you to Monsieur and Madame St. Alembert." Belfort nodded and smiled politely. The St. Alemberts remained several feet away, and the tension in the room pulsated between the married couple and their visitors. Jean-Luc slowly bowed, and Molly curtsied belatedly in an obvious gesture of support for her husband. Charnay continued, "The Comte de Belfort is my replacement."

To confirm his identity, Belfort pulled up his sleeve exposing his forearm's tattoo, *"Missi Dominici."* Jean-Luc knew that this Latin phrase, which means "emissaries of the master," identified the bearer as a paladin. These *crème de la crème* aristocrats were surrogates for the French king, authorized to act in his stead. What they say or decide carries the weight of the French crown.

Molly fought to maintain her composure. She knew that these men had come to use her husband in some way. Also, she was shaken by Charnay's haggard appearance. Eight years ago, he had been a handsome, driven, and courageous gentleman. Today, he personified brokenness and gloom. His once dark-brown hair now showed streaks of gray. Well, he is in his forties, thought Molly. She then turned her scrutiny upon the Comte de Belfort. He certainly lacked the grave persona of both Captain d'Alquier and Charnay. Instead, he demonstrated a rakish self-confidence that tickled her. His blond hair framed his handsome features. Wearing his chapeau at an angle that seemed out of place in colonial New York City, he radiated European fashion. Molly thought Charnay would have instructed him to wear it properly.

Jean-Luc asked, "How may I be of assistance, Excellency?" Being the scion of a lower-ranking French-Canadian aristocrat, Jean-Luc still felt compelled to render respect and support to the French government.

Belfort said, "We would like to speak with you in private."

Molly felt certain that her husband would reveal their trip to Montréal; she spoke up to preempt Jean-Luc's revelation. "I will leave you three to your discussions, but may I have a word with my husband first?" The paladins nodded politely and stepped over by the windows.

Molly whispered, "I will walk down the street to the bakery and return in twenty minutes. Please, don't say anything about us going to Montréal." Jean-Luc looked puzzled. Molly knitted her brows and asked pointedly, "Agreed?"

Eyeing the paladins, he nodded and said, "Agreed. Of course."

The visitors waited for Molly to gather her things and close the door behind her. The Comte de Charnay turned back to Jean-Luc, in French, "Bring us up to date on your activities with the group advocating independence from England."

Jean-Luc took a deep breath and replied in French, "Excellency, Events since you were here have turned deadly." Charnay nodded. "Three years ago, the British Army fired into a Boston mob and killed several. Public opinion is turning toward independence."

Charnay asked, "Did your group initiate this confrontation in Boston?"

Jean-Luc said, "No, the confrontation began when some street toughs began throwing snowballs at a sentry. But the distrust between the royal governor and the people is beyond repair."

Belfort asked, "What is your group's name?"

Jean-Luc said, "I am sorry, Excellency, but we do not speak its name. Nor do we use our real names during gatherings. We would face torture and execution from the English if our activities were discovered. Should discovery occur, our identities may yet remain undisclosed."

Belfort replied, "Understandable. How soon will the colonies declare independence?"

Jean-Luc said, "That is difficult to say, but I fear it is still years from becoming a reality. You see, a great many of my fellow citizens are conflicted over their loyalty to their king. My organization distributes information concerning His Majesty's government's abuses and Parliament's recent tax increases, but changing public opinion takes time. It is a process."

"I see," said Belfort. "What can you tell us about your organization's progress?"

"We have grown much stronger and now have working chapters in all thirteen colonies. We carry out actions independently of one another, but we have organized communication methods and maintain observers of the lobsterbacks' movements. When they are on the march, we learn of it quickly."

The paladins nodded and looked pleased. Jean-Luc continued, "We have established a courier system, and I believe that we have advanced the belief that each colony needs the other twelve and we must support the next in this cause. That is progress, and it will prove invaluable in the future. But it is only a start, Excellency. Do not underestimate the loyalty to the king and the population's identity as English. It is a mountain that will take time to overcome."

Charnay said, "Your report is most positive." He looked toward the window with a faraway look in his eyes and asked, "But when — *when* will the colonies break with England?"

Jean-Luc shrugged and held out his hands palms upward. He said, "Events are not entirely under our control. Parliament may relax their tax demands. That would result in a delay of the decoupling of these colonies." Jean-Luc checked the window for eavesdroppers. He looked Charnay in the eyes and asked, "May we rely on assistance from France if we declare our independence?"

Belfort said diplomatically, "France is rebuilding. Our army, our navy, our treasury — they all need replenishing. We fervently *wish* to support you, and will, when we are better positioned. You may relate to your organization that message."

Taken aback that the younger paladin had answered, Jean-Luc said, "I will certainly pass that on, Excellency." He glanced at Charnay, but the elder paladin looked away. Jean-Luc walked to the window and looked out. Noticing Molly returning. "It is wonderful that a nation as great as France is interested in our success. Is that all you wished to speak with me about?"

Belfort said, "It is important to hear direct a report like this." He then rubbed his hands together.

Jean-Luc asked, in English, "Are you cold? I could throw another log on the fire."

Charnay, heretofore passive in the conversation, asked, "Did you say, 'gold?' What gold?"

Jean-Luc blanched. He stuttered, "I, I asked if you were *cold*." An awkward silence followed. "Should I throw another log on the fire?"

Belfort studied Jean-Luc's reaction. He asked, "You almost fall in a faint when Geoff said the word *gold*. Is there something else you would like to tell us?"

"When his Excellency said 'gold,' it triggered a memory of the war. The word *gold* made me think that you may have come to Manhattan for that reason."

Charnay said, "Tell us about your memory."

Jean-Luc walked to the window and saw his wife approaching. He said, "My wife returns."

When Molly entered the office, the three men fell silent. Molly smiled and asked with forced pleasantness, "What have I missed?" She removed her cape and hung it on the coat rack.

Charnay turned to Jean-Luc and said, "We were discussing—gold."

"What is he talking about, husband?"

Jean-Luc looked flustered and at a loss for words. He swallowed hard and said, "I always wondered whether the gold was returned to the French king."

Molly turned to her husband and asked, "I still don't know what gold we are discussing."

Jean-Luc asked the paladins, "This *is* about the gold in the army pay chests, is it not?"

Bluffing, Charnay nodded.

Jean-Luc said to Molly, "The spring that followed our falling in love and before I came to ask for your hand in marriage, Major Rochebeaucourt—you remember Marc, don't you?"

Molly nodded and said with a hint of irritation, "Of course, I do."

"He sent me, Paul d'Espinassy, and two others on a secret mission to bury Fort Pontchartrain's pay chests to keep them out of enemy hands. I—" Jean-Luc looked down remembering his comrades. "I was the lone survivor of the mission."

Belfort said, "Tell us the story, if you please."

Jean-Luc closed his eyes. Long-suppressed memories flooded into his consciousness. He began slowly, "It was a Thursday evening in May [1], 1760, and...

Major Marc Rochebeaucourt watched his second-in-command, Lieutenant Paul d'Espinassy, lead three soldiers into his operations center located thirty miles to the east of Montréal. He was entrusting four of his old neighbors with a mission that required audacity, self-direction, and honesty. He turned to the officer in charge and said, "Paul, I want you to lead an important assignment." Paul and his three men, each under twenty years of age, listened stoically. "The tactical situation is dire. The enemy harasses our pickets and is constantly pressing our rear guard. We may not be able to hold out until reinforcements arrive from France."

"Is the war lost, Marc?" asked the youngest in the group, an 18-year-old militiaman named Jean-Luc St. Alembert.

"Never mind that, Jean-Luc" snapped Major Rochebeaucourt uncharacteristically. "Concentrate on what I am saying." He turned back to the appointed officer in

charge. "Paul, the enemy ships remain upriver. I have a sloop standing by. It is loaded with supplies and food. The sentries are expecting you."

Twenty-one-year-old Lieutenant Paul d'Espinassy had been friends with Rochebeaucourt since childhood. Paul had fought under Rochebeaucourt's command for over two years. These two men had endured perils together from Fort Carillon (Ticonderoga) to the Plains of Abraham (the Battle of Quebec) to the present. Paul leaned in to hear the details of the secret mission. With him were three trusted men who grew up on the same street in Montréal as Marc and Paul.

Jean-Luc St. Alembert was a handsome youth with dark hair and an athletic build, and he radiated self-confidence. Paul d'Espinassy considered him second in command of the detachment. Hervé Bissot was also eighteen and a reliable friend. Alexander Douglas was of Scottish descent but had been born and bred in New France. His red hair revealed his heritage, but the lad felt French through and through.

Seeing that he had the four men's attention, Major Rochebeaucourt said, "Sail to Fort Pontchartrain and deliver this letter to Colonel Bellestre. Then follow his instructions. I do not want you four lingering at the fort. By the time you arrive, they, too, will be threatened by advancing enemy units."

"I understand, Marc," said Lieutenant d'Espinassy.

Major Rochebeaucourt handed him the envelope and said, "Good luck. Do not allow this letter to fall into enemy hands."

Lieutenant d'Espinassy and his three subordinates saluted. D'Espinassy said, "We will not let you down, sir."

As the three younger soldiers went outside, Major Rochebeaucourt took d'Espinassy aside and said, "Paul, bury that money at the earliest opportunity. Too many bad things can happen if you attempt to bring it to Montréal. Select a location that will be easy to find. It may be years from now before we can recover the funds."

*A half hour later, Paul, Jean-Luc, Hervé, and Alex
arrived at the river and looked over the sloop that would be
their home for the next two months. Paul said, "Hervé, you,
Jean-Luc, and Alexander go below and check out the supplies
and gear."*

*While his men were below, d'Espinassy felt the envelope
in his pocket. Thinking that Major Rochebeaucourt had
not instructed him not to read it, he opened it and read the
contents: 'Colonel Bellestre, General de Levis, the
Commander of the His Majesty's Armies in Canada, orders
you to take all necessary actions to prevent the enemy forces
(approaching your location from the southeast) from
capturing your pay chests and fort's valuables. Entrust the
bearer of this letter. He has been instructed to hide His
Majesty's assets and to record their location. The crown will
dispatch agents to retrieve His Majesty's property at an
appropriate time.'*

Jean-Luc glanced at Molly for support. She nodded and gestured
for him to continue. Jean-Luc said, "When we arrived at Fort Pontchartrain du Detroit, it was sundown, Wednesday, June 4, 1760. We
accompanied Paul to the fort commander's office..."

*Lieutenant d'Espinassy, with his three-man detail behind
him, stood before the commander in Fort Pontchartrain's
headquarters. He saluted and handed General de Levis' letter
to Colonel Bellestre. After reading the correspondence,
Bellestre returned it slowly to its envelope. His face reflected
the reality that the war with England was lost. He turned
away from the young man who had brought him this dreadful
communication. Bellestre walked to the window and watched
thoughtfully as his soldiers labored to reinforce the walls of
the fort. He crossed his arms, looked down, and asked with a
sad voice, "What are your names, boys?"*

D'Espinassy said, "Sir, I am Lieutenant Paul d'Espinassy. I live in Montréal."

Jean-Luc said, "Sir, I am Jean-Luc St. Alembert, the son of Rafael St. Alembert. I, too, live in Montréal."

Hervé said, "Sir, I am Hervé Bissot, the son of François Bissot. I grew up two doors down from Jean-Luc."

Alex said, "Sir, I am Alexander Douglas. My father, William, died when I was a boy. I also live in Montréal."

"Ah, yes, I know your fathers. I remember you boys from when I lived in Montréal. You have travelled a great distance to deliver this letter." The sound of a distant explosion reminded all of the urgency of a fast transfer and departure.

"Return to your boat. My men will bring the fort's valuables to the wharf. Don't communicate with anyone. Just return to your boat—quietly."

Trying to sound nonchalant (because he was thinking of burying the treasure there), Paul asked, "What do you call the island in the river?"

"We call it Île aux Cochons. I have only gone there once. Legend says it is haunted by a red devil, but honestly what actually keeps me and others away are the rattlesnakes. The place is crawling with them."

"And yet you call it Hog Island. Are there actually hogs on the island?"

"Oh, yes—a sizeable herd; I ordered the farmers to place their hogs there to reduce the serpent population. The plan is working, but Mother Nature works slowly. The island is still home to many snakes."

Ninety minutes later, Bellestre's troops loaded three small chests onto the sloop. Lieutenant d'Espinassy saluted Bellestre and nodded to his men. Jean-Luc, Hervé, and Alex untied the mooring lines and pushed the bow of the sloop away from the wharf, jumped aboard, they raised the mainsail. As the sloop sailed away, Lieutenant d'Espinassy looked back at Colonel Bellestre and his soldiers, backlit by the campfires glowing from inside Fort Pontchartrain, as they returned to the palisade.

When the sloop was one hundred and fifty feet from Fort Pontchartrain's shore and floating in the darkness of the Detroit river, Lieutenant d'Espinassy said in a low voice, "Steer for the east side of Île aux Cochons. We shall bury the chests there. This river island will be easily located, thus making the king's gold easily recovered."

With Hervé and Alex working the jib sail, Jean-Luc pulled the tiller and turned the bow toward the island's boot. After a thirty-minute sail around the island's southern tip to its eastern side, the sloop's stem softly crunched against the island's sandy beach. Jean-Luc hopped overboard and secured the sloop to a tree stump.

Lieutenant d'Espinassy stepped ashore and said, "While you are off-loading the pay chests, I will locate a suitable site to bury them, pace it off, and record it."

"Sounds good, Paul. Let's get busy, boys," said Jean-Luc. As Alexander and Jean-Luc moved cargo out of the way they heard two knocks on the hull. They went topsides and saw a small man in the moonlight. Jean-Luc sensed trouble, as he figured that they would have to find a different burial site for the king's gold.

"Allow me to introduce myself. I am Le Nain Rouge. Who is in charge?" asked the small fellow in French.

Jean-Luc pointed to Lieutenant d'Espinassy and said, "That is him over there. I will take you to him."

Jean-Luc and Alex jumped ashore to escort the unwanted visitor across the rocky shore. In the moonlight, Jean-Luc took the measure of the small man. He was not a savage (that much he could be sure), and he conveyed a worldly weariness that made Jean-Luc think he would rather be elsewhere. They had not walked ten feet when the intruder stumbled

and fell. Jean-Luc helped him to his feet and asked, "Are you
hurt, sir?"

The small man brushed himself off and said, "Thank
you, but, no."

The trio walked another ten feet, and the small fellow
stumbled again and landed hard on his face. Jean-Luc and
Alexander again helped him to his feet. Jean-Luc said, "Allow
me to help you over these obstacles." He put his hand on the
Le Nain Rouge's jacket and held him up as they crossed the
beach to where d'Espinassy stood.

Jean-Luc said, "Lieutenant, we have a visitor. This man
wishes to speak with you."

Lieutenant d'Espinassy turned around and his jaw
dropped. "Who is this?" Before Jean-Luc or Alex could
answer, d'Espinassy pulled his pistol and pointed it at the
leprechaun-like intruder. Le Nain Rouge scowled, but didn't
look alarmed.

Jean-Luc said, "Paul, we can go elsewhere."

For a moment d'Espinassy did not answer. After several
tense seconds, he said "It is too late for that. He will tell them
we have been here."

"I told your soldiers who I was. They would have told
you, but you behave as a caitiff."

"We are here on official business."

"And yet, you are on my island."

Exasperated by the visitor's meddling, Lieutenant
d'Espinassy said with clear irritation in his voice, "Jean-Luc,
you, Hervé, and Alex are dismissed. I will deal with this hog
farmer. Thank you."

As Jean-Luc turned to leave, the small visitor grasped his
wrist tightly, pulled him to his level, and whispered, "You
have been pleasant. I have not observed that trait often in
strangers. Good fortune is coming. You will find three
abandoned ships on the north end of the Île d'Orleans. They

*are your wedding gifts from me. You still intend to marry the
auburn-haired girl, do you not?"*

*Jean-Luc felt as though a thunderbolt had struck him,
and he asked with a shaky voice, "Who are you? How do you
know Molly's hair color?"*

*Le Nain Rouge did not answer but resumed glaring at
Lieutenant d'Espinassy. He released Jean-Luc's wrist. Jean-Luc
stood and, though upset by what he had heard, returned to
the boat with Hervé and Alex.*

*Paul watched his men until they were out of earshot. He
said, "I am sorry you discovered us, but I cannot let you go."
Le Nain Rouge stood his ground defiantly.*

*As Paul pulled back the flint and both of them heard the
second click, Le Nain Rouge said, "I have no intention of
stealing your money. Actually, I will guard it until the rightful
owners come for it.*

*Paul felt his hand shaking. He had never killed an
unarmed person before. His finger tightened upon the trigger.*

*Within a second of being shot, the little man said
defiantly, "It is I who cannot allow you to return."*

*Not understanding, Paul hesitated. The little man
vanished before Paul's eyes. Shaken, Lieutenant d'Espinassy
blinked several times. "Have I imagined everything?" he
asked himself. He stood motionless for a minute, but then
snapped back to reality. He walked to the boat and said, "I
found two good spots—easily identified by the recovery
party." He turned and said, "Bring the pay chests."*

"What happened to the farmer?" asked Hervé.

*"Never mind that," he barked. Let us finish this and be
on our way." Lieutenant d'Espinassy, Jean-Luc, Hervé, and
Alex each held handles of the three chests and lugged them
across the beach. At the designated site, they dug a hole four
feet deep. After placing two pay chests in the earth, they
covered them with the spoil. Lieutenant d'Espinassy allowed*

them to rest upon their shovels. He then walked off seven paces, and standing in the moonlight made an annotation on his map. He turned back to his men and said, "I want the second hole here."

Jean-Luc, Hervé, and Alex quickly dug the second hole and covered the third chest with soil.

"Ouch!" cried Hervé.

"Pipe down. Voices carry in the night air," snapped Lieutenant d'Espinassy.

"What happened?" whispered Jean-Luc to Hervé.

"Something bit me."

"Let me look." Jean-Luc tried to examine the wound, but the moonlight was too faint for him to see. "I will doctor it after we get underway," said Jean-Luc sympathetically.

Lieutenant d'Espinassy nodded toward the sloop, and Hervé limped off. As Alex and Jean-Luc finished covering the hole and tamping down the earth with their shovels, Lieutenant d'Espinassy continued with his drawing on a piece of parchment. He wrote with the charcoal and accurately recorded the two locations. Jean-Luc and Alex watched their officer in charge pace the distance to the pay chests from the sloop and back. His map had to be as accurate as possible.

Alex leaned over to Jean-Luc and asked, "Did a rattler bite, Hervé?"

Mindful of the lieutenant's annoyance, Alex shrugged but looked over his shoulder toward the lieutenant as their officer paced off a final verification of distances.

"Ouch!" yelped the lieutenant. He looked down and saw a snake near his foot slithering toward the woods. "Ouch!" he yelped again. "Two of those bastards just bit me! "The colonel was not exaggerating about the snakes, was he? Clearly, that farmer and his hogs have not done a thorough job."

Jean-Luc could hear the snakes slithering in the dry leaves. He raised his shovel to strike one that came toward the

boat. He and Alex helped the lieutenant board the sloop.
Then, they pushed off the island's shore and raised the sail.
They sailed their boat to mid-river and anchored. The two
unbitten boys worked feverishly to save their friends. Working
simultaneously, Alex followed Jean-Luc's lead and did what
his more capable friend did.

They removed the victims' boots because snake venom
will swell the area around the bite. Next, they applied
tourniquets above the bitten areas. Then Jean-Luc and Alex
made cross-cuts and pinched the skin to force as much venom
out as possible. After about fifteen tense minutes, Hervé began
moaning, quietly at first, but in minutes the moaning grew
louder. Lieutenant d'Espinassy lay stoically silent with sweat
beads forming on his brow.

For the following hour, the boys kept wet rags on their
patients' foreheads. Jean-Luc could see that the situation had
grown dire, and that Paul and Hervé had little time remaining.

Hervé said, "My arm and upper chest are numb."

Alex looked at Jean-Luc with an expression both hopeful
and deeply concerned and asked, "What can we do?"

Jean-Luc slowly shook his head. "Pray for their souls and
pray that they do not suffer in their remaining hours."

Hervé succumbed first; complaining of blurred vision and
muscle pain, he pulled himself to the gunnel and vomited
overboard. He passed in that inglorious position.

Lieutenant d'Espinassy struggled to sit up. He took Alex's hand
and pulled himself to an upright position. Alex said, "Jean-Luc,
we should return to Fort Pontchartrain for medical help."

Before Jean-Luc could respond, an adamant Lieutenant
d'Espinassy said, "No! It will be obvious we off-loaded the
chests and buried them on the island. Hervé is dead, and soon
I will be. Sail into Lake Erie and do not look back at this
cursed island."

Jean-Luc reverted to their Montréal familiarity, "Paul, Alex is correct. We can do no more; the tourniquet is temporary, and it is all we can do for you."

"Jean-Luc, you are now in charge. Take the map from my pocket." Jean-Luc removed the small, rolled drawing. "You must see that this gets to Marc [Rochebeaucourt]." He said again, "Deliver that map to Marc." He died a moment later. Jean-Luc closed d'Espinassy's eyelids and wept.

Forty days later, Jean-Luc brought the sloop alongside the pier at Montréal. It was late afternoon when Jean-Luc tied off the boat and dispatched a soldier to headquarters with the news he had returned from Fort Pontchartrain. Major Rochebeaucourt came running to meet the sloop. Observing that the sailboat had only one occupant, Major Rochebeaucourt knew his worst fears had come true.

Major Rochebeaucourt asked, "Were you successful?"

Jean-Luc nodded sullenly. He stated the sad, but obvious fact, "I am the only one to make it back."

"What happened?" asked Major Rochebeaucourt.

Jean-Luc handed him the map and said, "This will show you the site of the pay chests."

Looking past Jean-Luc, Major Rochebeaucourt could see Paul d'Espinassy's fiancée, Danielle Langlois running toward the wharf. He also saw the fathers of Hervé, Alex, and Jean-Luc hurrying in his direction. He said, "Quickly, Jean-Luc. What happened?"

Jean-Luc said, "Paul and Hervé were lost during the first night at Pontchartrain. As we finished burying the pay chests on Hog Island, both were bitten by rattlesnakes. They died within hours. Alex and I buried them in unmarked graves on the mainland. Alex was killed later in an ambush by Indians when we steered too close to the north shore of Lake Erie."

"You did well, Jean-Luc. I will break the news to Paul's fiancée, Bissot's father, and Douglas's mother. Go with your father; he has been worried sick."

Jean-Luc exhaled deeply. He pulled a handkerchief from his pocket and wiped his brow. Molly saw that he was genuinely exhausted from retelling the ordeal, but the paladins were less sympathetic.

"That is an amazing tale," said Charnay, skeptically. "So that is how you came into your shipping business. I have wondered about that. You did not mention the pay chests to me when I was here in '65. Why is that?"

"When I first met you, you were dressed as a vagrant. I was intimidated and overwhelmed. I was surprised and in disbelief that someone of your status had crossed the ocean to meet with me. It did not occur to me that I should mention something that had happened long ago in a lost war—a mission filled with horrible memories. I have tried to put the nightmare of losing my friends out of my mind. If it were not for the thought of reuniting with Molly to keep me going, I do not think I would have survived either. Upon my return, I gave the map to Marc Rochebeaucourt and have not given it much thought until now."

Molly walked over to Jean-Luc. She whispered softly, "Of course, you are burdened with sorrow. I wonder how that small fellow knew about me. Well, what became of your benefactor?"

"The little man was with Paul when I returned to the boat. That was the last I saw of him." His inflection changed noticeably and said, "It was my belief that Paul was going to *silence* him."

Belfort asked, "So the little man kept his word and the three ships were waiting for you? Jean-Luc nodded guiltily. "After hearing this, we should recover the king's funds. Take us to Montréal to first find the map and then to Fort Detroit."

Molly quickly interjected, "We do not transport passengers." For emphasis, she said, "We are a cargo company."

Undeterred by the wife's declaration, Belfort asked, "Are you unable to transport us—or unwilling?"

Jean-Luc spoke up immediately, "For you, Excellency, we will make this trip an exception."

Molly said, "A voyage to Fort Detroit is time consuming—and dangerous. Husband, have you considered the portage around the great falls?"

Belfort turned to Jean-Luc and asked, "Given the obstacles, like this portage your wife mentioned, is it a manageable journey?"

Jean-Luc said, "It is manageable. We have a special vessel that will work for the portage."

Stifling her fury at her husband, Molly said, "Though my husband just agreed to this ill-considered journey, we would expect adequate compensation for a trip to the outer boundary of the *British Empire*, and what with the threat of capture and death that would be hovering over us daily—triple the amount of passage is about right, isn't it, husband?"

Jean-Luc's eyes widened, and he thought he needed to quiet Molly before she offended the French king's emissaries. Belfort at first made no expression. Clearly, everything he had heard about this woman was true! He finally said with a smile, "I think her price is perfectly reasonable. What do you think, Geoff?"

Charnay said dryly, "I agree, Rici. After all, the *four* of us will be hanged if caught by the *British* Royal Navy." That was Charnay's riposte to Molly's poke concerning their enemy's empire.

Molly said, "Major Marc will not still possess the map."

Jean-Luc considered her idea and mused, "Yes, he would have given it to General de Levis. This happened thirteen years ago. Who knows?"

Belfort said, "Regardless, we will interview Major Rochebeaucourt when we dock in Montréal."

◄—◆—►

MIAMI INDIAN TERRITORY

A skilled hunter and venerated warrior (though past his physical prime), Lone Eagle sat among the other Miami tribal elders. His group encircled a fire that illuminated the inside of the council lodge where the sachem had just completed a give-and-take conference on the threats and challenges facing their tribe. However, he was dreading the next topic—the Spring Tenderfoot Hunt. Beside Lone Eagle sat his close friend and fellow warrior, Hopping Bird.

The sachem said, "In three nights, the Miami peoples will send our sons beyond our boundaries on the annual young warriors' hunt. Since birth, these fifteen boys have been told by their mothers, aunts, and women of the tribe that they would be the tribe's future warriors, providers, and village elders. Much practice they have done for this first trek through enemy lands. The time to send them on this series of trials has arrived."

Lone Eagle glanced at Hopping Bird to see whether his friend felt the same reservations; he sensed his mouth going dry at the expected pronouncement from his sachem. Though the fifteen male teenagers came from respected families, Lone Eagle knew several of them to be rash in judgment, making any foray with them into another tribe's territory precarious. Unless a great change took place in some of these young men's hearts, these few hotheads represented a spear pointed at the heart of his Miami tribe.

The sachem continued, "The village shaman cast his enchanted stones, and as he read them, they indicated to him that Lone Eagle and Hopping Bird should lead our youth on this quest."

Knowing that the other elders had eyes on them, the two named adults did not grimace at the pronouncement (though they lacked enthusiasm for the assignment). The tribal elders nodded stoically at the appointments to show their approval. When the meeting concluded, Lone Eagle and Hopping Bird approached the sachem, and shaman by his side, to officially ask for the Great Spirit to watch over the boys and their adult leaders. They bowed their heads as the shaman stretched out his arms toward the sky and said "We pray to you, O Great Spirit, for success, and for the safe return of the seventeen Miami. We beseech your approval and guidance for our young warriors in their trials, and that they may return to a peaceful, secure village."

CHAPTER FOUR

MOLLY BUSIED HERSELF with preparations for departure. Nancy, her eight-year-old daughter, followed her about the house, assisting where she could by getting items from the chest of drawers as directed. Molly and Nancy packed Jean-Luc's clothes, the boys' garments, and their own. They then walked briskly to the warehouse to coordinate and supervise the loading of victuals and fresh water for the voyage to Montréal.

On board the *Marie*, Henry Charles kept Jean-Luc's boys close to his side. Henry worked Peter (6 years old) and Rafael (4 years old) to their capacities. Regardless that their father was the captain, Henry spoke to and employed the boys as he would little adults. Having been in this position before, the boys dutifully obeyed Henry.

Jean-Luc pointed up the wharf and said, "Henry, our passengers have arrived. After you show them their quarters, have Peter and Rafe show them where to stow their gear."

First Mate Henry Charles touched his cap with his forefinger to signal his understanding of his orders. He observed that his captain had loaded an impressive arsenal—enough to fight a small war. After all, he had helped load a dozen muskets, several swivel guns, and a half dozen small kegs of gunpowder. All in addition to the pistols stored near the captain's bunk and the four 4-pounders the ship always carried. The blond seaman asked, "Cap'n, pardon me for inquiring, but are you expecting trouble?"

Jean-Luc replied, "Simply being prepared. Why?"

"Thar' be enough gunpowder to send Neptune to hell twice over, and your children are aboard. Seems to me way o' thinking it be out of the ordinary."

"Jean-Luc smiled and said, "Regardless whether my family is aboard, we must be ready to defend ourselves, if the need arises. Besides, this voyage may have two destinations. That is why we are towing the *Kissing Rock*."

"Oh? I know of Montréal. Where be the second stop, Cap'n?"

"All I can tell you is that we may sail as far as the Niagara River together, but at that point, you will remain with the ship, and I will take the little boat from there." He placed his hand on Henry's shoulder and said, "I am counting on you to drum up small cargo runs to keep the crew busy, the *Marie* shipshape, and everyone out of trouble."

Henry looked puzzled and was a bit troubled by this, but said, "Aye, aye, Cap'n." Wishing to scratch an itch he had had for months, he asked, "Why did you name that old sloop, *Kissing Rock*? Seems *Flotsam* would be more appropriate."

Jean-Luc laughed at Henry's joke, and answered, "My wife named her. It is a flat rock that is special to both of us."

When Molly appeared from below deck, the pair changed the subject. She announced, "We have stored the rations, beer, wine, and fresh water. The barrels and other cargo are chocked and secure."

Jean-Luc placed his arm around her shoulder and squeezed. Preparing to go to sea was one of his greatest joys. Molly could see that he had gotten lost in his preparations, in part to take his mind off worrying about his father's health.

Jean-Luc said, "I forgot to mention, I picked up a present for Opie." Referring to his childhood best friend, an Ottawa warrior named Opechwan. As boys, Opechwan and Jean-Luc lived near each other and were inseparable companions. Jean-Luc smiled, remembering his many adventures with his Indian friend. "If there is any opportunity to see him, I want to be prepared. And I found something I know he can use and will enjoy."

"What is it?" asked Molly.

"I bought two dozen arrows imported from England. They are of the highest standard and were made for competitive archery. I am certain he will like them. They are highly accurate."

"I didn't know we were going to see Opechwan," said Molly skeptically.

"The Ottawas will be somewhere west of Montreal, and if we do go to Fort Detroit, we are sure to sail somewhere near his location. Since he was my best man in our wedding, I am simply being prepared. Twelve of the arrows have white fletching, and the rest have scarlet. I wanted to present him with a gift both beautiful and practical."

"But, darling, you don't even know whether you will have time for him this journey," said Molly.

"One never knows," said Jean-Luc grinning. "If we see him, I want to have a nice present."

Molly placed her head on his shoulder and snuggled. She worried about her father-in-law's illness, and she feared these powerful Frenchmen whom Jean-Luc felt obliged to succor. But most of all, she dreaded a destination far too close to Indians for her liking. Having briefly experienced Indian captivity in '59, she knew they enjoyed abducting colonial women and children. Molly shuddered at the trepidation brought about by the memory, and yet her husband's ebullience at returning to his Montréal home was contagious. And even Molly had to admit she would enjoy seeing Opechwan.

Henry Charles approached and said, "Cap'n, the ship is ready. Shall we cast off?"

Jean-Luc walked to the quarterdeck gunnel and peered over at the sloop, *Kissing Rock,* and its sturdy tow rope. Noting that the winds and tide were to his liking he said, "Yes, Mr. Charles, cast off."

Molly came around and took Jean-Luc's arm and placed it on her shoulder. As the two vessels floated away from the Manhattan dock, little Rafe came leaping up the steps and asked, "Father, may I give the command?"

Jean-Luc looked at Molly. She nodded and smiled at her youngest child for his zeal. Jean-Luc stooped, placed Rafe on his shoulders, and said, "The crew's waiting on you."

Rafe looked up at the crew standing on the footropes aloft and then over at Henry by the helm. Just as his nerves were setting in, the little boy cupped his hands to his mouth and shouted, "Make sail!"

The sailors aloft roared with merriment. Always happy to get a trip started with a laugh, Jean-Luc steered the *Marie* for the open water. With fair winds abeam and New York's rising tide swelling beneath their keel, the St. Alembert family gathered on the quarterdeck for what Molly referred to as a "tous ensemble." Thus, the St. Alemberts joyously began their voyage to Montréal. Not realizing that their future held sacrifice, new challenges, friendships, and terrifying dangers, Molly and Jean-Luc set sail intending to grant his dying father's request that his son come home.

CHAPTER FIVE

MOLLY AND EIGHT-YEAR-OLD Nancy bustled around the galley helping the ship's cook, Cuillerée, prepare the evening meal for the crew and passengers. Bright-eyed Nancy asked Cuillerée, a strongly-built forty-year old biracial sailor from Jamaica, "Does getting a tattoo hurt?"

Shocked that her daughter had asked him such a personal question, Molly started to scold Nancy. In truth, Molly had always wanted to inquire into the seagoing tradition of tattoos.

Unoffended by the personal nature of the question, Cuillerée laughed at her curiosity. He said in a fib, "They did not hurt much."

Nancy asked, "They? You have H O L D F A S T on your knuckles? You have more tattoos?"

Cuillerée answered, "Aye, wee one. Thar be Neptune holding a shellback between me shoulder blades. You knows what a shellback be, don't ye?" Nancy shook her head. "Why it be a bulky turtle, that's what."

Nancy put her hands on her cheeks and blurted out, "May I see it?"

At that point Molly interjected, "Nancy, no. You have gone too far."

Blushing, Nancy looked down and said, "Yes, ma'am."

To extricate the girl from her mother's censure, Cuillerée said, "I got these letters when I war' a topman. A reminder they be to hold tight the ship's lines. They have served me well my years aloft. I got Neptune and the shellback tattooed after I crossed the Equator. Of course, that be before I came into the employ of my current captain. Tattoos are tradition to them that makes a life of the sea."

Molly watched Nancy soak up this information which in truth, she also found new and fascinating. However, she said, "Nancy, tell your father and our passengers that dinner will be in fifteen minutes." Molly waited several moments for Nancy to exit the galley. She turned to Cuillerée and asked, "Does a teardrop tattoo under the eye have meaning?"

Cuillerée stopped stirring the porridge. He looked her in the eyes and said slowly, "It indicates a killer, ma'am. Seen someone with that tattoo has the Cap'n's missus?"

Molly said, "I have."

"It can mean more than jes' killing, ma'am. Often times it says the killer is in an organization with illicit purposes."

Molly said, "I will keep that in mind. Thank you, Cuillerée."

Later, as the guests filed into the Captain's Quarters, Charnay and Belfort took the two end seats at the table.

The middle child, Peter, said in protest, "My Ma and Pa sit in those chairs."

Jean-Luc quickly said in deference to the paladins, "Peter, they are our guests and are welcome to sit there."

Charnay, who realized that overseas missions could be jeopardized by such mistakes, said, "You are correct, Peter. Thank you for setting us straight." After a nod of his head to Belfort, the paladins changed chairs.

As Molly and Nancy plated the food for their guests, Molly said, "Children, go outside and see if Mr. Charles needs you for anything. I will feed you after the adults are finished."

In unison, they said, "Yes 'm."

After the door had closed, Belfort asked, "Encountering the savages of North America is something I am looking forward to this trip. Are we likely to come in contact with them?"

Jean-Luc looked at his wife to gauge her reaction to the query; he then said, "It would not be possible to avoid them after we have passed Montréal."

Belfort said, "Excellent. I wish to gain first-hand knowledge of this 'noble savage' I have read about."

Molly asked, "Did you just refer to them as *noble*? What sentimental codswallop."

Horrified, Jean-Luc said, "Molly!" He turned to the young paladin and said, "Please excuse my wife. She does not intend offense."

Belfort waved off Jean-Luc's objection and said, "I wish to hear her views." He turned to Molly with curiosity, "Have you had experiences with the savage in the wilderness? You do not like them?"

"Not like?" repeated Molly. She looked out the porthole reflecting on her answer. "It is true I will cross the street to avoid one." Molly then said, "Now take my Mama and Papa for instance; they loathe Indians."

Jean-Luc rolled his eyes, but Belfort was hungry for information. He had sincerely been looking forward to meeting the noble savage he had heard about in the halls of Palais de Versailles. Indeed, France's leading philosophers Rousseau and Voltaire had written extensively about morality and man living in nature versus in civilization.

Belfort asked, "Why does your father loathe the savage?"

"Fourteen years ago, the Huron killed my baby brother and captured my mother. Her captivity separated our family for more than four months. During that period, I, too, was a captive of two Micmac Indians—though only for a few hours. While neither my mother nor I experienced rape, which is the customary fate of women in Indian captivity, our experiences were certainly unpleasant enough."

Belfort said, "These savages live in the forest and in a state of nature, do they not? A philosopher would argue that they know neither good nor evil. Therefore, the Indian is ignorant of vice, if you will." Molly listened with her hands together under her chin in a sign of attentiveness. Belfort said, "To me, the Indian is amoral for that reason."

Jean-Luc said as he stirred his porridge, "An interesting view."

Molly couldn't accept the soppiness of the philosopher's unrealistic argument. She said, "Rape is only the beginning for a captive. My folks' reason for loathing the Indian encompasses their fiendish delight in torturing prisoners."

Defending the Indian, Jean-Luc said, "But, darling, civilized man at times tortures to obtain a confession or some other information."

Molly retorted, "An Indian tortures his victim for the delight in seeing a helpless enemy suffer hellish agonies. Extracting information is not their motive."

Charnay queried, "Would you agree that the English and French settlers corrupted the Indian with trade goods?"

"From what I have observed," said Jean-Luc, "trade goods such as steel knives and axes have made the Indian's life much easier."

Belfort said, "All right, I grant you that point, Jean-Luc, but Rousseau would say that inequality in the societies are the result of the Indian now wanting the trade goods, but unable to produce them himself. Rousseau believes that once the dynamic of accumulation begins, the Indian must follow or be conquered."

Molly said, "Listen carefully to what I'm saying; the Indian's tribe discourages any display of compassion. Philosophy has little place in the forest when one is tied to a stake to be tortured for the savages' amusement."

Belfort said, "Again, I concede that your argument is convincing. And yet, I must point out that the 'civilized' Europeans have burned a great many heretics at the stake—a painful death by fire either way, no?"

"You are missing my meaning," said Molly. "They burned religious heretics in an erroneous effort to save their souls by purification. The fire was laid in such a way that smoke inhalation killed the victim, and not from the burning of their flesh."

Charnay said with a twinkle in his eye, "It would seem you are losing this debate, Rici."

In irritation, Belfort said, "Either way, it's a horrible death, as I see it."

Molly said, "That is disingenuous. When an Indian tortures, he not only does *not* want you to die quickly, but he will intentionally stretch out the hellishness of your last day on earth for his pleasure. Death ends their amusement and robs them of their theatre." Molly angrily poked at her food and started to take a bite. She stopped, pointed her fork at Belfort, and said, "You will come into contact with Indians on this trip. Do not get separated from us and do not allow yourself to be captured."

Charnay said, "Well, this discussion has been enlightening, has it not, Rici?"

"Most enlightening, Geoff. I would not imagine that Monsieur Rousseau has ever been tied to an Indian's stake."

Charnay said, "Or debated an experienced colonial such as Madame St. Alembert!"

Belfort said, "I could conclude that it is all philosophical drivel. However, I will be attentive to the savage's behavior and keep an open mind on their nobility." Belfort took a sip of wine, held the glass up to the light in a reflective posture, and asked, "And what is your experience with the Indian, Jean-Luc? Surely growing up in Montréal has afforded ample opportunity to interact with them."

Jean-Luc glanced at Molly and saw that she was focused on his answer. He said, "Well, Excellency, it is true that my experiences are more positive in that regard than my wife's. My childhood companion was an Ottawa boy. At that time, they lodged near Montréal, and I have spent hours in the Ottawa village and he in my home."

"Interesting," said Belfort. "Where is your friend now?"

"I do not know. His older brother was the chieftain, Pontiac, who led an Indian coalition on the warpath against the English colonists. Whether or not Opechwan took to the warpath in support of him, I do not know. But if the opportunity arises for me to see him on this journey, I will jump at it."

"What memories of this Indian's friendship do you recall fondly," asked Charnay.

"Opechwan knew when I would complete my chores. Since he did not have what we regard as chores, he usually came by in the late afternoon." Jean-Luc glanced at Molly to gauge her reaction. "We did what little boys do—we raced each other, we carved objects of amusement with our knives, and we talked. I remember we used to talk and talk."

Now her interest was piqued, and Molly asked, "What did you talk about?"

"He had questions of me and I had questions of him. We spoke of my Christian God and he spoke of his Manitou. We spoke of the future. I had the impression he was overhearing adults in his village discuss these issues."

Molly had met Opechwan and liked him. She added, "Opechwan stood by your side at our wedding. He has been a good friend. I have this wonderful memory of the two of you walking down the road after we escaped from your uncle. You had just promised to come for me after the war. The memory still makes me smile."

Belfort asked, "Your uncle held you and Molly captive? Why?"

Charnay interjected, "His uncle is the scoundrel, François Bigot —the former Intendant of New France."

Jean-Luc said, "It was not just the three of us, but also Molly's parents and his Excellency, Captain d'Alquier. Uncle François planned to execute all of us. Molly came up with this crazy idea that involved a wedding with Captain d'Alquier officiating." Jean-Luc and Molly started laughing.

Molly said, "Well, he was a captain in the navy. Of course, it was a stall for time. We were still too young to marry."

At the mention of Captain d'Alquier, the paladins looked at one another. Belfort asked, "But why did your uncle intend to kill you?"

"Captain d'Alquier was investigating my uncle's embezzlement. I, too, had become aware of the scope of my uncle's graft and had refused his invitation to join his illegal activities."

Charnay quickly added, "I spent six months in Switzerland negotiating the extradition of Bigot to France to stand trial."

Belfort asked, "Just out of curiosity, how did Captain d'Alquier die?"

Molly, collecting the dirty plates, stopped and said, "Some English sailors from my ship were trying to find me and approached the house where his uncle was holding us."

Jean-Luc, warming to the story, jumped in and said, "Captain d'Alquier had just married Molly and me in a faux ceremony."

Molly said, "When my shipmates approached, panic erupted in Bigot's henchmen. Captain d'Alquier killed one of them with the man's own pistol. Then he and Intendant Bigot attempted to escape English capture. There was a shootout with the sailors, and d'Alquier was killed. Bigot managed to mount a horse and ride off before my shipmates could stop him."

An animated Belfort looked at Charnay and said, "Geoff, do you realize what this means? This information must be transmitted to His Majesty."

His remark meant nothing to the St. Alemberts, but Charnay did feel buoyed and nodded.

Molly and Jean-Luc walked out the door and down the companionway to the galley. Molly stopped and said, "Dear, the messenger that came to our door, do you remember his tattoo?"

Jean-Luc nodded and said, "Yes, he had a teardrop under his eye. Why?"

"The more I think about him, the less confident I am about his news concerning your father. Cuillerée says that the teardrop means that he has killed someone."

Jean-Luc said, "I did not trust that man, but we have not been to father's in ages, and we should visit him anyway. And we did agree to transport our passengers to Fort Detroit."

CHAPTER SIX

A S THE SHIP neared the wharf at Montréal, Nancy, Peter, and Rafe scampered to the foredeck. Molly ran after them, because they could distract their father at the ship's helm. Knowing that Jean-Luc would be preoccupied with the docking, Molly rounded up the children as the crew prepared to secure the ship. She wanted to debark the moment the gangplank lowered. Molly had spent many evenings during the trip getting the children excited about seeing their grandfather and preparing them for his serious illness. Their two passengers joined them and chatted amiably with her and the youngsters.

Jean-Luc, who had grown increasingly agitated after the vessel passed Quebec, called down to Molly, "I will join you shortly. I want to have a word with Henry." Turning to his second-in-command, he said, "Depending on my father's condition, we could berth in Montréal for two days or up to a week. Bring the sloop alongside and secure it. Tomorrow, begin transferring supplies to the sloop so that we can sail at a moment's notice."

Henry said, "Aye, captain. Consider it done."

Jean-Luc smiled grimly and patted him on the shoulder. He knew that he could rely on Henry. Jean-Luc handed Henry a piece of paper and said, "This has my parents' address. Should you need me, I can be reached there."

"Don't you worry none, skipper. Your family needs you. We'll get her ship shape."

Jean-Luc led his group ashore. With the two French aristocrats by his side, he moved with purpose up rue Saint-Sulpice. Molly and the children walked behind the three men. Jean-Luc's concern for his father's condition placed him in a solemn state of mind. When they passed a squad of redcoats marching in the other direction, all conversation stopped.

Only two blocks from the quay, they passed the striking gray stone Notre Dame Basilica on their left. As they turned left on rue Notre Dame, Molly pointed out to Nancy and her brothers the church where she and Jean-Luc were married.

Little Peter gazed at the three statues over the arches and asked, "Who are they, Mama?"

Molly smiled at his curiosity and said, "The one on the left is Mary, the mother of our savior. St. John the Baptist is in the middle. To the right is Mary's husband, Joseph." Squeezing his shoulder, she said, "That was an excellent question." Addressing all her children, Molly said, "Montréal was founded in 1642 by French missionaries led by Paul de Chomedey. It was originally named *Ville-Marie* in honor of our savior's mother."

Jean-Luc exchanged a knowing glance with his wife. For the benefit of the paladins, Jean-Luc pointed out the *Place d'Armes* on their right. It was his former drill field, and it was where he and the remnants of General de Levis' army surrendered Montréal and the northern half of New France (Canada) to the British. Remembering the pomp of fifes and drums and billowing flags arrayed over the cobblestones, he shook his head at the sad memory and gut-wrenching humiliation he felt that day. All three men became somber at this reminder of France's defeat thirteen years earlier.

Arriving at his father's door, Jean-Luc rapped three times. The elder St. Alembert answered the door and, upon seeing his son and son's family, smiled and exclaimed, "Jean-Luc? What a wonderful surprise!"

Jean-Luc's and Molly's jaws dropped. Jean-Luc stammered, "Father, I was told that you were ill!" The three grandchildren hugged their "Papa," and he hugged and embraced them in a huddle fashion. Then he stood and shook his son's hand with enthusiasm and then hugged Molly firmly.

Molly waited for the commotion to die down, and for the right moment, and then said, "Papa, we received a letter saying that you were gravely ill. The bearer said you sent him."

Purely overjoyed at the unexpected appearance of his son, daughter-in-law, and grandchildren, Sieur St. Alembert ignored the ominous implication and said cheerfully, "As you can see, I am quite well. Come in, come in. We will sort it out."

Nancy and her two younger brothers bounded through the front door. Laughing at their youthful exuberance, Sieur St. Alembert turned back to the adults. He offered his hand to the men accompanying Jean-Luc and said, "My name is Rafael St. Alembert. Welcome to my home."

After the paladins were introduced as French business associates, Rafael invited everyone inside where the cozy house had two fireplaces burning. The senior St. Alembert ensured that the accompanying voyagers felt his gracious hospitality and that they could relieve their fatigue with food and drink.

Two doors down, Rafael's neighbor felt less than thrilled that Jean-Luc had returned. That neighbor was Jean-Luc's former cavalry officer, Marc Rochebeaucourt. The forty-year-old had, by chance, been looking out his window just as the St. Alembert group passed. Stunned by the sudden appearance of his former neighbor and subordinate, his mind raced back to that night in '60 when he had ordered four men on a secret mission deep into the lake region to prevent the enemy army from capturing the fort's pay chests. Starting in '63, Rochebeaucourt had begun making regular trips to the Île aux Cochons to pilfer money out of the pay chests.

Rochebeaucourt felt compelled to take the money from the buried chests to cover his wife's spending habit. That wife, Gabrielle Langlois Rochebeaucourt, was sitting impatiently across the room from the window fidgeting in anticipation of their discussion (actually marital spat is more accurate) to continue.

"Please stop tapping your foot," snapped Marc Rochebeaucourt as he allowed the drapes to fall from his fingers. He refrained from mentioning the St. Alemberts' arrival because he knew that the presence of Jean-Luc in Montréal would send his wife running to the St. Alembert house to welcome her former boyfriend home.

"You seemed to have blacked out or something, dear. Why did you stop in mid-sentence?" asked Gabrielle. "Did you see a ghost?"

Rochebeaucourt said, "Gaby, your bills have *again* reached the point where I can no longer manage them. We will now have to sell something to cover your latest wasteful purchases."

"Marc, you knew when you married me that I like nice clothes. Would you rather that I dress like a scullery maid?"

"Of course, not, but you continue to purchase new clothes and have not even worn the ones you brought home last week."

"Dear, if you want me to look like a plow horse, just say so. If you want me to look like a thoroughbred, then I must do what I must do. I do not understand your hysterics. In the past, you went away, earned the money, and returned to make everything right with the merchants."

"Gabrielle, you must understand, that is no longer possible. The funds I once used—are depleted. Besides, the trips into the interior are always difficult and dangerous. And each time I have returned, I have been met with a mountain of new unpaid invoices. You cannot go on spending money like this. We simply no longer have it."

Gabrielle began to sob. Spoiled as a child, she had grown up to be a spoiled, childish woman. Not a natural beauty, Gabrielle felt that she must deck herself out in the latest fashions to attract the attention that she so desperately craved. The possibility that she could no longer buy the pretty dresses and millinery that drew appreciative glances from men and the envious glares of women filled her with genuine sadness.

She said, "You know that I tend to spend when you are away. Please do not leave me alone in this house."

"I do not know. I need time to think. Right now, I must travel to my lumber mill."

"What are you going to do? When are you leaving?"

"Within the half-hour, Gabrielle."

"What? I was not aware of this trip."

"I must look over the property and determine how I can satisfy our debts. This, I must do at the saw mill."

"But that means you will be gone for a week or more," said Gabrielle teary-eyed.

"Yes, I suppose it does," said her unsympathetic husband. "With our income from out west consumed, I must decide where the money is coming from to pay for your latest purchases. This time you have gone too far. I must pack and leave right away."

"Do not leave me alone in this house, Marc. It is when you are gone that I am lonesome and become depressed. It is then the spending urges *begin*."

Marc shook his head sadly and said, "We cannot have it both ways, Gaby. Either I go to the saw mill, or we fail to pay the invoices. The trip is difficult enough. I cannot stay, and you cannot accompany me. I do not know what to say to you. We cannot afford the luxury of me keeping you company. And I must go right away." Fifteen minutes later, Rochebeaucourt pulled the door behind him, walked to the stable, and nervously looked over his shoulder again and again as he cinched the straps of his saddle. With a final glance to ensure that no one was approaching, he spurred the animal into a gallop and rode down a back street to avoid anyone from St. Alembert's house seeing him.

Back in the St. Alembert residence, Rafael stroked his chin as he pondered who could have sent the letter that supposedly came from him. He finally said, "Someone wanted you to sail to Montréal, *or*, they wanted you out of New York."

Molly realized that this was a good time to herd the children upstairs for a rest, to clean up, and to allow the men some time to assess the situation.

Sieur St. Alembert poured four cognacs and then served them to his male guests. Jean-Luc paced slowly around the room, thinking.

Charnay asked his host, "By the way, where does Major Rochebeaucourt live? Jean-Luc mentioned that his old cavalry officer used to live near him."

"That is true; and he still does. Marc has done well with his business interests," said Rafael. Nodding toward Jean-Luc, he said, "Jean-Luc, the Rochebeaucourts will want to see you and your wife."

Belfort said, "And we would like to meet them."

"Of course. First thing in the morning, I will invite them over. But, of course. I must warn you that Gabrielle will become quite animated when she learns that Jean-Luc is in Montréal." Belfort nodded in understanding and shot a knowing glance at Jean-Luc.

The following morning, Sieur St. Alembert knocked on the front door of Marc Rochebeaucourt. Gabrielle answered the door and said, "What a pleasant surprise."

Sieur St. Alembert said, "Gabrielle, my son and his family arrived quite unexpectedly yesterday. Is it possible for you and Marc to come over and say 'hello?'"

Gabrielle looked confused, but then said, "Jean-Luc? He is here?"

"Yes, we would like for you and Marc to come over."

Gabrielle refocused on Rafael and said, "Jean-Luc is here? I will freshen up and come right over." She shut the door in Rafael's face. Realizing that she had closed the door on her elderly neighbor, she quickly reopened it and, "I am so sorry, Monsieur St. Alembert. I will be right over."

Rafael nodded, turned, and walked away. A moment after he walked through his doorway and pulled the door behind himself, he heard someone knocking rapidly. Upon opening the door, Gabrielle was smiling demurely and attempting to mask her breathing from her having run over. He said, "Come in, Gabrielle." He turned and called, "Jean-Luc. Molly. You have a visitor."

Expecting to see his old cavalry commander, Jean-Luc walked into the foyer. Gabrielle squealed with delight and hugged her old flame tightly.

"Gabrielle, I—," said Jean-Luc awkwardly.

"It is *wonderful* to see you, Jean-Luc," said Gabrielle in a flirty voice.

Molly, Belfort, and Charnay walked in next. Molly cautiously said, "Hello, Gabrielle."

"Hello," answered Gabrielle in a muted reaction. She could not bring herself to call Molly by name.

Molly walked to Jean-Luc's side and took his arm.

Now uncomfortably close to her old rival, Gabrielle took a step back. The symbolic retreat exposed her uneasiness in Molly's presence.

Molly said, "Jean-Luc, introduce our guests."

Feeling a bit awkward himself, Jean-Luc said, "Uh, Gabrielle, may I present Monsieur Brown and Monsieur Smith. They are traveling on business."

Impressed with the strangers' deportment, Gabrielle correctly sized them up as men of substance. She curtsied and said, "*Enchanté.*"

Rafael led the group into his parlor. After everyone had taken a seat, a period of requisite chit-chat ensued.

During a pause in the conversation, Charnay said, "Jean-Luc has spoken highly of your husband. We would enjoy meeting him."

Gabrielle said, "Unfortunately, Marc left town yesterday on business. I do not expect him back for several weeks."

"That is too bad," said Belfort.

"Yes, it was sudden, and I, too, was surprised. But the trip is for business and that means profit, and you know how men are. He feels we need more to be successful."

The room fell into an awkward silence. Charnay looked askance at Gabrielle for a moment, but then said, "We wanted to meet Major Rochebeaucourt. Jean-Luc has spoken many times of the major's courage and calm demeanor under fire." The older paladin turned toward his partner and made an expression that suggested Marc's sudden departure had not come as a surprise to him.

Only Jean-Luc observed this silent communique. When he saw Belfort nod in agreement, he thought, "I hope *for Marc's sake* we find those pay chests undisturbed."

The visit continued. Molly eventually excused herself to return to the kitchen for refreshments.

Gabrielle said, "Molly, I will help you, if you would like me to."

As the women entered the kitchen, Molly asked, "Tell me about your children?"

"Sadly, Marc and I have no young ones. My doctor believes the hunger period during the '59 siege affected my ability to bear children." Gabrielle's eyes teared up, and she looked down in obvious embarrassment.

Molly put her arm around Gabrielle's shoulder. "Would you like one of my little monsters?" She held out her handkerchief to her guest.

Gabrielle laughed at the idea, and then blew her nose. "I did not think I would ever like you, Molly, ever since you and your beautiful auburn hair charmed Jean-Luc out of the pool of Montréal's eligible bachelors! But the passage of time has healed the wound. Thank you for making me feel accepted and welcomed in the St. Alemberts' home."

The remainder of Gabrielle's social call went smoothly, even when the children bounded downstairs to meet their parents' visitor. And Molly was thoroughly enjoying Gabrielle's sophistication and engaging personality.

When little Rafe began to tug at his mother's dress, Gabrielle realized that time had gotten away from her. She said, "I must be going. I know that you have preparations to complete since you are sailing tomorrow." She stood and turned to go. At the door Gabrielle said with a mixture of joy and sorrow, "Bon voyage." Gabrielle then gave Molly a heartfelt hug that caused Jean-Luc to smile. She curtsied to the paladins and said, "I will see you when you return, I hope."

Charnay said, "You may rely on it. *Adieu*, Madame."

That evening, Molly, Jean-Luc, and Rafael discussed the pros and cons of leaving the children with their grandfather, because Molly insisted on accompanying Jean-Luc into the Great Lakes' hinterlands. Torn emotionally by the thought of leaving the children with Rafael, she considered the impact on the children of being without their parents for over two months.

Rafael said, "Really, I think Jean-Luc will be fine; but, if you must go, the children will be fine here. I will manage beyond your expectations."

Looking at her husband, Molly said, "From Fort Niagara onward, there would be no one to watch your back."

Rafael said to his son's surprise, "It will be a wonderful opportunity for me to get to know my grandchildren."

Jean-Luc said, "Are you sure, Father? They can be a handful."

Rafael slapped his son on the back and said, "We will have a delightful time together. Do not worry about us."

CHAPTER SEVEN

MARCH 16, MIDAFTERNOON

THE FOLLOWING MORNING, Jean-Luc got his boats on the river
early. The winds did not cooperate, and the Marie was frequently "in irons." Jean-Luc and the crew had their hands full
tacking repeatedly in the disagreeable conditions simply to make modest headway.

Molly stood by herself near the forecastle—an area topside near
the bow. She watched Montréal grow smaller as their ship sailed upriver toward Lake Ontario. Jean-Luc, Henry and the other crew members had seen her standing there before and knew not to disturb her
when she was deep in thought.

With the wind blowing Jean-Luc's dark hair about, Molly said
under her breath, "nobody should be that handsome." Jean-Luc looked
steady and in command; but knowing her man as she did, she could
see that he was struggling to maintain a command presence. Molly
turned back to face upriver and then considered their French passengers. She felt that the older one, Charnay, showed genuine concern for
Jean-Luc by listening to him and allowing him to speak about whatever topic the young husband wished to discuss.

Molly reached down and picked up a belay pin from the rack. She absent-mindedly turned it in her hands as she grimaced at the memory of their meeting with the visitor with the teardrop tattoo. Molly believed that his actions were more than a mean-spirited prank.

Molly slowly returned the belay pin to its rack and turned to face downriver. Her mind shifted to the news that she wanted to break to her husband. For the next five minutes, she allowed herself to enjoy the beautiful scenery of the river foam in the ship's wake. Canada is beautiful, she thought. Yet it also seemed to her equal parts raw beauty and raw danger. Molly turned around and regarded Jean-Luc a moment and wondered what his reaction would be to her news.

She called, "Jean-Luc, dear, may I have a word with you?"

Jean-Luc answered, "*Toute de suite*." He then called to Henry, who was standing on the mainsail's footrope and holding onto its spar, "Henry, I need you to take the helm for a moment." Henry smiled and waved. He slid down the ratlines and was standing beside the skipper seconds later.

Jean-Luc walked over to his wife and asked, "Yes, dear, what is it?"

"I have something to tell you," Molly said. Her husband cocked his head, indicating that his interest was piqued. She took a step in and took his lapels and rubbed them in her fingers. "I'm with child, darling."

Jean-Luc felt exhilarated. His broad grin expressed his positive reaction to the news. But he forced himself to remain composed. Though he felt like shouting for joy; he then grew serious (at least mock earnestness) and asked, "Are you sure?"

Molly rolled her eyes up and to the side playfully. She said, "Aunt Flow didn't visit me in Montréal and—" she held up her arms with her palms open, and continued, "Nothing since. I am *weeks* overdue."

"How long have you known?" he inquired.

"Oh, I began to suspect something a week ago, but with, well, you know, that unpleasantness hanging over our heads, I chose not to say anything to you until now."

"Have you considered names?" asked Jean-Luc smiling.

"Well, if it is a girl, I am partial to Elizabeth."

Unable to contain himself, Jean-Luc said, "Or perhaps Marguerite?"

Molly wrinkled her nose, but forced a smile indicating to her husband that Marguerite wasn't on her short list. "And if it is a boy?" asked Jean-Luc.

"Well, I was thinking of Jean-Luc." Her husband grinned from ear to ear. "But I like John and Luke, also," she added as she rubbed his head good-naturedly. "You have been a wonderful father to our children, and I cannot wait to see you with a new baby."

Jean-Luc said, "This is wonderful news. You have made me very happy." He kissed her on the forehead and walked to the helm with a noticeable spring in his step.

Molly called after him, "It is just between us for now."

Jean-Luc smiled and waved. He resumed the helm from Henry, who immediately scurried up the ratlines and again took his station on the mainsail spar.

Feeling pleased with herself and her husband's reaction, Molly turned around and began humming. It seemed that the foul winds at Montréal were behind them and it would be good sailing from here.

MARCH 16, SOUTHWESTERN BANK OF LAKE ERIE

Lone Eagle looked at the fifteen Miami youth seated on the forest floor before him. His fellow warrior (and childhood friend) Hopping Bird, stood beside him. Lone Eagle slowly moved his eyes over each fifteen-year-old's face in an effort to detect doubt or trepidation. Their hopeful expressions shone with anticipation of a great adventure, but without a full understanding of how dangerous the world was away from the tribe. This is a good sign, he thought.

Lone Eagle said, "Once we begin, we will move through the lands of the Traders ("Ottawa"), People of the Peninsula ("Wyandot"), and Genuine Men ("Lenni Lenape"). We shall move like the Bobcat — we shall walk without noise, with our eyes scanning the forest for danger *and* for opportunities to put an arrow into a bird or animal. We will need fresh sustenance, for the food we bring will not be enough. We shall also move like a snake—without noise—and without tracks. For us to return safely from this hunt, no other tribe can suspect we are on their lands. Should our enemies detect our presence, you will have the opportunity, whether you desire it or not, to earn acceptance into the tribe's Circle of Warriors. Like the snake, we seventeen will move stretched out, when we stop to rest, we curl up, facing outwards, and always ready to fight an enemy."

Lone Eagle paused and looked into the faces of his fifteen neophytes. From childhood, they had heard the terms bobcat and snake. They knew each animal's strengths, and why Lone Eagle wanted those attributes in his hunting party. He continued, "For us to be successful, to return home with our heads held high and with food to share with our village, we need to avoid enemy warriors. Any questions?" With no youth raising his hand, Lone Eagle said, "I have asked Hopping Bird to speak. Give him your ears as you have given them to me."

Hopping Bird stepped in front of the youth and said, "Before we depart the lodges of the Miami, I will inspect your preparations." Having previously instructed the youths to bring certain items in certain amounts, he initiated their first test—attention to detail. "Display your arrows. Separate them by purpose."

The boys knelt. Each laid out exactly 24 arrows in three separate piles: six wooden bunts with rounded ends for injuring (or knocking senseless) birds and small animals, wooden self-points (economical and easily made arrows with tapered ends), and twelve flinted arrowheads. Before moving on, Hopping Bird stood over each boy, and upon inspecting his arrows, nodded to indicate his satisfaction. Hopping Bird returned to the center of the boys' array and said, "Now open your food pouches." The boys unfastened their leather bags, which contained a mixture of corn flour and maple syrup. This food was so nourishing that a mere handful would sustain a warrior for a day. Satisfied that each youngster had the required 25 handfuls that he had been instructed to carry, Hopping Bird nodded to Lone Eagle, though he remained expressionless in the presence of the boys.

Hopping Bird was glad that he would not be required to verbally chastise a student. He then instructed them, "Hold up your water bladders." The boys obeyed once more. Satisfied that they were prepared and had followed their guidance, Hopping Bird said, "You have done well."

Lone Eagle returned to the front and said, "Gather your things." The boys scurried to do as they were told. He then said, "Remember the following hand signals." Lone Eagle and Hopping Bird proceeded to demonstrate the most common gestures that they used on the warpath; the final gesture was a downward-turned palm moved in a circle, to send the group to hiding in the grasses. "We will depart shortly. You eight will follow me," His left hand indicated the boys intended. Then his right hand swept slowly to the right. "You seven will follow Hopping Bird."

Lone Eagle led the neophytes into the forest in single file. Both he and Hopping Bird felt the oppressive burden that their tribal leaders —the elders and the sachem—had placed on them. Initiating this perilous journey, they would be afforded numerous opportunities to observe the tribe's future leaders and defenders. Upon their return, he and Hopping Bird would relate to the tribal council their observations of which of the boys had demonstrated the bravery, character, and wisdom to be a tribal leader one day.

Lone Eagle signaled for the long single file to gather around him. "Tomorrow, we will enter lands claimed by the Wyandot. Today, we hunt and eat, for we will fast tomorrow." He pointed to a youth named, Chava, or in the Miami tongue, Fertile Earth. Lone Eagle said, "Chava, you are to lead this day's hunt."

The fifteen-year-old stepped forward boldly. Lone Eagle held out a blackbird feather that marked the temporary leader. Chava confidently slipped it into his headband.

Hopping Bird said, "Look around. What signs of game do you see?" While Chava underwent this public trial, the others remained dutifully silent.

Chava took his time and scanned the forest trees for clues. His eyes settled on several trees that had small, short, but distinguishable scratches on their trunks. After noticing the same on other nearby trees, he said, "There are chipmunk in this area." Hopping Bird and Lone Eagle exchanged silent glances. Chava said, "Friends, I will gather wild oats from the lakeside, I want you to spread out in a circle and be still. We will use our bunts on the chipmunk. Remember to aim at a chipmunk with a tree trunk behind him so that your arrow will bounce back to you if you are off-target." The boys nodded, and quietly took their positions. Having hunted chipmunks before, they knew just how far back to hide.

Hopping Bird followed Chava to a marshy area near the great lake, Erie. Soon, the young leader found what he was seeking, and plucked a wild oat stem. This he would use to call the chipmunks into the hunting circle.

Hopping Bird asked, "Do you know how to make the call?"

"I am not very proficient at it, but I will try," said Chava.

"Let us save time. I will demonstrate." Hopping Bird split the reed with his knife. After kneading the grass between his fingers until he was satisfied, he gently blew into the strands and made a loud, high-pitched whistle sound. "Now, you do the same with the reed you have, Chava."

With Hopping Bird coaching him, Chava practiced and soon mastered the technique. They returned to the hunting circle. Before taking his spot behind a tree, Hopping Bird scanned the area for the others. Knowing that they were hidden nearby, it was a positive sign that he could not detect any of them.

Chava then blew into the wild oat reed. The resulting sound was as good an animal call as any Hopping Bird could remember. Chava continued to make the sound he learned for luring chipmunks; the hungry Miami youths waited patiently. After several minutes, first one chipmunk showed himself, then several more, then several more, until finally a dozen critters cautiously entered the encircled area. The chipmunks looked about warily and held up their tiny ears to detect the sounds that had drawn them to the clearing.

On Chava's war whoop signal, the young hunters stood and

emitted their own child-like versions of a blood-curdling war cry. Startled, the chipmunks scurried en masse for safety in the trees. With the chipmunks now treed, the boys shot their bunted arrows time and again. When struck by the blunt projectiles, the injured chipmunks fell from the trees and landed at the young hunters' feet.

Sensing their eventual doom if they remained in the trees, the chipmunks scampered down the trunks in hopes of surviving the projectiles by scattering. Chava and his mates responded by wrapping their arms about the tree trunks and blocked the frightened critters' path. The chipmunks retreated up the tree trunks once more. Successfully thwarting their escape attempt, the Indian boys renewed their deadly volleys. As the dead and injured chipmunks fell to the forest floor, it became apparent that the young hunters would eat well this evening.

That night, Chava chewed his food with a new confidence in his abilities. Thinking about his new skill with the oat reed, he knew he could feed himself, a wife, and a papoose. He looked around the campfire and watched his mentors enjoying their chipmunk meal and felt a warm glow within his breast. Chava knew his trial had gone well.

PART II

A Debt Paid

CHAPTER EIGHT

THE *MARIE* WITH its smaller boat, the *Kissing Rock*, in tow approached the point where the great lake, Ontario, drains into the St. Lawrence River. The former French Fort Frontenac, now in British hands, sat on the north bank. It strategically blocked all river traffic between Lake Country and the St. Lawrence and Cataraqui rivers. Built by the French in 1673, the fort was mostly destroyed in 1758 by the English during a siege led by Lieutenant Colonel John Bradstreet. Now, only a small contingent of redcoats kept watch. The armistice had lured them into complacency, and they hadn't even reinforced the garrison's defenses.

The soldiers stopped their chores long enough to watch and wave a greeting to the passing ship, because until the ship reached a certain point and continued on its way, they had hopes it would be a supply ship. Jean-Luc and his crew, though wary of the redcoats, returned in kind the friendly gestures. Profoundly disappointed when they realized that the ship wasn't stopping at their location, the soldiers returned to their chores.

Belfort and Charnay had been chatting privately and strolling the poop deck since breakfast. Without drawing attention to themselves, they noted that the redcoats had a stack of trimmed trees that were clearly set aside for rebuilding the fort's exterior walls. Belfort and Charnay further noted that the fort's interior buildings had been rebuilt and appeared to be in good condition.

Addressing Belfort, Charnay said, "I remember reading war correspondence when Frontenac was lost." He turned to Jean-Luc and asked, "Have our enemies renamed it?"

Jean-Luc said, "Not to my knowledge, but they will. Even in New France, the fort was never considered a first-class facility. Forts Pontchartrain du Detroit and Niagara always dominated the government's priorities. It is a pity actually. As you can see, if it had held out, one avenue to Montréal would have been sealed."

Belfort slapped him on the back and said, "You would make an excellent general."

Jean-Luc smiled sheepishly but then glanced around for his wife, but he did not see her anywhere topside. He assumed that she was in the cabin. With the idea of a new baby occupying his mind, he had barely considered his great fortune that wind was blowing across the ship's course. This beam reach is the ideal point of sail for a fore-and-aft-rigged vessel. Thus, it allowed them to make good progress up the river.

As their ship entered the lake, he changed course, which meant that they were now running before the wind. He knew landlubbers, a Yankee term for a non-seafarer, would think that this would be the ideal point of sail. Yet seasoned sailors knew that it could cause problems for a fore-and-aft-rigged vessel. Spreading the foresail and mainsails out "wing-and wing" (one to starboard, the other to port), allowed the ship to go reasonably fast (but not as fast as a beam reach). However, a slight change in course or a slight change in wind direction would cause the boat to jibe: the boom of the mainsail would swing rapidly to the other side. This could be dangerous for the crew. Jibing can also damage the rigging because the sails are exposed to the full force of the wind during the maneuver. Thus, a bad jibe could damage the rigging. Thus, Jean-Luc now must focus his full attention on the wind and on his compass. Jean-Luc knew that as long as this condition persisted, neither he nor the crew would get a breather. Fortunately, the Marie responded appropriately to its skillful handling and sprinted headlong west by southwest.

The paladins, impressed by the captain's adroitness, returned to the helm. Belfort asked, "Do you not employ charts?"

"Of course," said Jean-Luc, "when I have them. For this voyage, I am relying mostly on memory and seamanship." Belfort looked puzzled. "A seaman can identify shallows by watching how the surface water behaves. If you have sailed long enough, you can navigate the most treacherous waters just by reading the currents, ripples, and eddies." Belfort nodded as though he understood what Jean-Luc meant; but in truth, he was a landsman and really didn't. Charnay observed, listened to Jean-Luc interact with his crew, and then walked away smiling.

Two hours later, Jean-Luc's concern over Molly's behavior drove him to summon Henry to take the wheel. He wanted to ensure that she was not hurt or worse, and her absence all afternoon was troubling him.

Jean-Luc entered the cabin and saw his wife on her knees in the dark scrubbing a spot on the deck, her eyes closed, and her head down. He asked, "Molly?" His wife didn't stir. "Molly, what is wrong?" Again, no response. He rushed to his wife, knelt beside her, and placed his hand gently on her back. He rubbed softly in small circles (the way she liked him to).

Without looking up, Molly murmured, "I lost the baby." She collapsed into his arms.

THE SAME DAY

Lone Eagle signaled his young charges to halt. The boys knew from experience this would be their camp for the evening. Without prompting, they spread out in a large circle and faced outward. Lone Eagle walked among his charges, making minor corrections to their positioning. Hopping Bird had gone ahead, to ensure that there were neither large beasts nor a Wyandot hunting party in the area. As they were still near a piece of land that the Miamis and Wyandots still fought over, he wished for one more night without the stresses of moving through enemy lands.

After a short period, Hopping Bird returned and found Lone Eagle sitting with his back against a tree. He approached him and said, "I detected no enemies."

"Good," said Lone Eagle. "After tonight, we will be especially vigilant. I want the boys to have a hot meal. They worked hard today and should be rewarded."

Lone Eagle supervised the boys as they stripped the flesh from the forest creatures, gutted them, and impaled them with deadfall skewers. He enjoyed the boys' ribbing one another about the numerous hunting mishaps and shot arrows that didn't bounce back as expected. Lone Eagle announced that Miakoda (Moon Power) and Tadewi (Gentle Wind) were the boys responsible for building tonight's fire.

After all of the chipmunks had been eaten, the boys lay against a log. Their stomachs bulged, and a wonderful feeling of self-satisfaction enveloped them. Hopping Bird walked a short distance into the woods and looked in on the sentinel.

Chava asked Lone Eagle, "Would you tell us a hunting story? There is time before sleep comes to us. We would enjoy a story, Lone Eagle."

An excited murmur erupted from the boys, and Lone Eagle could see there was no denying Chava's request. He said, "I have a story from my last hunt. I was alone in the forest west of the river that runs beside our village." The boys sat up and leaned forward anticipating Lone Eagle's exciting account of pursuing forest game. "I had killed a stag and had him hanging from a branch. I drained him and removed his entrails. I set about carving the meat, when— " he looked into each boys' face, "when I heard the leaves rustling. The sounds were coming from two directions. Whatever or whoever they were, they wanted the deer."

"What did you do?" asked Miakoda.

"I hid in the bushes and waited. You can imagine my relief when two raccoons emerged and climbed upon a tree stump under the stag.

They began gnawing on my deer, unaware of my presence. I would have shot them both with my arrows, but I believed that if they had smelled my fresh kill, other beasts had as well. I allowed the raccoons to act as my sentries, and so I allowed them to eat. Soon enough, the raccoons began to squeal when two wolves approached. Now, I *had* to act. I shot an arrow into one wolf, spun about and, before the other could attack, sent an arrow into the second."

Tadewi asked, "Did you eat the wolves?"

Lone Eagle said, "There was no time. As soon as I vanquished them, a Black bear growled loudly and came into the clearing. He had approached my camp when my attention was on the wolves. To my good fortune, he wanted, not me, but the deer, and charged toward it. With one swipe of his paw, he knocked both raccoons off the stump. I shot an arrow into his flank. Then two more arrows as fast as I could draw my bow. The bear limped a short distance to lick his wounds."

Chava said, "You had more food than you could ever eat. It happened all so fast."

Lone Eagle said, "You are correct, Chava. I prayed in thanks to the Great Spirit for surviving those encounters. I returned to my village for help in bringing in the dead bear. The village women celebrated the bounty with a feast in my honor. The Great Spirit looked upon me with favor that day."

Miakoda said with respect, "I want to hunt wolves and bears, too."

Lone Eagle sounded a cautious note, "Never take on more enemies than you can handle, Miakoda. I was fortunate to see my family again. The encounters with the wolves and bear happened. I reacted without thinking. And the raccoons may not be there as sentinels the next time. I owe those raccoons my life."

As darkness enveloped the forest, the happy band of boys slipped into a deep sleep; the fifteen slept a contented sleep that results from a full day of hunting, food preparations, and storytelling.

Tomorrow, Lone Eagle and Hopping Bird would lead the boys into the lands of the Wyandot. That, too, was part of their trial.

CHAPTER NINE

MARCH 17, 7:15 P.M.

JEAN-LUC SAID sympathetically, "Oh, Molly. He continued to rub her back for several moments, and then said, "Here, allow me to help you to a chair."

After a period of silence, Molly said, choking back tears, "I was sitting, and," he continued rubbing her back, "my flow began, and—I knew—I *knew*." Then her anguish overwhelmed her, and she broke down sobbing.

Jean-Luc said in a soothing voice, "We will keep trying." He frowned as he reminded himself, stop trying to fix things—Molly doesn't like it. Her rebuke that would have typically taken place never came. This is a bad signal concluded Jean-Luc. He said, "Let me help you into a chair." Molly didn't resist and slowly responded to his assistance, and sat down without looking up or speaking. "I'll tell Cuillerée to not expect you in the galley tonight." Again, Molly didn't respond.

As Jean-Luc shut the cabin door behind him, Belfort noticed his expression and asked, "Is something wrong, Jean-Luc?"

"I am afraid that my wife is ill, Excellency. If you will excuse me, I must provide instructions to my men in the galley." Belfort nodded, and Jean-Luc scurried below to speak to the cooks.

Charnay approached and asked Belfort, "Is something the matter?"

"Actually, yes, but we must bide our time in learning the details. It has to do with the wife."

That night as Jean-Luc, Belfort, and Charnay ate their evening repast, there was little conversation (and no questions were asked concerning Molly's absence from the table), that is, until Jean-Luc said abruptly, "There may be a slight change in plans."

"Oh?" asked Charnay. He successfully masked a touch of unease.

"My wife is unwell and requires a physician. I am going to put in at Fort Niagara."

Belfort said, "Both Geoff and myself are schooled in medicine. Perhaps we can help?"

Shaking his head, Jean-Luc said, "I do not think Molly would want that. But if you are concerned about the delay, please be assured that we will not linger at the fort a moment longer than necessary. I am not anticipating a lengthy stopover."

There was a knock at the cabin door. Jean-Luc stood and walked over to answer it. Upon opening it, a sailor said, "Skipper, Henry wants you to know that we will be near Fort Niagara in the morning." Jean-Luc nodded and shut the door.

The following morning went routinely, but Jean-Luc instructed Henry to guide the *Marie* to a position a half mile north northwest from Fort Niagara. This positioned the ship outside of, but near, the Niagara River's channel.

When Jean-Luc went to his cabin to check on Molly, she asked, "Why have you anchored, husband?"

"We are going into Fort Niagara to see the doctor."

After a moment, she said, "I don't want a doctor."

"I am taking you to the fort, and that is final."

"But there is nothing the matter with me. Doctors just put leeches on you and make you feel worse." Knowing that her husband had decided the matter, Molly ceased protesting.

Twenty minutes later, Molly and Jean-Luc, the paladins, and four crewmembers sat in the *Marie*'s skiff. The crew lowered them carefully into the water with the davit. No sooner were they unhooked than the four crewmen began a smooth, cadenced rowing. The skipper's lady was ill, and this concerned everyone aboard. Henry noted that the early spring winds had produced whitecaps. He hated that the choppy waters would make his skipper's short trip to the doctor unpleasant.

Looming like a gray block of civilization in a world of dark green and brown natural beauty Fort Niagara loomed in the distance. Under the gloomy sky, the stone walls appeared intimidating, uninviting, and impenetrable from an attack from the water (or from any other direction for that matter). On the land side, these same stone walls had three separate, spaced, defensive stone walls protecting the fort from a land attack. Any hostile force that penetrated the fort's defensive system of three stone walls would be rewarded with cannon firing hellish grapeshot. The defenders knew very well that Native Americans did not conduct frontal assaults, and the fort provided excellent protection for its inhabitants and control of the river.

Belfort asked, "Jean-Luc, is this fort another example of one France built but is now controlled by England?"

Jean-Luc nodded solemnly. Belfort began to appreciate how personally the French Canadians had taken the fall of New France. He continued holding his wife close to him, and his expression reflected his concern.

Charnay studied Madame St. Alembert. Her eyes were dark circles, her face expressed sadness, and her shoulders were slumped. He said sympathetically, "It will not be long." Molly nodded feebly.

As the skiff struck the land below the escarpment that elevated the fort from the lake, the men helped Molly from the vessel. Though she tried to walk on her own, she did so only with great difficulty. The steep dirt road made her husband's assistance necessary. The road led to the wooden walkway — *La Porte des Cinq Nations* (the Gate of Five Nations), so named by the French to honor their allies, the Iroquois Confederacy. The wooden walkway led to the main stone portal of Fort Niagara.

The guards admitted the visitors after Charnay explained in his excellent English that they needed to see the doctor. Jean-Luc had asked Charnay to do the speaking, since his own French accent was still quite thick.

The first English officer to notice the visitors walked over and said, "Welcome to Fort Schlosser. May I be of assistance?"

Charnay said, "This lady needs a doctor."

The officer asked, "Are you settlers?"

"No, we are merchants with goods for trade."

That answer satisfied the officer, who then said, "Unfortunately, our physician is away for another week." He pointed down the street and said, "His assistant is in and might be able to help, depending on the problem."

"Thank you," said Charnay in his faux Cornwall accent. The officer walked away.

At that moment, an Indian woman hailed Jean-Luc from across the parade ground and came running over. At first, Jean-Luc looked confused. He was unsure of who she was. He could see the Ottawa totem inked into her skin, but now he believed he *should* know her name and felt embarrassed.

"Do you not remember me, Jean-Luc?" The young woman spoke French and looked coyly disappointed. Before Molly's husband could answer, the flirtatious Ottawa said, "I am—"

Jean-Luc answered in French, "Star Dancer! I did not recognize you at first." The Indian girl whose village he had visited frequently years before had matured into a stunning woman. And it quickly became clear that this woman, who once had a girlish crush on Opechwan's friend, still had powerful feelings for Jean-Luc.

"*Oui! C'est moi!*" She moved forward to give her old friend a flirtatious nose to nose greeting.

Jean-Luc glanced nervously in Molly's direction to gauge her reaction. Had he eyes in the back of his head, he would have seen Belfort and Charnay stifling snickers. Noting that Molly was not reacting to

Star Dancer's romantic signals made him realize just how out of sorts Molly was feeling. Under normal circumstances Molly would have punched out this vixen for coming on to her husband.

To dissuade further flirting from the comely Indian, Jean-Luc quickly said, "Star Dancer, I would like you to meet my wife, Molly." The Ottawa maiden did not even look at Molly, and Molly remained impassive. Jean-Luc quickly changed the subject and asked, "Why are you so far from Montréal?"

"My tribe moved west 12 years ago when the hunting became scarce and," she lowered her voice to a whisper, "our tribal friend moved to New York." Star Dancer then asked, "What is wrong with this woman?"

"We came to this fort hoping to find a doctor," said Jean-Luc, avoiding the inappropriate query. Out of the corner of his eye, he saw that the two Frenchmen were quite entertained by his situation.

Jean-Luc asked, "Where is your village now, Star Dancer?"

"My people returned to the lands beside the river, Maumee, where we dwelled before our move to Montréal."

"Then you are still far from home," said Jean-Luc.

"Yes. I accompanied our shaman, Noshi, He and I seek his needed herbs, and when we have obtained them, we will return to our village." Star Dancer then asked, "You also are far from home. Why?"

"Yes, Manhattan. That is my home now."

"Oh, I thought you had come for the wedding."

Jean-Luc shook his head and asked, "What wedding?"

"Opechwan's wedding—I just *knew* you would come."

Jean-Luc asked enthusiastically, "When is the ceremony?"

Star Dancer said, "It is in twenty-one moons. Noshi and I must conduct our business quickly and begin our return trip." She looked at Molly and could see Jean-Luc's woman was not well, and if Jean-Luc's woman was indisposed, she figured to have some time alone with Jean-Luc. Star Dancer said, "Noshi can cure your wife. I am certain of it."

"Do you think so?" asked Jean-Luc.

Star Dancer nodded enthusiastically and said, "I will take you to his lodge. It is outside the fort's outer wall."

When Molly and her entourage arrived at Noshi's teepee, Star Dancer motioned for everyone to remain outside; she then entered through the flap. Fasting and meditating, Noshi looked up, though he didn't break his silence.

Star Dancer said, "Noshi, I encountered an old friend." He did not react. "It is *the* friend of our sachem, Opechwan." Noshi's eyes widened a fraction, but that was enough for Star Dancer to know her words had made an impression on him.

The medicine man slowly began to stand, but was having difficulty due to the amount of time spent sitting. Star Dancer quickly lent a hand to help her older companion to stand (though he needed the aid of his rod). Noshi limped outside and walked up to Molly. He glanced at Jean-Luc; and though his expression revealed nothing, he was stunned by the changes brought by aging thirteen years. He greeted Jean-Luc with a simple open palm, but thereafter returned his attention to Molly.

Charnay tapped his colleague on the shoulder and they discreetly backed away, giving the couple their privacy. Star Dancer did not need to hear either, and she also stepped away respectfully (besides, she knew Jean-Luc's woman would remain with Noshi).

Molly had been listless all day, but now she began to inch closer to her husband as she realized that she had been brought to an Indian shaman. Noshi stepped forward and studied Molly up and down, but he focused mainly on her eyes. Molly did not understand or like this examination. Indians of any tribe made her uncomfortable ever since Huron raiders had murdered her baby brother, kidnapped her mother, and burned their Mohawk River cabin. And stories that well-meaning neighbors had told of Indian atrocities had added to her distrust of the red man. Noshi motioned for Molly to enter his teepee.

Jean-Luc said, "I will not be far away, dear."

Molly reluctantly let go of his hand, nodded, and unenthusiastically followed Noshi through the flap. The shaman motioned for her to sit on a blanket beside his small fire. He did not sit initially, and now Molly, summoning inner strength, studied this healer and her situation.

She did not feel threatened and felt great reassurance that her husband was within earshot. Noshi, she noted, had quite a serious demeanor (even for an Indian, as they rarely allowed the white man to know their thoughts or see them in laughter). He also had a withered right leg, which was several inches shorter than the left. Noshi saw Molly looking at his leg but made no sound. From what she had heard, she understood that a tribal man who could not defend the village might choose the path of the medicine man. What bothered Molly, when her initial observations reached his face, was Noshi's war paint. She caught herself recoiling in discomfort.

Noshi noted her unease. He knew that he must gain Molly's trust before he could succeed in treating her. He said, *"Je parle Français. Et vous?"*

Molly had learned French from her Acadian mother, and Molly and Jean-Luc often spoke to each other in French at home and at work. Hearing the medicine man speak French, and not the guttural sounds of the Ottawa language, Molly exhaled in relief. She answered, in French, "Yes, I do."

Noshi said, "Your husband brought you to me."

Molly noted that this medicine man was choosing his words carefully. Her life experiences had made her wary of Indians, but she felt in her bones that this man truly wanted to help her.

Noshi asked, "Are you injured?"

"Only my spirit."

Noshi grunted in a universal sound of understanding. He suspected as much.

Molly said, "My spirit is at war with my body." Molly paused in mid thought, and Noshi waited patiently for her to continue. "For two days I cannot walk, I cannot function, and I feel I my life is spinning out of control."

Noshi did not speak, and his stoic expression masked his feelings from Molly. In truth, Noshi had labored mightily to cure demons from a couple of his tribesmen. However, he was wise enough to know those methods had little applicability to this woman seated before him. From a leather pouch, he took some shredded dried leaves and proceeded to brew Molly an herbal tea. Molly found that the tea smelled potent but not offensive.

As Molly sipped the tea, she felt an awakening within her—an awareness. This shaman's tea had brightened her outlook on life. "Well, that was easy," she thought. Several more minutes passed in silence.

Noshi finally said, "Why?"

Molly felt strengthened by the medicine man's treatment. She asked blithely, "Why what?"

Noshi refilled her cup with a second dose of his brew. "Drink." He watched passively as Molly blew on the liquid to cool it, and he observed her clinically as she sipped the entire drink. He finally broke the long silence and asked, "Why is your spirit at war?"

"Because—we find ourselves on a difficult voyage."

Noshi said, "Stand." Molly felt some stiffness as she struggled to her feet, but she eventually did as instructed. He then said, "Place your foot out and squeeze here." Noshi slowly extended his own foot and squeezed his calf muscle to demonstrate.

Molly squeezed her calf as instructed, but she felt puzzled and asked, "What does this prove?"

Noshi said, "Your spirit is only as strong as this part of your leg." Molly's expression told him that she did not comprehend the correlation. Noshi said, "*Your* leg is strong."

Molly said in halting words, "Yes, I—I climb the ratlines every day to sit in the crow's nest. It clears my mind. I like to ponder things up there." Now Noshi was stumped. Molly said to clarify, "Ratlines are rope ladders on ships."

Noshi slowly spread his hands apart and said, "Your leg is strong, so I believe your spirit is strong, too."

Molly said, "I think I understand."

"Yet your spirit remains in conflict. What *else* troubles your spirit?"

The last subjects Molly wanted to broach with the medicine man were her star-crossed pregnancy and her suspicions of the paladins. She did not answer.

Noshi said, "Finish your drink." Molly nodded unenthusiastically but did as instructed. "Now, sit."

Again, Molly obeyed. Then Noshi sat across from her and waited patiently by the fire for his charge to reveal her true reason for her inner conflict.

Minutes passed in silence. Noshi watched a tear form in Molly's eye and begin its unhappy ride down her cheek. To Noshi, that was a good sign. Molly's chest heaved a heavy sigh, and she placed her hands over her face. Noshi remained patient.

After a deafening period of silence, Molly opened up to the medicine man and said in slow, measured words, "I was—with child." Noshi nodded. Molly wasn't at all sure she wanted to continue this line of treatment, nonetheless at that juncture she admitted, "But weeks later, my flow reappeared."

Noshi nodded again. There was another long silence. Noshi wanted more information but wouldn't force his patient. Finally, he broke the silence and asked, "How long after you left your home did this occur?"

Molly said, "Four weeks—I cannot remember exactly."

Noshi pondered Molly's new information. He slowly reached for his small kettle to pour Molly another cup of his potion.

Molly held up her hand and said, "No thank you. I have had enough."

Noshi slowly returned the kettle to the fire. He then took a leather pouch, opened it, and removed six dried leaves from his collection of medicinal plants. Molly watched his every move carefully, and (not fond of Indians in general) reluctantly concluded that she began to value his sincere efforts to help. And besides, his tea provided a pick-me-up like she had never experienced. Noshi carefully arranged the six leaves onto an elevated, heated, flat metal surface. The leaves began smoldering, but they never ignited. Molly's nose wrinkled at the smell emitted by their pungent tang, but she was not alarmed when the medicine man began to chant and hold his arms outward beseeching the Great Spirit. His song droned on for several minutes. At that point,

Molly began to feel sleepy and closed her eyes. She deceived herself when she supposed she was just resting them. In short order, she fell into a deep sleep. This sleep was her first in days. Noshi covered her with a blanket, stood, and walked outside.

Jean-Luc hurried over. He asked, "Is she better?"

Noshi shrugged. He liked Jean-Luc and knew that his sachem liked him, too. Noshi had not spent a great deal of time with this man, but he had observed Jean-Luc as a child many afternoons competing against the tribal boys in foot races, shooting arrows, and throwing spears, sticks, and any other activity boys do. Noshi said, "Your woman spoke of a lost papoose and a dangerous trip."

"Oh?"

"She is strong in both the body and the spirit. But within her these two strong powers are in conflict. There is more to learn, but she may never say what it is."

"Then, how can you heal her? You do not know what it is, and you are telling me my wife may not know either."

"Noshi cannot heal until she reveals this fear."

From inside the teepee came a muffled scream followed by whimpering. Noshi and Jean-Luc threw open the flap and rushed inside. Molly lay slumbering beneath his blanket as Noshi had left her, and she appeared to be talking. Noshi and Jean-Luc knelt beside her. In English, she said in a whisper, "The shot went between my legs." Molly's face reflected the anguish she was holding inside. "Someone wants to kill me," she whimpered.

Jean-Luc and Noshi looked at each other. Noshi did not understand English and did not comprehend her words. Jean-Luc translated her words and added, "That happened eight summers ago." He leaned in and placed his ear close to his wife's mouth. He asked in English, "Molly, who tried to kill you?"

Molly rolled onto her back and continued her sleep talk. "You are hurting my arm."

"Who is hurting you, Molly?" asked Jean-Luc in a whisper.

Molly's face contorted in anguish. Jean-Luc desperately wanted her to continue, but Molly fell silent. Noshi's tea and smoldering herbs had put her into a deep sleep.

Noshi stood and walked outside. Jean-Luc followed a minute later. Then Noshi sat on a log near his lodge and reflected on what had just happened. For a period, Jean-Luc paced outside the wigwam, with Noshi close by straddling a log. The paladins continued to keep a respectful distance.

Growing restless with the time this cure was taking, Belfort nodded at Charnay, who then approached the worried husband. Putting his hand on his shoulder, he asked, "Is there anything we can do?"

Jean-Luc shook his head sadly.

The following day at mid-morning, Molly stirred and sat up. Jean-Luc said, "Good morning, dear."

Molly asked, "How long have I been asleep?"

"I would guess fourteen hours," said Jean-Luc. "Feel any better?"

"Yes, a little. I needed the sleep." Molly looked around and saw Noshi sitting near the flap of the teepee.

Noshi was wearing a false face mask to reinforce his patient's need for the spirits to intervene with powerful medicine. The carved wooden mask, Molly observed, had a hideous scowling expression and angry eyes. It was decorated with long strands of horsehair. Normally, his assistant, Star Dancer, would also don a false face and participate in his chanting, but Noshi prudently did not involve his nubile aide in the ceremony.

Noshi motioned for Jean-Luc to step outside. As Jean-Luc lifted the flap, the medicine man added, "She and I must speak, and no other ears must hear."

Jean-Luc nodded and departed. He approached the paladins and said, "The medicine man wants to speak with Molly in private. Let us take a walk." Belfort frowned slightly, but Charnay nodded in agreement.

Inside, Noshi began to chant in his native tongue while he shook a turtle-shell rattle. After several minutes, he began to move in painfully slow dance steps about the teepee. When he halted his dance, he placed his hand on Molly's head and said, "Your spirit spoke while you were asleep."

Molly wasn't sure that was a good thing. She asked warily, "What—did I say?"

"The spirit and your body are warring."

"I do not understand. What did you put in my tea?" Molly put the back of her hand against her forehead. "I want to go back to sleep," she said softly, but if she were being honest with Noshi, what she really wanted was to be free of this medicine man's questions.

"The drink made possible for your spirit to release the wickedness that you have trapped inside. Why?" Noshi shook the rattle and began a chant. His song lasted several minutes. He then stopped as suddenly as he had begun. Noshi waited patiently for Molly to confront the trapped demon.

"I cannot remember what I said last night. I was delirious, probably," whispered Molly in protest.

Noshi said pointedly, "No, that is the coward's path."

Molly turned away from the healer. His words wounded her pride. She said in weak protest, "I am *not* afraid. How can I possibly remember today? My mind wasn't right last night."

Noshi said, "You are afraid of someone—of that I am sure. Your spirit knows this person. If you will not speak of it now, if you will not tell me or your man, then this event of eight summers ago that churns your insides—could take future papooses."

That horrified Molly. Every fiber in her body wanted to flee the teepee and escape the medicine man's disturbing statements.

Noshi raised his arms skyward and asked, "Do you feel the Great Spirit even now? Great Spirit, help this woman eliminate this buried memory." He brought his hands down, turned to Molly, and said, "Allow the Great Spirit to sit at your side with His arm around your shoulder. Together, it is possible to resolve this conflict so that you may have inner peace."

Molly felt both unconvinced and inwardly glad that Noshi understood her pain.

"Someone tried to kill you. Allow the truth to come out."

Molly gasped. "How could you possibly know that?"

"Your spirit answered the summons last night. Your body does not want this war, but the body is no match for the memory. The body must yield—*you* are now the instrument of its submission."

"Now is not a good time," said Molly weakly.

"Do you want to see your children again?"

A tear ran down Molly's cheek as she affirmed, "Of course, I want to see my children again."

"Someone tried to kill you, and you *know* who it was."

Molly put her hands to her face and said, "No! No, I don't know. It was dark. I never saw the person's face."

Noshi insisted. "Your *spirit* knows."

Molly put her face in her hands and said, "Noshi is correct." She stood and walked to the flap. She looked down and studied her upturned palms. Even her hands seemed to be beseeching her spirit to name the mystery assailant of eight years past. She faced Noshi and said with regret, "I know who it was. I have—always known."

CHAPTER TEN

MOLLY WALKED OUTSIDE Noshi's lodge. Her eyes needed to adjust to the bright sun, and she had to squint for several moments. As her eyes became accustomed to the conditions, she spotted Jean-Luc. With him stood that Star Dancer person. Several steps away, the paladins conversed among themselves.

When Star Dancer saw Molly, she giggled and calculatedly moved into Jean-Luc's personal space. This action surprised Jean-Luc; and when he realized Molly was observing, his face turned bright red. He looked truly uncomfortable.

Star Dancer had selected a bad time to test the rejuvenated wife. With her ire rising, Molly started to cross the area to where this temptress was trespassing on her turf. Star Dancer, keeping one eye on her competition, began to realize that the object of her childhood infatuation had a vibrant partner, not a weakling whose husband could be easily wooed away.

Jean-Luc proactively extricated himself from Star Dancer's grasp and hurried over to embrace his wife. "Are you feeling better, darling?"

Molly nodded. Jean-Luc wrapped his arms around her. For the moment, Molly forgot about the flirtatious rival, but after several seconds passed, she remembered and began wiggling to get free and at Star Dancer. Jean-Luc wisely kept the two separated, and Molly finally relented and snuggled within Jean-Lu's embrace. Deep down, she knew that her husband had not given his attractive childhood friend any encouragement. Deciding not to make him any more uncomfortable than he already was, Molly embrace Jean-Luc tightly in the midst of their allies, and then kissed him on the lips. Normally a reserved couple, they would never have engaged in such a public display of affection if the events of the last seventy-two hours (not to mention the last sixty seconds) had not happened. The kiss had the intended effect on Star Dancer. Humiliated, she ran into the forest to avoid Noshi's admonishment.

Molly glanced at Charnay, and their eyes met for a moment. Turning quickly back to her husband, she said, "I feel much better. This experience has made me a believer in Indian medicine." Her husband beamed. He felt relieved that Molly's health had been restored. But Molly had undergone a radical transformation inside the teepee, as her traveling companions would soon discover.

Charnay had noticed Molly's expression when she glanced at him. Feeling a knot in his gut, he sensed she had come to a profound realization. His countenance darkened, and a sense of helplessness overcame him.

Belfort noticed his ally's altered countenance and asked, "Is there anything the matter, Geoff?"

Charnay grew pale. He said, "We cannot fail, Rici." He reached into his pocket and felt his small pistol. "Paladins do not fail—twice. You have seen how the king reacts to failure. He will throw me back into the Bastille. This time for good."

"What is this talk of failure, my friend? We will not fail. Besides, you did *not* fail the first time. Your influence on this couple has been positive for France. That is an impressive accomplishment. Do not hang your head. This aspect of our mission has filled me with optimism."

Before departing, Jean-Luc gave Noshi a bolt of imported English cloth for his aid in restoring Molly to health. The medicine man looked pleased with his gift. Molly, well known among the crew for her distrust of Indians, said sincerely, "I am grateful for what you did for me. I am leaving your lodge a changed person. I thank you, Noshi."

Jean-Luc motioned that they needed to depart. A different attitude toward the clock descended over Jean-Luc, who was newly motivated by the news of Opechwan's nuptials, and now felt there was little time to lose. Molly and the paladins accepted this and walked with purpose back to the skiff.

Charnay was quiet, but Belfort assumed that it was his doubts about the mission. Feeling like a sea captain aboard a sinking ship, Charnay was prepared to sacrifice himself when the wife's inescapable confrontation occurred.

When the skiff bumped the mother ship, a flurry of activity began for the next leg of the journey. Henry took a long look at his employer's wife and said, "It is great to see color back in your cheeks, ma'am."

Jean-Luc chipped in, "The fort physician was away. She saw a *medicine man*." The crew laughed good-naturedly. But given Molly's past outlook, Jean-Luc was amazed that she would allow herself to be treated by an Indian healer.

No one, not even her husband, was aware of the mental burden Molly had uncovered. And amid the flurry of activity to prepare the ship to get underway, no one noticed when she slipped away to the storeroom where the small arms were stockpiled. Alone with her thoughts, a resolute Molly selected two pistols, loaded them with great care, and locked the door. She reflected upon Jean-Luc's fealty to France, but her time to be tested had arrived. Her face bore the expression of someone about to enter the arena. Nervous, but yet determined to proceed, she ascended the companionway, entered the open deck, and walked to her cabin. Stopping at the door, she motioned to Henry that she wanted a word with him.

Henry hustled over and asked, "Yes'm? What can I do for you?" He was a little taken aback by Molly's gravity, especially so soon after coming aboard. And the crew were still in good spirits over her recovery. This change in the skipper's wife troubled him.

Molly said, "Henry, please inform our older passenger that I would like to speak with him."

Henry said, "Aye, ma'am, I'll go straightaway." Wondering what the Frenchman had done to get on her bad side, Henry scooted across the deck to complete his errand.

Molly entered her cabin and took a seat at the small table. She sat with the window behind her, to ensure that the sunlight reflecting off the lake would cause the room to appear even darker and the light behind her brighter. She gripped the pistols below the table to hide them from sight. Moments later Molly heard the expected knock on the door and she said, "Come in."

Charnay walked in and shut the door behind him. In an attempt to seize the initiative (or to put the wife off-balance), he said assertively, "I am not accustomed to being summoned." Molly did not respond, nor did she seem intimidated. Trying a different tack, he asked, "Something wonderful must have happened in the teepee. We are all relieved that your health is better."

Molly said with an edge in her voice, "Something wonderful did happen in the lodge." Charnay's eyebrows arched in anticipation. "I was able to resolve some issues that have been weighing on my mind."

"That is good to hear," said Charnay, trying to sound upbeat.

"Yet the medicine man believed that I would fall ill once more unless I resolved a third issue that is weighing on me. His medicine put me into a trance—a trance that shed a clarifying light on an eight-year-old mystery."

"Oh?" Charnay shifted his weight.

"Yes, you see, someone tried to kill me eight years ago. Jean-Luc and I never discovered who. We assumed it was a robber or a dock ruffian. Let us say, *that* is my third issue."

Charnay said, "Eight years is a long time to go without knowing."

"It is, and it weighs on a person's thoughts. The medicine man convinced me that not knowing was impacting my health."

"For that, I am truly sorry, but what does the unfortunate incident have to do with why you asked to speak to me?" The paladin was seeking to put the woman off balance.

"As I recall, you were in Manhattan during that tumultuous period. I know that you remember, because it was I who smuggled you out of Manhattan." Molly shook her head slowly. "Tax riots, the navy confiscating colonial ships, tax collectors being tarred and feathered. There was a great deal happening around us."

"I remember well." Charnay placed his hand inside his cloak and gripped his pistol.

Molly said, "Drawing your pistol would be unwise under the circumstances, don't you agree?" Charnay removed his hand and it went to his side. Molly slowly raised her two pistols into view.

Three loud knocks interrupted Molly's line of questioning.

Jean-Luc and Belfort walked in. Jean-Luc's jaw dropped when he saw his wife holding two pistols on Charnay. "Molly, what is the meaning of this?" he shouted.

Molly said calmly, "We are clearing the air on something that happened eight years ago. Noshi made it quite clear that I need to resolve a mystery that has been eating at me since that night on the dock, when a musket ball passed through my dress."

Looking confused, Jean-Luc glanced at Charnay and asked, "I remember well. How is it related to the count?"

Molly turned her attention to Belfort, who had placed his hand inside his tunic. She said, "Please remove your hand from your tunic and stand beside your colleague," she motioned with her pistol.

Charnay said, "Do as she says, Rici." Belfort slowly complied.

Molly now had one pistol trained on each paladin.

Belfort said, "Please put the pistols down. We can explain."

"No, thank you. My papa always said to bring a gun up quickly but put it down slowly. I am just following his advice." Molly turned to her husband. "We had just gotten to the good part, dear."

Again, Jean-Luc tried to reason with his wife. "Molly, there must be a misunderstanding."

Molly said, "Husband, this is part of the medicine man's cure." Turning back to the paladins, she said, "To return to the matter at hand, the Indian predicted that I *did* know who took that shot, but that, in his words, 'my spirit was at war with my body.' He believed that I did not *want* to know, but that not knowing was causing my health to deteriorate. But why would I not want to know, I asked myself. Last night, when his potion began affecting me, a clearness descended in my sleep." She looked Charnay directly in the eye and said, "It was *you* who attempted to take my life that night."

Jean-Luc blurted out, "That is not true, is it, your Excellency? Tell me that is not true. Please."

Charnay was now the one off balance. Feeling trapped, his instincts took over and his mind raced. He tried mightily to invent an alibi that would clear him. He had witnessed the grit this woman possessed: first, at the quarry when her husband's life was in peril, and second, when she sprang him from jail and smuggled him out of New York City. He did not doubt she would kill them both.

Molly said, "No denial? I have asked a simple question, and I am waiting for your answer; know that I will kill you if you simply stand there in silence." Molly cocked her pistols. To the Frenchman, the four clicks sounded like an executioner's query whether this prisoner had a last request. "I have buried the memory of you twisting my arm before you boarded that ship."

Charnay felt a terrible emotional mélange of anxiety, shame, and primal fear. Instinctively, he ruled out the option of shooting his way out this situation. He said slowly, "I did pull the trigger that night." He closed his eyes and waited for the musket ball to rip through his chest.

Molly asked, "Are you expecting to die?" Charnay opened his eyes but did not respond. Molly continued, "You've never met my father; but he taught me, 'the truth will set you free.' Know that had you denied it, you would be dead now."

"In '65, I was sent to speak with your husband and to avenge Captain d'Alquier."

Still aiming the pistols at the paladin's chest, Molly said, "We were with Captain d'Alquier the morning he was killed. He, Jean-Luc, and I were fighting the same enemy."

Surprised by Molly's statement, Charnay asked, "What enemy? *You* were with the English Navy!"

"I was, but the enemy you ask about was a certain corrupt Intendant of New France named François Bigot. The captain, Jean-Luc, and I were his prisoners."

"I am well aware of Bigot's criminal enterprise, because d'Alquier's mission was to investigate him. I am beginning to understand—"

Belfort thought that he saw an opportunity and said, "Geoff spent seven years in the Bastille because he did not kill you that night. The king neither appreciated his reluctance nor his use of judgment."

"And what is your version, monsieur le comte?" asked Molly.

"I believed that it was counterproductive to kill Jean-Luc's wife. It never made sense to me. But—"

"But what?" blurted Jean-Luc who was feeling let down by this emissary.

"But the king is not someone you argue with, Jean-Luc. I am a soldier; I am not a cold-blooded killer. I could never commit murder, and I have come to accept that is why my shot missed that night."

Belfort said in supplication, "This man suffered terribly for disobeying the king. When I located him months ago, he was an inmate lying in prison straw amongst common criminals. He has been stripped of his title, incarcerated, and—"

"And yet here you are. How did you get out of this prison you say you were in? Are you planning to finish the job?" asked Molly.

Belfort said, "I convinced the king that he was needed on this mission, that he had established a relationship with your husband, that France needed this brave paladin back on the job." Noting Molly's expression remained skeptical, he said, "We have witnessed how you and Jean-Luc love each other and support one another, and, it is obvious that for France's foreign policy to succeed, we must work with both of you and do our best to keep both of you alive. From previous experience, that is challenge enough, do you not think so?"

Molly glanced at Jean-Luc for an assessment. Jean-Luc said, "I think they are sincere. Think back, they have supported us in everything. They have had ample opportunity to do us evil."

"Agreed," said Molly, and she slowly lowered her pistols' flints into their frizzens. The Frenchmen breathed a sigh of relief and smiled nervously. With a hint of sarcasm, Molly said, "I feel safer already."

Charnay said, "Same here."

After leaving to walk the deck, Charnay said, "It is well that this discussion took place. The wife's participation is important."

Belfort nodded and in his best imitation of a sailor's dialect said, "Let us just recover the king's treasure and put North America in our wake."

CHAPTER ELEVEN

MOLLY AND JEAN-LUC climbed over the gunnel of the twenty-five–foot sloop, *Kissing Rock*. Henry held the skiff close, using the boathook skillfully and allowing the Frenchmen to safely board. Molly went below and verified that the food, water, other essentials, and muskets were aboard. She also noted the bolt of cloth and the keg of nails that Henry had stowed in the corner, for giving the impression that the four were on business as traders. She pulled up the disguised floorboards, where they intended to stow the French payload.

Jean-Luc joined her below deck and quickly inserted the dagger board in its slot amidships. This 3- by 24- by 60-inch plank would serve as the sloop's keel. The dagger board can be raised and lowered to adjust the sloop's draft as needed. It can even be removed when the sloop is beached or entering shallow water. Jean-Luc had designed and built this sloop with coastal smuggling in mind, so that it could traverse brown water, leaving a pursuing revenue ship with the options of discontinuing the pursuit or running aground.

Charnay moved to the bow and fastened the jib to the bow's mast stay. He then untied the line securing the sloop to the parent schooner, but he held onto it. Belfort climbed atop the cabin and hoisted the mainsail half-way. Thus, he could raise it quickly when instructed. Molly had returned to the cockpit and held the tiller.

Jean-Luc came topsides and said to Henry, "We will be gone about three weeks—maybe four. Sail the *Marie* northward. Do some fishing and hunting, but do not allow anyone to become separated while ashore. Indians would love to take your weapons, clothes, and valuables. Return in three weeks and rendezvous with me. I may be delayed a week or ten days."

"Aye, skipper. We'll see you when you get back."

Jean-Luc put his hand on Henry's shoulder and said, "I am aiming for three weeks, my friend."

On Jean-Luc's signal, Henry raised the boathook and Charnay dropped the tether. Charnay gave the schooner a shove that pointed their bow away. Jean-Luc said to Belfort, "Hoist the main sail." He turned to Molly, who had glanced upward at the masthead fly to learn the wind's direction, "After we clear the ship, point us toward the Niagara River. We are already facing the channel's entrance, and I noticed that the approach was well marked when we went in the first time."

Molly guided the sloop in a safe arc around the mother ship, and on a leeward reach, the boat gathered speed. Molly kept one eye on the compass and one eye on the bow to keep them aligned, and she steered toward the river. The stem sliced through the lake's whitecaps and gave off a robust wake. When they passed Fort Niagara, they had a good head of speed. Though the distance to the point where they would egress the river was but a few miles distant (and the great Niagara Falls only a few miles after that), all four aboard were imagining the famous falls and wondering if it would look as dreadful as they imagined it.

Belfort said, "Another overcast day! Is that all Canada has for weather? The gray even reflects off the water's surface."

Charnay laughed and said, "Rici, we cannot do anything about the climate here; and if anything, it is more agreeable than the weather in Normandy."

Belfort said, "The weather in Normandy, Geoff? You grew up in

Alsace." Turning to Jean-Luc, he asked, "Let us change the topic, how did you meet your wife?" Jean-Luc and Molly glanced at each other and broke into wide grins.

Charnay said, "This is going to be interesting."

Jean-Luc said, "We met on a riverbank near Quebec, but *we fell in love* underneath a capsized canoe that same night in the middle of the St. Lawrence River."

Belfort said, "Sounds cold and wet and not very romantic."

Molly said, "And yet it was quite romantic, Jean-Luc was trying to take care of me and wanted me to get safely cross the river,"

"And why were you on the river at night?" asked Charnay.

"The seminary students from the cathedral were going to attack the English artillery on the opposite side of the river. They were intent on driving the enemy cannons from the plateau."

Belfort asked, "And how did you happen to be on this particular riverbank?"

Molly laughed and interjected, "Well, General Wolfe wanted me to get inside Quebec."

Not really wanting to emphasize Molly's role in the war, Jean-Luc quickly said, "The students' attack never happened. We were still a great distance from the English when they panicked; there was wild firing of muskets, and everyone dashed back to the canoes." Seeing that the paladins were interested in their story and that their expressions did not darken at Molly's mention of General Wolfe, he thought it safe to continue the story. "Molly showed up in the middle of this chaos at the canoes and knocked me into the river."

Molly giggled and said, "As he fell, he grabbed me—we both went into the river."

Belfort asked, "This is getting good. How did you find yourselves under a canoe in the middle of the river?"

Jean-Luc said, "Those canoes could not take the abuse the frantic holy men heaped upon them. The one Molly was in began to leak badly and was filling with water. Finally, it capsized midway."

Molly said, "Jean-Luc dove into the dark river to save me. First, I surfaced underneath the canoe, and then Jean-Luc came up. It was just the two of us under there - alone. He was so handsome and dashing. For a few moments, I allowed myself to behave like a smitten coquette and simply put the war out of my mind."

Charnay said, "Quite a story. There must be more. We would like to hear it."

"It will have to wait, your Excellency. I can see Joncaire's Post in the distance. And the rapids are not far after that. This docking may be tricky, so we must be vigilant."

Belfort asked, "How far distant is this huge cascade I have heard so much about?"

"Six or seven miles past the post. This boat will have a steep hill to overcome, and then the most difficult leg of the journey will be behind us."

Twenty minutes later, the paladins scrambled to their positions. Jean-Luc provided skillful instructions to his inexperienced crew. Molly guided the boat up to the wharf, where three men stood prepared to help tie the boat's lines to the dock. All aboard then jumped ashore.

A barrel-chested man wearing a fur cap and well-worn working leathers walked over. His brown hair and a full salt-and-pepper beard, blew in the breeze. Molly guessed that he was in his forties. Jean-Luc introduced himself. As they shook hands, the man warily eyed the sloop.

He said, "I'm John Stedman. I run the operation." He nodded at the *Kissing Rock* and said, "That's an unusual boat you have there, mister. We don't see anything but bateaux around these waters. That's all we're rigged to handle."

Jean-Luc asked, "Where I come from, a bateau is not of much use. But you *can* haul us up that slope, can you not?" He then cocked his head as if to ask 'how much is this haul-out going to cost.

Stedman stroked his whiskers as if deep in thought and said, "The boatlift can easily manage her out of the water and onto the flatbed, but you will have to unstep the mast. My crew hasn't never done it and wouldn't know where to begin."

Jean-Luc said, "We will have it down in minutes."

"And I'm going to have to figure out how to keep her from sliding off the flatbed."

Jean-Luc said, "If you do not mind, I can help with that, too. Do you have lots of dunnage?"

"Dunnage ain't a problem."

"Good. I will show where and how to chock the hull and just as importantly, where *not* to."

"Sure, there is plenty stacked over there, and I can put three men to assist. But with all the extra that is involved, I'll have to charge more for *this* portage."

For the next few minutes, Molly watched her husband negotiate the give and take of striking a deal. When Jean-Luc and Stedman concluded their negotiations, she knew that a firm accord had been struck. Molly approached Stedman and asked, "What kind of slope are we facing here?"

He stroked his beard and respectfully gazed at the hill in front of them. He said, "Missy, that be a thirty-six degree rise, and it runs for three hundred feet. The haul uphill always tuckers out them animals. I will have to rest my oxen for a spell at the top."

"How many hours would you say before we are back in the water?"

Again Stedman stroked his chin and said, "I'm guessing six—give or take. You're staring at a nine mile slog. You up for that, or would you want to rent a horse?"

Molly smiled and said confidently, "I'll be fine."

After the sloop was loaded, Jean-Luc, Belfort, and Charnay worked fast. A short while later, the *Kissing Rock* was chocked and securely tied down. Jean-Luc and Stedman walked around the flatbed, checking the arrangement and the knots until both were confident that the sloop rested securely on its transport. Stedman nodded to his teamster. The man cracked the whip and the oxen began their trek up the slope.

Molly and Charnay walked to the right of the sweating, straining animals. To the animals' left stood the teamster. Jean-Luc and Belfort walked on each side by the rear wheels. They carried wooden chocks to slip behind the rear wheels in an emergency. Should something happen to the sloop, they would be stranded. They could not chance a runaway flatbed if the oxen faltered.

A third of the way up the hill, the team driver felt compelled to whip two of the oxen who he deemed weren't giving the required effort. He effectively motivated his beasts, and the sloop renewed its journey to the summit. The oxen, wagon, and sloop completed the short, but strenuous, journey up the escarpment without incident. As Stedman predicted, the team driver gave his animals a lengthy break with the flatbed fully chocked and resting on level ground.

During the break at the top, Molly walked to the precipice overlooking the river and gazed down at its roaring rapids. The whitewater looked wild and untamed from where she stood. Jean-Luc came up to her and said, "Do not worry, we will not be in any rapids. Where we put in is above the falls and there is no whitewater there."

Molly looked skeptical and asked, "Are you sure? They go for as far as I can see."

Jean-Luc smiled and put his hand on her shoulder. "I thought you might be thinking about the children."

Molly put her head on his shoulder and said, "I have been thinking about them. I am trying not to cry. I miss them terribly. I hope your father isn't going crazy."

"I miss them, too." He looked down at the rapids and said, "I promise you, we will recover the king's money, attend the wedding, and sail back to Montreal as fast as possible."

Before renewing the slog, the teamster and Jean-Luc rechecked each wood support and tie-down. With the load secure, the teamster cracked his whip to renew the portage. The oxen strained to get the awkward and top-heavy cargo back into motion. The flatbed's timbers creaked in sympathy with the animal's straining. Fully obeying the Law of Inertia, the wheels reluctantly and slowly began to turn. A cacophony of grunting coupled with snorting emanated from the beasts. The level leg of the portage appeared easier for the ox teams.

Two hours later, the oxen entered a portion of the road that had a fall off on each side. It was known as Devil's Hole. After the boat crossed this dangerous stretch, the teamster gave his oxen a second breather, though this one would be shorter.

Molly observed quite a number of wooden crosses. "What happened here?" she asked.

The man frowned at the memory, but said, "Ten years ago, hundreds of murderin' Seneca attacked a wagon train led by Mr. John [Stedman]. They was unhappy about losing their portage business." The paladins looked wide-eyed at the crosses. Neither had experienced Indian warfare. "Take a long look at them graves. Know that Indians don't much like a fair fight. There was hundreds of them agin' twenty-four. Mr. John and two others somehow escaped the butcherin' and ran to the fort. Twenty-one souls that day didn't escape. Around these parts it is called the Devil's Hole Massacre."

Shocked by the teamster's vivid account, Molly said with sympathy, "That's dreadful."

The teamster continued, "Soon afterwards, the regulars from Fort Schlosser sent out a rescue party, but the Seneca chopped them up, too. Ugly stuff it was." Thinking he had been too graphic, the teamster felt contrition and said, "'Beggin' your pardon, ma'am. I didn't mean to be sanguine."

Molly nodded and said, "Think nothing of it. I asked, after all."

The teamster nervously glanced at Jean-Luc, who though unpleased the story had frightened his wife, wasn't put out with the man. The ox driver added, "No need to be worried, ma'am. The region is peaceful now. No 'hostiles' for miles and miles." He pulled out a piece of folded paper from his pocket and, after unfolding it, showed the four travelers a map. "You can see, we're over halfway there. You can be on your way in a few hours." He pointed SSW and said, "The great falls are about two miles in that direction. You won't want to miss seeing them."

Another hour passed. The teamster pointed to his right and said, "If you walk over there and look down, you can see Niagara Falls. I never grow tired of it. It is a view you don't want to pass up."

Though Jean-Luc and Belfort couldn't abandon their duties as emergency chockers, Molly and Charnay did make the side trek to take in Mother Nature's spectacle.

Charnay seemed particularly struck by the display of his Creator's imagination. He pushed his hat back and said, "*C'est magnifique, non?*"

In awe of the falls, Molly could simply said, "Oui, c'est tres beau." As they gazed upon the thundering falls, she turned to the dark paladin and asked, "If you had known how the last seven years would go, would your shot have missed?"

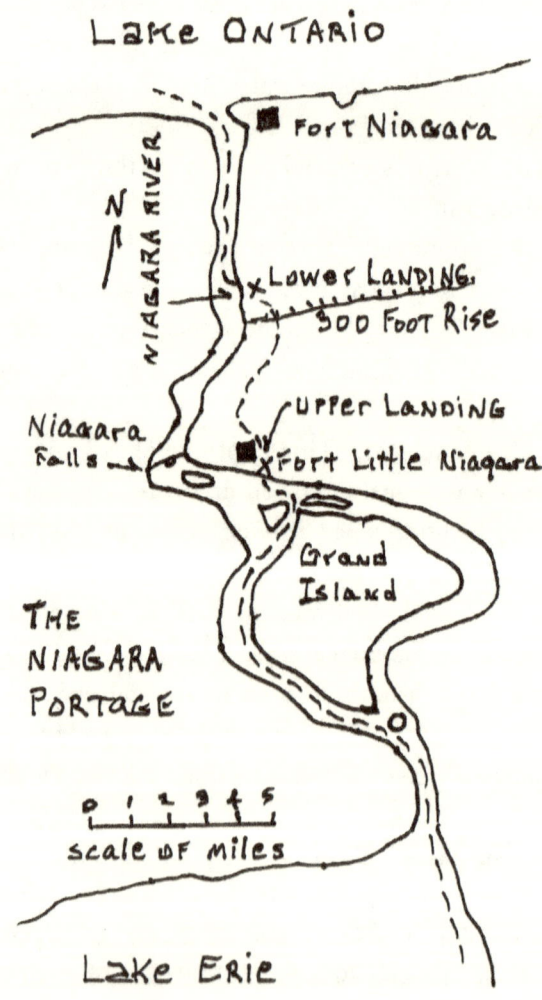

"Madame, I *am* obligated to obey my king. However, shooting a woman is not something I am able to do. In addition, I believed that His Majesty would be better served by having you at Jean-Luc's side. Obviously, His Majesty disagreed. But given the same options to further His Majesty's interest, I would still defer to my better judgment. So—yes, I would make the identical decision. And this journey has only reinforced the wisdom of my choice."

"And yet, your shot came within inches—albeit a little off the mark." Molly couldn't resist poking the paladin.

"It did that," said Charnay, looking away. He then added, "*Vive le roi*," employing the gallows humor Molly had come to expect from him. Molly reached down and picked a wildflower and sniffed it. Several seconds ticked off as the pair watched the water cascade. Breaking the silence, Charnay said, as he gazed at the horizon, "I fear that Jean-Luc will now regard me in a different light."

Molly said, "I accepted your explanation. And though my husband hasn't said so, he must have accepted it given that you are still alive." Charnay grimly smiled at Molly's own brand of gallows humor. She leaned in and whispered, "Jean-Luc respects you a great deal. He sympathizes with what you have endured for employing better judgment than your monarch."

"I knew when I entered my king's circle that loving France more than its flawed sovereign might one day become a problem."

As they rejoined the group, Charnay replaced Rici, allowing his compatriot to trot over to take in the vista of the cascading waters. The shadows lengthened, and the sunlight flickered through the treetops. Soon, the forest, road, and dark green environs would be lit by only the stars. Thinking that the worst was behind him, Charnay had no inkling of the terror that awaited his party on the next lake.

CHAPTER TWELVE

MONDAY, MARCH 22, 7 P.M.

THE TEAMSTER REGARDED first the trail and then the waning crescent moon's capacity to light their way. This small slice of moon presented little reflective surface for providing light. It told him that the dangers of proceeding outweighed the creature comforts offered at Fort Schlosser. He called Jean-Luc over and said, "If we had ninety minutes more of daylight, we could make the fort, but it is too dangerous to continue."

"Agreed," said Jean-Luc. He and Belfort chocked the wheels and jumped onto the flatbed to check the tie-downs. The teamster tended to his animals' needs while the three men divvied up guard duty. The voyagers, not to mention the beasts hauling the cargo, were exhausted, and they contentedly slept under the stars in the cool night air.

TUESDAY, MARCH 23, 5:50 A.M.

Molly was awakened by a hand on her shoulder. She opened her eyes and saw Jean-Luc kneeling over her. Molly said, "Hey, handsome, how about giving a girl a kiss." Jean-Luc grinned but then looked around to see if anyone was watching. Seeing no one, he gave his wife a good morning kiss. Wanting to roll back and sleep some more, nevertheless, Molly threw off the covers and went to work. With the breakfast fire started, she turned her attention to preparing the morning meal.

By 8:30 a.m., the teamster had his oxen, flatbed, and people up, fed, and back on the road. The boat and flatbed creaked as it rolled toward an abandoned, rundown military structure. Though two separate structures rose up to greet the voyagers, the teamster pointed to the nearest and said, "That's the old French installation, Fort du Portage. It never amounted to much." Further down the road, but in sight, sat a newer post. The teamster said, "*That* is old Fort Schlosser." He spat in the dirt, wiped his mouth on his sleeve, and continued. "Once garrisoned by the regulars, it's now operated and maintained by Mister John's men. You won't find much in the way of creature comforts, ma'am, but we keep enough fellers on hand to lift that little boat of yorn back into the river real easy like."

Since the teamster had addressed Molly, she said, "That's all we need, isn't it Jean-Luc?" Turning back to the concessionaire, she asked, "I have seen many rapids; and the great falls, though wondrous, fill me with the dread that we could get caught in the current and go over the precipice. So, just how safe is this re-entry point?"

Feeling tempted to frighten the lady for some light-hearted joshing, he succumbed to the enticement and said, "This here area will be far enough up river from the falls that it won't be a problem for you, unless—"

"You were about to say something else. What aren't you telling us?" Molly gave the teamster a stern look.

The teamster said warily, "Like any good mariner, afore you shove off, make sure the wind is cooperating. That's all. It would be a real bother for us to have to scramble about and save you from going over the falls." He leaned in and whispered, "It ain't like it never happened, before." The teamster spat on the ground as an exclamation point.

Entering between the wide, wooden palisades, the teamster deftly drove his flatbed straight to the boatlift with impressive skill. He knew he had impressed his patrons. With false modesty, he said, "It was easy, but only 'cuz I've done it many a time."

In short order, the *Kissing Rock* had been lifted from the flatbed and gently lowered into the Niagara River. Jean-Luc's crew immediately boarded to prepare the sloop for departure. Jean-Luc and Belfort stepped the mast so efficiently that the teamster and boatlift operators looked on in admiration. Then, the men hooked the sails and raised them a short way up the mast and forestay.

Molly jumped ashore and slipped the teamster a monetary reward for good service. Then, she unexpectedly put her forefinger on his chin and swiped down with a giggle. The expression on his face was priceless. This good-natured gesture, observed by his co-workers, elicited wild hoots and ribbing comments, causing the rugged teamster to blush crimson. Molly smiled demurely and walked back to the sloop.

Jean-Luc asked, "What was all that about?"

"Oh, I just got even with our driver for thinking it would be good fun to spook me."

As the sloop's bow swung to the SE, Molly turned and waved to the teamster and his co-workers on shore. Belfort and Charnay raised the main and jib sails and tightened the lines until Jean-Luc expressed satisfaction with the sails' trim. The *Kissing Rock* sped up, glided by several small isles, and approached an island large enough to be mistaken for the mainland. The teamsters called it Grand Island.

Having turned the tiller over to Molly, Jean-Luc said, "Steer for the channel two points off the starboard bow. It is the channel we want, and it has good depths and few obstacles."

Belfort scrambled back into the cockpit and sat next to Jean-Luc. He said, "I want to learn more about the natives. I am surprised that we have seen so few since we left Montréal."

Jean-Luc said, "Unless there are trade negotiations under way, the red men keep to themselves, and actually everyone likes it that way."

"And why did you refer to them as red?"

"It's not what you think. Early colonizers encountered natives heavily tattooed with red ink designs. It doesn't refer to their skin shade as many believe. The Indians in this region tattoo themselves, but not necessarily in the red as did the coastal Indians of one hundred years ago."

"I see. And as a youth, one of your friends was an Indian boy. How did your friendship begin?"

"Opechwan has been my friend for a long time. I was hunting in the forest near my father's home twenty years past and stumbled upon an Indian boy trying to get away from a black bear. He had climbed a tree, but the bear was about to climb that tree. It wouldn't have been long before the animal reached him. I shot the bear. When Opie dropped out of the tree, he said his friends had run to their village for help and left him. Then, Opie's father came running, and when he saw the dead bear —he treated me as his son's rescuer. He said Opie owed me his life. Opie was relieved and grateful. He put his arm around my shoulder and smiled from ear to ear. He was fun to be around, and always has been. We soon became close friends. I spent a great deal of time in the Ottawa village."

"Did the other Indians accept you?"

"They did. Opie's father was the sachem. When he pronounced me a friend of the Ottawa, acceptance by the tribe was assured. Let me tell you, there is no middle ground with an Indian. You are either his friend or his enemy. As I matured, I understood that being a friend of the Ottawas had it privileges *and* its obligations."

"What kinds of privileges and obligations?" asked Charnay, who had taken an interest in Jean-Luc's conversation with Belfort and had seated himself by the tiller.

"I learned that the Indians and the European traders did not understand one another. The Ottawas could not separate the trading relationship and the social relationship. To them it is impossible. Whether you are the buyer or seller, the Indians thought of it as a relationship with a friend."

I am beginning to see the misunderstanding," said Charnay. "You do not try to profit from your son's labor or charge a friend's daughter for the food she consumes as a guest."

Jean-Luc nodded and said, "That is right. To the Ottawa, a person shares freely with family *and* kinsmen. With other villagers the same is true, given the understanding that they will reciprocate in the future. You can see that European traders trying to maximize their profits and beat the Indian in the deal would offend them."

"How did the fur trade ever get started, with this inherent miscalculation?"

Jean-Luc said, "The two sides adapted. In my case, I learned to share what I had when I visited Opie in his village. In return, safe passage in the forests and shared meals with his family were my benefits."

"And if a trader was considered an enemy, how did they treat him?" asked Belfort.

"If the fur trader chose to act greedy, like an enemy, they would treat him wholly different. Lying to and stealing from an *enemy* are sources of pride to an Indian. And remember this, the Indian of teenage years is the most dangerous."

"But they are the least experienced in battle, are they not?" asked Charnay.

"That is true, but a teenager must pass three tests to become accepted as a warrior, and each is pressured to earn this designation early." Jean-Luc looked at Molly when he said, "And if he is a warrior, a proven hunter and fisherman, then his desirability as a husband is high." He smiled broadly and winked at his wife.

"Don't you wink at me," Molly said in mock sternness. She harrumphed, turned, and looked downriver. "Look, isn't that the next lake?" Molly pointed upriver and the men looked where she indicated. "Is that Erie I see in the distance?"

"It is Erie, because I can see the English fort on the west bank. In that case, we are down to the final two hundred miles," joked Jean-Luc.

Belfort said, "Pray continue. I wish to learn about the Indians. What are these tests an Indian must pass to become a brave."

"Remember, from childhood, the Indian boy practices the skills he will need. His first test, he must steal the horse of an enemy. He has practiced stealing and stealth techniques since a child. Next, he must touch the body of a living enemy."

Charnay said, "A difficult feat I imagine."

Jean-Luc nodded and said, "In my opinion, it is the most difficult. And the final test is to kill an enemy. Some of these acts are rewarded with an honor feather."

Molly said, "Well, that's something I have never heard of. What is an honor feather?"

"Those feathers in their hair are not there for decoration. They are awarded by their sachem for doing what I have just described," answered Jean-Luc. "The more feathers he has, the deadlier the adversary."

"Well, you have given me much to reflect on," said Belfort running his fingers through his hair.

"What is the likelihood that we will encounter these savages?" asked Charnay. "It seems odd that we have only seen a few of these red men, and that they were in Montréal."

"There are reasons for that. One is that the game they hunt flees when the European enters the forest, and they, too, must retreat to where their food has fled. Another reason is more worrisome—we may not know that they are present, but if they are in the area, *they* would know where we are. They make certain to see us, even though we cannot see them. They could be watching us even now."

Both Belfort and Charnay looked about with a new (more worrisome) awareness of their surroundings. The beautiful scenery and the wild environs through which they passed now seemed less scenic and more ominous.

As the *Kissing Rock* entered Erie's waters, it sailed under the guns of Fort Erie, one of the British Empire's newer fortifications. The bastion's *raison d'etre* was to control the entrance to the Niagara River, and by extension, the portage and access to Lake Ontario. To the strategically savvy paladins, it was clear that the Lion of Britannia had strengthened his hold on the Great Lakes region and the fur trade. To the two agents of the French king, the newly built forts made any contemplation of reviving France's empire in the Canadian wilderness much more difficult to accomplish.

The sloop's heading took it along the southern shore, and ultimately across the paths of four canoes.

CHAPTER THIRTEEN

MONDAY, MARCH 25, 9 A.M.

OLLY STEPPED OUT of her small galley, and following her husband's adage of "one hand for the boat and one hand for yourself," she worked her way to the bow. She enjoyed the wind blowing her hair, the boat's stem rising and falling as it carved effortlessly through the water, and the exhilaration of speed. She observed the lake's waters tossing and foaming from the hull passing through them. Molly liked the *Kissing Rock* for these reasons. She stood there awhile, alone with her thoughts, when some dark objects in the distance caught her attention. Memories of her days on the *H.M.S. Pembroke* flooded into her consciousness, and she recalled with a smile Putty Gordon's threat to the lookout, "If I see a ship from the deck before you– you will spending another four hours in the Crow's Nest."

Molly called over her shoulder, "Movement on the water ahead. Looks like canoes."

Belfort asked Jean-Luc, "Canoes? That would indicate Indians, correct?"

Jean-Luc said, "Not necessarily. Fur traders use them, too."

Charnay asked, "Could they become a problem?"

Jean-Luc leaned forward to peer around the bulkhead. He nodded grimly and called out to Molly, "Dear, go below and retrieve the muskets and gear. I stowed them in the starboard compartment."

Anticipating this, Molly already had begun inching amidships. Shortly after entering the small cabin, she brought up four muskets. Though working with little room, she and the paladins quickly loaded them. As they took the precaution of preparing for a fight, the sloop plowed ahead, Molly glanced repeatedly at the dark rain clouds. When a thunderclap boomed and raindrops began to fall, Molly and the paladins tried to shield the muskets from the precipitation.

Molly said, "Husband, in a few more minutes, our muskets will be worthless."

<hr />

Lone Eagle watched with concern as the odd-shaped vessel glided toward them. Having already deduced the weather implications of the dawn's red sky and his uneasiness about the strengthening breeze, he signaled Hopping Bird to turn the canoes for the shore. Not knowing the duration or intensity of the rain, he didn't want his hunting party to be on the lake during a thunderstorm. Besides, he frowned on the idea of encountering the small sailboat without better knowledge of its purpose. He didn't want to provoke a fight with jumpy Europeans while he was shepherding learners on their first serious hunt. The boys had seen the sloop, and a pair of them grumbled about the directive to head for shore.

Chava and Miakoda voiced their unhappiness. They wanted to attack the small ship and steal its property.

"There are many of us, and the boat is small," said Chava in protest.

Miakoda chimed in, "Chava is correct, Lone Eagle. Give us this occasion to earn honor feathers and become warriors."

Lone Eagle did not respond to his carping charges, but did give Chava and Miakoda a withering glare that discouraged dissension in the boys who had not as yet voiced unwanted opinions. He thought, if

I were with fifteen adults, then I might attack the boat... but I must return these boys to the tribe.

From inside the cabin, Molly asked Jean-Luc, "Are the Indians paddling toward us?"

Jean-Luc looked closely through the telescope off the port side to scrutinize the canoes. He lowered the telescope and said, "No, they have turned and are heading for the south shore." Jean-Luc then looked at the storm clouds massing in the western sky and said, "The Indians do not want to be on the lake when the squall hits." Jean-Luc slowly closed his telescope. He said to Belfort, "I am sorry, Excellency, but your desire to observe the savages will have to wait a while longer."

"May I?" asked Belfort as he held out his hand to use Jean-Luc's telescope. Extending the telescope, he observed the Indian canoes for several moments. Belfort adjusted the focus and said, "Only two in the group have feathers in their hair—does that mean anything?"

Jean-Luc thought for a moment. "That *is* odd. The feathers designate who in the tribe has earned warrior status. I would expect a larger number in a group that size." But the distance separating the vessels made it difficult for the St. Alembert group to observe the Indians in detail. For now, the two groups were going their separate ways, and that was as both party's leaders wanted.

The breeze now whipped into the occasional strong gust, and the sloop began to roll and heel at angles that foretold that movement about the deck would soon become difficult. When one particular gust sent Belfort falling into his partner, Jean-Luc said, "It is better to act before the storm arrives." He looked about the lake and said, "White-caps have formed." Knowing that soon the small white-tipped waves would give way to rollers, he thought it best to have the sloop prepped to ride out the storm.

Jean-Luc said, "Reef the mainsail."

Charnay glanced at Jean-Luc and asked, "Is that what you want?"

Jean-Luc nodded grimly and then yawned involuntarily. Charnay pulled Belfort's sleeve and said with an urgent tone, "Help me with this." Before he went forward, Charnay said to Jean-Luc, "You are spent. Get some rest, and we will man the boat."

Jean-Luc said, "I would prefer that my wife man the tiller, and just one of you remain with her. That person should man the sails."

Charnay nodded and said, "Then I will stay with your wife, and Rici can join you where it is dry." Then he tugged on Belfort's sleeve and said, "Let us get the boat ready." The two men scrambled forward, clinging to the handrails, and stood precariously atop the heaving boat's small cabin to untie the halyard from the mast's cleat. Charnay worked using only his right hand and allowed the mainsail sheet to slide slowly through is fingers.

Jean-Luc said, "Lower the mainsail only about two thirds and tie it off."

"Will that not be too much sail for the conditions?" asked Charnay, confused.

"Because you are also going to replace the genoa with a storm jib, and if the mainsail is completely down, we would lose control of the boat. Next, lower the genoa and hank on the storm jib."

Overhearing her husband's directive, Molly retrieved the storm jib from the sail locker. Hustling topsides with the sail, she exchanged it for the genoa that the paladins had just hauled down.

Belfort and Charnay worked feverishly to hank the storm jib onto the forestay; and after they raised it, they tied the halyard sheet to the mainmast cleat. The fear of falling overboard focused their minds on keeping a firm grasp on the deck handrails in the strong wind and strengthening waves. The sloop's deck returned to a controllable angle, and the boat surged ahead with good speed despite employing far less canvas than before. With those critical tasks complete, the paladins returned to the cockpit and sat down. Charnay tried not to huff and puff in front of the others. He put his hand on Belfort's shoulder and squeezed it good naturedly.

Feeling relieved that the mainsail reefing and sail switch had gone without incident, Jean-Luc stood up and said, "Darling, you have the tiller."

Belfort said, "It seems wrong that I stay dry inside the cabin while your wife manages the boat alone."

Molly forced a smile and said with faux confidence, "I can manage. Really."

Tired, Belfort nodded gratefully and carefully moved below to get relief from the tossing deck. As he passed Molly, she noticed that the skin on his arms that had red marks like wasp stings would leave. The wind and rain promised to make Molly and Charnay miserable.

Exhausted, Jean-Luc looked uncertain with his decision, but he waited patiently for her to finish tying the cords of her rain bonnet tightly under her chin. Then he released his grip and transferred the tiller to his wife and stepped toward the cabin. All could see that. Jean-Luc was long overdue a break from the helm.

With one foot in the cabin, he turned and said, "Sail across the waves at an angle." Molly managed a smile and nodded. Jean-Luc looked around at the boat's preparations, and said as a reminder, "If you need me, just call."

Molly sat and began to steer with her right hand while holding onto the gunnel with the left. As the wind and waves strengthened, she kept Jean-Luc's admonition in mind. For the next several hours, she steered the sloop at an angle, cutting across the waves as her husband instructed. Molly knew that the one silver lining to being wet and miserable was that the boat was making terrific time and distance in the blustery conditions.

Molly focused on the ballet between the rollers and the sloop's hull. But inevitably, the occasional wind gust would catch them off-guard. When it came, the sloop heeled another ten degrees, sending the resting men inside rolling out of their berths and landing on the deck with a thud. Charnay looked at Molly with a concerned expression. Molly chided herself for not cautioning him against tying off the sheet in these conditions. She held her tongue since it would have been better had Charnay been prepared to let out the boom and storm jib sheet to luff off the wind blast and keep the sloop at an even keel. Had he done so, the gust would have had minimal effect.

Charnay held onto the handrails to keep himself aboard. The boat then snapped back after the gust blew through. He quickly untied the sheets but kept them wrapped about the capstans so that he would correctly handle a future similar occurrence. Charnay struggled to maintain the proper sail tension; but as the situation stabilized, his responsibility in causing the close call dawned on him.

Adding to his embarrassing lapse, Jean-Luc called out with understandable sarcasm, "What is the problem up there?"

Charnay turned crimson in embarrassment, fearing that Molly would expose his poor response during the nautical crisis.

Molly responded with a marital skill honed over thirteen years, "Everything is under control, dear. Go back to sleep."

Charnay looked at Molly. His expression conveyed both his regret and gratitude. Molly nodded. After that steering fiasco, she returned the sloop to a close reach and had it once again slicing across the wave crests. Her confidence returned, and she soon had the boat in a smooth rhythm once again.

Just as the mistake's effects faded, Lake Erie conspired with the wind to play another nasty trick. A second rogue wave slapped against the hull and the follow-on roller overpowered the stern as the sloop sat in the swell of two large waves. Molly stared with wide-eyed terror as water flowed over the transom and into the boat. The specter of sinking filled her mind as lake water began flowing into the boat. Molly shrieked, "Jean-Luc!" She grabbed the oaken bucket and bailed feverishly with her left hand while gripping the tiller to steer away from the wave's crest. Charnay also began bailing.

Jean-Luc shot up from his berth and leapt toward the hatch, where he was met with a foot of water swirling about the deck. As if God were her co-pilot, the wave lifted the boat's transom into the air. Jean-Luc held onto the companionway's railings, but Molly and Charnay were tossed forward and hit the deck hard when the sloop landed with a bone jarring splash.

"What did you just do?" asked Jean-Luc accusingly.

Charnay said in Molly's defense, "It wasn't her fault. That foul wave came out of nowhere."

The boat's stern went temporarily airborne on the next wave and sloshed much of the water over the scuppers and out of the steering compartment. Molly and Jean-Luc's eyes met, and they realized how close they had [all] come to death. Molly turned quickly to look toward the bow and adjusted the tiller to return to her 'close reach' course. Jean-Luc took the bucket and bailed the last of the water. When he turned to return to his berth. He stopped, looked skyward with a thoughtful expression, and ran his fingers through his hair. He said wryly, "I do not understand why I would have thought there was a problem. Anyway, it looks like the storm is passing over."

As he walked below, he said over his shoulder, "You are doing a good job."

Molly sensed his teasing tone. Her anxiety level lowered conspicu-ously. Despite the pelting rain, she smiled at Charnay. She whispered, "Enjoy the rare praise."

What little water remained raced through the boat's scuppers and flowed overboard. Just as Molly and Charnay breathed a sigh of relief, several lightning bolts zigzagged in white flashes across the dark, steely sky. Molly swallowed hard, knowing that lightning is a danger of the highest order to a lone boat on the lake's surface. She said to Charnay, "We're not out of danger quite yet. The mast is the highest point for miles around and could attract a strike."

Charnay asked, "What will happen if lightning strikes the boat""

"Well—neither the mast nor the sloop would survive, Excellency. A strike assuredly would run down the mast and punch a hole in the boat's hull. We would sink within a minute."

Charnay's eyes widened as he looked first at the sky and then around for some sight of land.

When the anticipated thunderclap boomed astern, Molly sighed audibly.

Charnay asked, "What?"

Molly said, "The storm has passed over us and is now to the east.

Do you remember the Indian canoes turning tail and heading ashore?"
Charnay nodded. "You have to admire their knowledge of the weather's
signs. I would have preferred to have sought a sheltered area to anchor
and ride out the storm, but then that would have placed us too close to
the Indians, and I didn't want that."

As the tempest subsided, Molly remained at the tiller. The rain slack-
ened to a soft shower, the wind fell off, and the waves settled down. When
the whitecaps died out, it was safe for her to look in on Jean-Luc. She
found him sleeping like an angel. Even Belfort managed to catch some
shut-eye, despite the hair-raising drama Molly and Charnay endured.

Molly felt proud about her turn at the helm. She had capably steered
the vessel through a squall, showing remarkable stamina in miserable
conditions, and guided the boat safely over the waves. Despite the boat's
rising and falling, and the miserable spray that flew into her face when
the stem smashed downward into the lake's surface, the sloop was for-
ging its path across Erie's waters. She resumed her reliance on the compass.
She felt confident that, providing they maintained their current speed,
they would be close to the mouth of the Detroit River in the morning.

As the gray day slipped toward darkness, Molly began to grow
afraid of sailing in the dark. She feared that she wouldn't be able to see
a floating log. Fortunately, she had the comforting memory of her old
deck officer's admonition to rely on her training. She smiled at the memory of her time as a powder monkey on a frigate during the war. She had
mastered her fear than, and she could do so again on this lake in the
darkness.

The *Kissing Rock* continued westward under Molly's steady hand,
but she was definitely wearying from the cool wind flowing over her
wet clothing. When Jean-Luc and Belfort emerged from the cabin to
relieve them on the helm and the sails, she and Charnay were spent.

At sunset, Jean-Luc nodded to Molly to observe the pink sky
spreading across the lake. Molly recalled the adage, 'Red sky at night,
sailor's delight.' She said, "Husband, I would like to get out of these wet
clothes and stand on land. Put ashore for a spell, will you?"

Jean-Luc nodded empathetically and tacked for the south shore.

CHAPTER FOURTEEN

WHEN THE *KISSING ROCK* approached the strait and a large river island loomed before them, Belfort asked, "We must be close to the pay chests, no?"

Jean-Luc said, "We are still about 30 miles from *Île aux Cochons*. We will sail the east passage, trying to keep a river island between us and the far shore. Let us hope they shield us from enemy observation. The Detroit River is a strait that connects the two large lakes, St. Clair and Erie. Your buried pay chests lie on an island near the head of the strait at Lake St. Clair. As you can see, the strait is quite wide here — almost four miles wide. The natural depths of the strait are about thirty-five feet — more than sufficient."

The paladins and Molly walked forward and stood near the bow. Molly turned around and asked, "What can you tell us about this island?"

"It is the *Île de Bois Blanc*, and it is the largest we'll encounter. At its northern end, there is a perfect anchorage. I used it last time. But now, we must sail against the current and navigate with only moonlight."

Belfort asked, "What can I do?"

"If you would be so kind, your Excellency, would you sit by the bow and watch for floating debris?"

Charnay said, "I will do that also."

With the moon illuminating the course, Jean-Luc steered the sloop up the eastern channel and past several small islands. Two and a half hours later, the paladins lowered the anchor off Île de Bois Blanc's northeast shore.

━━━━◆━━━━▶

Lone Eagle and Hopping Bird stood on the shore of Lake Erie. They and the boys had travelled far and were deep inside Wyandot territory. He glanced back at the boys drying their clothing over the small fire that he had reluctantly allowed them to build. Hopping Bird tapped his shoulder and pointed to rising smoke in the distance. Lone Eagle nodded and gave the hand signal for the boys to extinguish their fire. He then asked Hopping Bird, "Should we send them to steal from the Wyandots?"

Hopping Bird shrugged, but then said, "This is our purpose. It is why we have brought them into the forest. We shall see who among them can act decisively in a do-or-die situation."

Lone Eagle turned and walked to where the boys were drying their clothing. "Wyandots are in these forests, less than a morning's walk away. I have seen their lakeside campfire to our east. Let us hope that they have not seen ours."

The boys stopped their small talk, turned, and listened intently. Everyone knew now that a false move would mean death. Chava slowly and deliberately extinguished the fire and spread the embers about for cooling.

Tadewi asked, "What do you want of us, Lone Eagle?"

Lone Eagle said, "Two volunteers will approach the Wyandots to silently observe. I want them to tell me how many of the enemy there are."

With disdain in his voice, Chava said, "That is not difficult."

Hopping Bird, standing to the side, said, "And take some object without the Wyandots knowing."

The Miami youth looked at one another. For a moment, no one moved; but then Chava stood. Miakoda, realizing that he must defend his own position as a top prospect, also stood and walked over to take a place beside Chava.

Lone Eagle said, "We have our volunteers. Let us approach the Wyandot camp without delay."

Two hours later, the Miamis, in single file, halted a hundred yards from the Wyandot camp. The Miami's could smell the enemy's campfire, where meat was being dried to make jerky. At that point, Chava and Miakoda approached furtively, with Lone Eagle a short distance behind them to observe their actions.

The trio crept forward with stealthy skill and halted to watch the lone Wyandot cooking some fish over a fire. Using hand signals, Lone Eagle cautioned his two charges there may be others in the area and they were to observe the enemy camp awhile. Though they nodded, Lone Eagle's brow furrowed over the thought the boys might act rashly. But the boys had been trained well, and they waited... and watched. For another hour, the Miami trio observed. Lone Eagle concluded that it was unlikely that the Wyandot had companions in the vicinity, and he nodded to the boys. His signal gave them permission to approach the campsite.

Chava, Miakoda, and Lone Eagle inched to the camp periphery. Lone Eagle held his breath as Chava reached through the bushes, attempting to pilfer the man's hunting knife. With only Chava's forearm exposed, his hand grasped the handle and pulled it into the bush. Lone Eagle (and the boys) smiled at the successful incursion. The Wyandot warrior's attention was fully on his fish cooking above his fire. The four actors in the play were within yards of one another.

Now it was Miakoda's turn. He would prove Chava's equal, but when he crawled under the bush near where the Wyandot's gear sat, he found nothing within reach. Lone Eagle deemed the situation too risky and expected Miakoda to silently withdraw. If only Miakoda had withdrawn, he would have reported that the young man had used excellent judgment. But Miakoda did not withdraw. Rather, he waited until the Wyandot turned his back to add wood to his fire. Miakoda tiptoed from the bushes to the Wyandot's quiver. He slowly withdrew a single arrow.

Beads of perspiration dripped from Lone Eagle's brow. There was no way his young student would succeed, and his eyes darted from the Wyandot to Miakoda and back. His hand slowly moved to his knife and he unsheathed his blade.

As Lone Eagle anticipated, the Wyandot looked around. Miakoda froze. The Indian's surprise turned quickly to anger, and he moved for his knife. Arriving where he had placed his knife, it was not there, Miakoda turned to flee. However, the Wyandot was agile. He seized Miakoda by his wrist. Reacting to his instincts, the Wyandot ripped the stolen arrow from Miakoda's grasp.

A second before he plunged the shaft into the teen's chest, Lone Eagle leaped from the brush, put his hand over the enemy's mouth, and thrust his knife into the Wyandot's back. The enemy's grip on the boy's wrist loosened, and he sank to the ground bleeding profusely. Lone Eagle, a veteran of many such battles, placed his foot on the Wyandot's back and pulled his bloody knife free. Miakoda bolted away from the clearing and ran into the forest. He didn't stop running until he came to the clearing where his friends lay in wait.

Though Hopping Bird did not see the deadly encounter from his hiding place, he knew that his friends had been compromised. Using hand signals, he motioned for the other teens to move back to the lake, where they had grounded the canoes.

Before departing the Wyandot's camp, Lone Eagle picked up the purloined arrow. Then he, Chava, and Miakoda ran through the forest, weaving their way through the dark green vegetation. Moments later, they met up with the others at the canoe site. The other boys crowded around Chava and Miakoda and congratulated them profusely. Chava beamed with pride, but Miakoda grew sullen and withdrew. He walked to a tree and sat.

Hopping Bird herded the boys into the canoes. Just as the last teen became situated, Hopping Bird gestured to Lone Eagle that he wanted a private conversation with Miakoda. As Lone Eagle walked across the shore, every boy looked upon him in awe. Only Miakoda, in sullen humiliation, stared out at the lake.

Hopping Bird asked Lone Eagle in a whisper, "What happened?"

"The Wyandot discovered Miakoda. He showed bad judgement leaving his concealment. The Wyandot was about to kill him. I had to intervene."

Hopping Bird said, "I understand."

Lone Eagle walked over to Miakoda and sat down beside him. He said, "Miakoda, listen to me."

Miakoda said, "I just want to be alone; I failed."

Lone Eagle knew he had to boost Miakoda's spirit. He said, "One instance of poor judgement does not define you. There will be more opportunities for you to express your courage and leadership."

Miakoda picked up a small stick and scratched the ground with it as he mulled over Lone Eagle's words. Finally, he asked, "Will the Wyandot's suspect the Miamis?"

Lone Eagle wasn't going to lie and said, "I believe so." The implication was clear to both of them—the Wyandots would take to the warpath, to seek revenge on the killer's tribe. Someone from the Miami tribe will be ambushed and killed to avenge the Wyandot warrior's death. Someone from the village will die a horrible death because a young Miami acted recklessly.

Miakoda said, "I am in your debt. Lone Eagle saved Miakoda's life."

Lone Eagle said, "Miami's take care of their own. You would have done the same for me."

Miakoda glanced up and smiled. He said, "I will make you proud of me this hunt, Lone Eagle. You have my word."

Lone Eagle said, "Let us rejoin the others."

SATURDAY, 5:45 A.M.

Molly sat cross-legged in the bow of the sloop. She was wrapped in a blanket and held her musket in her lap. The bill for the arduous journey had come due. Her body ached, she missed her children terribly, and the morning's chill in the air made her tired bones wish that they were in her Manhattan featherbed. And yet, she had stayed awake in the final watch over the sloop (and its inhabitants). Though it had been a struggle to remain awake, she did her best to enjoy the quiet in the cool, morning air. She took the opportunity to enjoy watching a flock of mallard ducks that had swooped in low past the boat and landed one after another in gentle splashes off the starboard beam.

In the mist ahead, she could barely make out some blurry shapes. Then, several canoes broke through the river mist and glided southward. They contained two trappers per canoe. The men appeared strong, focused, and capable. She noticed that the canoes carried no hides. Thus, they must have just departed from Fort Detroit late yesterday.

A trapper in the lead canoe called out to her. "Settlers?"

Molly shook her head and said with a friendly tone, "Traders."

"I figured. No settlers ever came in a vessel like that one. Good thing that. Otherwise them regulars would most likely be on you like a duck on a June Bug." He then asked, "What have you to trade?"

Molly answered cautiously, "Cloth—mostly." The trapper returned to paddling.

Jean-Luc sat up and rubbed the sleep from his eyes. Get got up from his berth and looked out the companionway. He asked, "Who are you talking to, darling?"

She pointed to the canoes moving downriver and said, "These waters are too busy for us to move undetected. Since the regulars will be hearing about us, I propose we stop in at the fort for supplies."

Jean-Luc nodded. He reached over and awakened the French aristocrats. He said, "We could encounter English soldiers at any time. You may want to brush up on your accents."

By first light, they had the sloop's main sail up and began making headway upriver. At mid-day, the wind shifted direction. Now blowing out of the north, it forced the *Kissing Rock*'s crew to repeatedly tack to make modest headway. It was difficult and frustrating, and the distance covered was underwhelming. Their alternative was to anchor until the winds blew from a favorable direction. But Jean-Luc's persistence paid off; and by late afternoon, Île aux Cochons loomed into view.

As their destination came into view, the treasure hunters could see the sun disappearing behind the trees. Jean-Luc said to Belfort, "Excellency, everyone is exhausted, and I just do not envision us digging up the treasure this evening."

Belfort said, "Agreed. I have been thinking of your story, and since your friends were bitten in the darkness, I think it's smarter if we went ashore in the morning."

Molly said, "We have some time before the sun goes down. I could cook a hot meal if one of you gentlemen would start a fire on the beach."

As Charnay lowered himself over the side into knee-deep water, he asked Jean-Luc, "It has been thirteen years since you were here. Do you think the hogs have been effective in eliminating the snakes?"

"They certainly have had enough time," said Jean-Luc laughing.

The following morning, Jean-Luc, Belfort, and Charnay went ashore. Jean-Luc stopped before three scraggly pine trees and looked about with a slightly puzzled expression.

Charnay asked, "Is something the matter?"

"The trees have grown. It threw me off for a moment. They not only look different, but I remember there being only two here," said Jean-Luc.

Belfort said, "Take your time. It has been thirteen years since you were here, and it was nighttime."

Jean-Luc mopped his brow and turned to catch a glimpse of Molly standing by the boat. She waved, and the exchange helped him to relax. He studied the area around the three trees. He knelt in front of the pines and scooped up a handful of soil. He allowed the grains to fall slowly between his fingers. Jean-Luc stood and announced, "The pay chests aren't here."

Belfort with a hint of irritation asked, "What makes you think that?"

"The soil has been disturbed — someone has been here," said Jean-Luc.

Charnay stepped forward and said, "We have travelled far. Let us verify your theory, shall we?" He placed his shovel's blade in the dirt and shoved it into the earth. He began tossing dirt to the side.

Jean-Luc said, "I will help you, Excellency." He, too, began digging, and they quickly deepened the hole. Molly observed from the shore with keen interest. Not discovering any pay chests after digging down three feet, Jean-Luc said, "It is not here. I was afraid of this." He turned to Molly and shook his head. Molly's shoulders slumped in response to the discovery.

Agitated, Belfort asked, "Are you certain that this is the correct tree?"

"There is a way to verify it," said Jean-Luc. Then he surprised his companions by stepping off seven deliberate steps to the east. He went to one knee and studied the ground. After concluding that the ground had not been disturbed, he placed his shovel's blade against the ground and forced it into the earth with his foot.

Leaving the sloop to see what was happening, Molly walked up with a pistol, and with Belfort and Charnay walked over to Jean-Luc. Molly could tell her husband was finding it hard to dig. His expression showed that this hard going comforted him, because he believed that it meant that the third chest hadn't been poached. It only took a few dozen shovelfuls of dirt before his blade struck something hard. Jean-Luc fell to his knees and brushed dirt away with his hands until a metal box lay fully exposed. Jean-Luc broke open the lid with his shovel. The pay chest hasps had rusted and didn't want to work. Jean-Luc pried open the lid, revealing a large cache of gold coins. Jean-Luc stood and slapped his hands together to knock off the dust. He looked over to the prior hole and said, "We can be certain now that our first hole was the correct location."

Charnay asked, "If French government agents recovered the first two, why not the third?"

Belfort nodded. "He is correct. It does not make any sense." Jean-Luc ran his fingers through his hair as he mulled over the enigma.

Molly felt as confused as the paladins. She looked at her husband and asked, "Jean-Luc, what do you think happened?"

CHAPTER FIFTEEN

SATURDAY, MARCH 27, 1773

JEAN-LUC GLANCED at his wife and then returned his attention to the gold coins in the earth below his feet.

Molly said, "I know you have a theory."

"I do—and it is growing more plausible. I believed that Marc's disappearance was purely coincidental. But now I am suspicious."

Charnay said, "Explain, if you please."

"Rochebeaucourt and d'Espinassy were friends."

"How does that effect the missing pay chests?" asked Belfort.

Jean-Luc said, "When the lieutenant handed me the map to give to Marc, I put it in my pocket. I did not look at the map for a week and a half. I viewed it only after Alex was killed in the ambush. The first thing I noticed was that the third pay chest wasn't delineated. But I dug the second hole, and I knew where it was even though Paul did not record it on the map"

Molly said, "I understand. When you gave the map to Major Marc, he did not know of the third pay chest. Was Paul going to double cross him?"

Jean-Luc said, "It looks that way to me."

Charnay asked, "But you could have reported it. Why did you not?"

"My arrival touched off chaos that night. Paul's fiancée and the parents of my dead comrades were descending on the boat. Marc was anxious. Right away he sent me with my father. And believe me, Montréal was frenzied in the days prior to the surrender," said Jean-Luc. He knelt and scooped a handful of gold coins. He stared thoughtfully at them and then allowed them to fall one by one between his fingers. He looked up and said, "With my last mission completed and the war lost, my thoughts were on Molly."

Molly said, "That's sweet."

"Reuniting with her was my focus. I was not thinking of an omitted detail on the map."

Molly said, "So Paul intended to cheat his partner. If they were going to split the two chests between them, Paul would only have to return here alone at some future time and would have doubled his take."

Belfort said, "We should interrogate Monsieur Rochebeaucourt. It is well that we recovered this pay chest, but we shall account for the missing ones before departing Montréal, and I think he is the one with answers."

Molly said, "It was a good thing that you didn't mention the third pay chest, because it, too, would have been lost. At least the king will have one returned."

Belfort and Charnay nodded.

She said as an afterthought, "The gold will be excellent ballast for the trip home."

Jean-Luc and Charnay each took a handle and lifted the chest from the hole. As they turned to carry their load across the island's sand to the shore, Molly said in an alarmed voice, "Everybody freeze."

Slithering across Belfort's left shoe was a four-foot snake with a heart shaped head and gray diamonds running the length of its brown body. Belfort's eyes widened and beads of sweat popped out of his brow. Molly cocked the pistol and pointed it at the snake's head.

Charnay said in a soft voice, "Do not pull the trigger, Madame. It is a mother, and she has recently given birth." Molly's finger moved off the trigger, but she didn't release the flint into the frizzen and kept the pistol pointed at the snake.

Jean-Luc said, "I must have disturbed her, or them, while digging one of the holes." He pointed and said, "Look, there are more."

Charnay said, "Look!"

A dozen baby snakes slithered into view. The four treasure seekers did not move.

Molly said in a whisper, "Young snakes can kill, too." The four-footer slithered away but then stopped. Her babies then surrounded Molly and her companions. With their pistols out and ready to shoot a lunging serpent. Molly's eyes moved from snake to snake. Moments later, she glanced at Jean-Luc. His face had blanched, and it was obvious he was still frightened of rattlesnakes. No one spoke as the serpents coiled up four feet away. She said to her husband, "You are right to be wary, dear, you have seen what their poison can do. It appears we aren't to move."

A twig cracking underfoot in the woods provoked the four to turn toward the sound. Emerging from the woods ten feet away was a small man about forty-two inches tall. His hair and beard were red, his teeth were pointed, and he was wearing a felt sun hat. He appeared to have recently awakened, because there was straw on his clothing and in his hair.

"You startled us," said Molly.

"Are you afraid of snakes?" he asked. He then knelt and motioned for the mama rattler to come to him. She stopped at the little man's feet and allowed him to pick her up.

Molly asked, "Are you one of this island's swineherds?" He shook his head slowly. "Are these your snakes?" He nodded slowly.

Jean-Luc blurted, "I know you. You were present the night we buried the chests in the sand."

The dwarf again nodded. Speaking French, the dwarf asked Jean-Luc, "Did you find your ships where I said they would be?"

"Yes, I did, and—thank you," said Jean-Luc with a forced smile.

Molly's mind raced, and it occurred to her that this little person could be the spirit who haunts the Great Lakes. Molly turned to the dwarf and asked, "What are you intending to do with your serpents?"

"Oh, we guard the treasure, but alas, our efforts have been insufficient." Molly recoiled and stepped backward. The little man chuckled. "Are you afraid of me? Your expression says yes." He petted the rattler's head and smiled.

Molly instinctively placed her hand on a small cross around her neck. She asked, "Are you Le Nain Rouge?" The dwarf looked surprised. "Yes, you are he!" With anger rising in her breast, Molly slowly removed the cross from her neck. The red dwarf watched her with interest. She then held it at arm's length toward him.

The snake in his hand hissed and the red headed dwarf seemed confused. "It appears we are at an impasse," he said.

Molly said, "It appears so." She glanced back at Jean-Luc, but he remained oblivious to her predicament. "I am willing to part company peaceably, if you are."

"And yet, your friends are stealing the last of my treasure," said the red dwarf with sadness.

Molly said, "We aren't stealing. This gold has an owner."

Belfort spoke up. "The gold belongs to the King of France."

"I know," said the little man perking up.

"You should not object, then, to us returning the gold to the king's treasury."

Charnay relaxed his defensive posture, slowly returned the flint-lock to its pan, and straightened his stance. He said, "Do you recognize me, Roger?"

The little man began to shake visibly. His voice cracked as he asked, "How do you know my name?"

"Because I, too, am from the Rhône Region. I am Geoffrey, Comte de Charnay. You once served, or should I say, 'betrayed,' my great-grandmother, did you not?"

Belfort swished his pistol back and forth and asked, "You know one another?"

"As a boy, my aunt told me about him," said Charnay. "You see, he once was part of Maison de Charnay. Her trysts with the king would never have been spoken of again, but for Roger here. When other courtiers heard of the king's conquest, they let the servants know that there was a reward for the woman's name. He knew of her affair and whispered it into the ears of my great grandfather's enemies for the *money*." Turning to Le Nain Rouge, he said, "You did not hesitate a second, did you, Roger? He did not want to shame his wife, for he loved her despite her failings. How, then, did you land in this primeval spot, Roger?"

Le Nain Rouge said, "My daughter and I, innocent girl though she be, were hexed by two angels who responded to the countess's prayers. They sent my daughter and me to New France to suffer in the snows until the curse ends or our time is commuted. The holy messengers hinted that I may help or harass humans I met for good or for ill. See, monsieur," he said pointing to Jean-Luc, "I helped you thirteen years ago, did I not?"

Jean-Luc said with hesitation, "You did."

Le Nain Rouge asked, "Are you four with the other man that came for the king's gold?"

Charnay said, "We know not to whom you refer, Roger. I am not in the mood for a riddle."

"He was here only days ago. He cleaned out the second box. I didn't like him. He was rude; and now that I know that he is a thief, I feel better about the hex I placed on him."

Charnay remembered the circle of serpents and asked pointedly, "Roger, are you forgetting something?"

"Pardon me, monsieur le Comte, I will dismiss them *toute de suite*," said the dwarf. He waved his hand toward the woods, and the serpents, one by one, began to slither toward the dwarf who held their mother. Le Nain Rouge gently placed the mama rattlesnake onto the ground and watched proudly as she and her dangerous brood slithered into nearby bushes.

"We intend you and your pets no harm," said Molly.

Le Nain Rouge asked, "Monsieur le comte de Charnay, would you pray for my daughter and me? We have faithfully carried out our instructions." Charnay nodded unenthusiastically. Le Nain Rouge turned to Jean-Luc and asked the same question. Jean-Luc also nodded.

Le Nain Rouge said, "I have two of the best advocates possible." He doffed his cap melodramatically, and vanished.

Jean-Luc said, "Let us leave Île aux Cochons. I will fill in the earth and cover up the signs that the soil has been disturbed. Get aboard and I will join you in a few minutes." Molly did not respond. Jean-Luc looked at her and asked, "Was that a ghost?"

When his spade work was finished, Jean-Luc walked to the river's edge and found Molly waist deep in the river holding a rope attached to the bow. The paladins had hoisted the anchor aboard and had partially raised the sails. With the sails ready to hoist, the paladins held off until Jean-Luc climbed over the gunnel and Molly pulled the stem away from the isle. Jean-Luc offered Molly his hand. After she placed her hand in his, he pulled her aboard.

As the *Kissing Rock* picked up speed, Molly broke into a wide grin and said, "We did it. We found the pay chest."

"Well, one of three," said Charnay matter-of-factly.

The sloop rounded the island's boot and Jean-Luc steered her for Fort Detroit, which loomed ominously on the distant riverbank. He whispered to Molly, "I am glad you came along."

Molly smiled and said, "Me, too." She thought back to the island and her meeting with the little man and his snakes. She then looked across the river at the distant frontier fort and asked, "What's next?" The paladins heard her query and looked at Jean-Luc.

Jean-Luc said, "We will pick up supplies at the fort and then head for the Ottawa village and the wedding.

SUNDAY, APRIL 1, CHIPPEWA TRIBAL COUNCIL

Chief Ahmik looked into the faces of his assembled councilmen. He had been dreading this conference, even though everyone knew beforehand its purpose. The council had convened to decide who among them would accompany the sachem and his daughter into Ottawa country and attend the momentous wedding. These two tribes had bitterly competed for land and resources longer than anyone sitting there could remember, and the rivalry had only intensified when the Ottawas returned to the Maumee River Valley on their southern border.

Chief Ahmik was dreading the conference because he expected that his hot-headed war chief, Migisi, would ask to be among the wedding delegation. And as certain as the impending sunset, Migisi sat sullenly near the entrance of the council lodge. Ahmik opened the council by lighting the tribal calumet. The Chippewa traditionally opened councils by passing this decorative peace pipe among the attendees. Ahmik lit the tobacco and took two long, deep draws of the pungent smoke. He slowly passed the calumet to the councilman on his left, who replicated his action. Each elder did the same until the calumet made the rounds. Then Chief Ahmik took the calumet from his kinsman and placed on its stand. Thus, this pleasurable activity opened their solemn gathering.

"We are here to make a decision." The tribal elders listened respectfully. "My daughter is marrying outside our tribe. The ceremony is in the Ottawa lands three moons to the south. I wish all could accompany me, but life in the village goes on. We must have sufficient warriors and their women to protect our lodges and tend to the crops."

Taima (Ahmik's friend since childhood) said, "Several elders in this council would be a good delegation to the Ottawa nation. It is Ahmik's daughter; he should select our delegation."

Migisi spoke up to denounce Taima's suggestion. He said, "The Ottawa are our enemies. Not only the sachem but his war chief should attend. We must project strength to the Ottawa. I will select three of our best braves, and we will safeguard the sachem while he is in the lodges of the Ottawa."

Taima nodded thoughtfully, but he did not back down (to Ahmik's relief) and said, "This marriage will end the enmity between the Ottawa and Chippewa. And Migisi, you were once engaged to the bride. The new husband may not appreciate this and may interpret your presence as a challenge. That would not be in the Chippewas' best interests."

With rising anger in his voice Migisi said, "It is our tradition that the war chief accompanies the sachem to an enemy's village. If Ahmik is to powwow with the Ottawa, the war chief should be present."

The gray-haired Taima said, "This is a wedding, not a powwow." Migisi glared at him, and the deep tension between Taima and Migisi was palpable.

A heretofore silent council member said, "It is tradition for the war chief to represent us. Perhaps Migisi should go."

To defuse the emotional gathering, Ahmik said, "Does anyone else wish to speak?" Ahmik paused to give all a chance to indicate that they wished to speak for or against Migisi's ideas. Sincerely wishing that the council had overruled the war chief's request, the father of the bride reluctantly picked up the calumet and said, "It is decided, our war chief will escort the sachem."

◄—◆—►

TUESDAY, APRIL 9, 6 P.M., MAUMEE RIVER MOUTH

Though the *Kissing Rock*'s unique design had stirred a great deal of interest, the visit to Fort Detroit for supplies had gone without incident. Having sailed all day, the St. Alemberts and their passengers arrived as the sun behind the forest cast the longest shadows across the lake's shore. After dropping anchor, Belfort tried again to achieve a consensus for his inclusion.

Belfort said to Jean-Luc, "I would enjoy attending your friend's wedding. An Indian wedding—it would be unique. Do you think your friend would object if I accompanied you?"

Molly and Jean-Luc looked at one another in disbelief that the subject hadn't been raised earlier, given Belfort's stated interest in native culture.

Jean-Luc stammered, "I would like to take you, it is just that," he stopped and looked beseechingly at Charnay.

In support of the idea, Molly said, "If the comte de Belfort came along, we *would be safer* on the trail."

"I am thinking of the boat: its security, that is," said Jean-Luc.

Charnay, hesitant to urge restraint, said in a measured voice, "The gold aboard cannot be left unguarded, and if I alone remain behind, that is inadequate security. Rici, this boat represents our only way to return to civilization, not to mention the king's treasure. The St. Alemberts have earned the right to attend their friend's wedding without feeling guilty." He placed his hand on the younger paladin's shoulder and added, "But, if you really want to go, I will watch the boat while everyone is away."

Belfort's brow furrowed. He turned away in thought. After several moments, he faced his colleagues and announced, "Our New York hosts have brought us deep into the North American wilderness to recover the king's gold. We have been successful. They should have the opportunity to see their friend and attend his wedding. I will forego the pleasure of watching a native wedding and will remain with you, Geoff, and the boat."

Jean-Luc said, "Thank you, Excellency. I know that monsieur le Comte de Charnay is grateful for your sacrifice."

Charnay allowed a smile to crack his normally serious expression and said, "Rici, you and I will have a wonderful time conversing, fishing, and discussing the politics of Versailles." He turned to Jean-Luc and said, "Enjoy yourselves and do not worry about us."

The following morning, Molly and Jean-Luc set out early for the Ottawa village. At sundown, they arrived and were greeted by a surprised and delighted Chief Opechwan.

CHAPTER SIXTEEN

OLLY LAY IN her bedding watching a large bead of water as it traveled down the rope; it gathered in size until it came to the end two feet above a clay jar and dropped, "Kerplip." I enjoy the sound of rain, she thought, why is tonight different? A few seconds later there followed another water bead, "Kerplip." Now even raindrops were annoying; they sounded foreboding. Molly opened one eye and looked up at the rope system that her host had constructed to control leaks. Enduring fitful sleep, she had studied his system for hours. While she marveled at the ingenuity, the dripping noise nevertheless made getting to sleep difficult.

Molly sat up, pushed her auburn hair out of her eyes, and stared at the rain jar. She cocked an ear and listened for footsteps. Hearing none, she returned her attention to the jar. She considered moving it, but that would only create a new problem. Though the gentle shower had fallen throughout the night, only small amounts of rain managed to enter the teepee's smoke hole. The resident's solution to this problem was to place a series of rope loops below the opening to catch the rain and have it run down his lines and drip into a container. The solution worked well, and the dripping sounds apparently didn't bother anyone else. Molly rolled onto her back and felt the armed musket she placed there (just in case).

Smelling an unpleasant odor, she wrinkled her nose and tried breathing through her mouth. The teepee smelled of a mixture of smoke and the animal fat that was stored near the entrance. Molly didn't have to ask about the fat, because she knew that her host used it as a skin rub to keep away biting mosquitoes and pesky no-see-ums.

As she settled onto her back, she felt something digging into her. "Ouch," said Molly under her breath. Mindful of the early hour, she rolled over quietly, pulled her blankets away, and felt beneath them. Jean-Luc slumbered quietly alongside her. She spied a small pebble, which was probably the culprit. She flicked it away. Satisfied that she had resolved the issue, she smoothed out the blankets and snuggled under them once more. But now her feet felt chilled, so she quietly inched closer to her husband and placed them against his calves.

"*Mon Dieu*," gasped Jean-Luc. With a wide-eyed expression, he rolled over, and asked Molly in whispered French, "What are you *doing*?"

Molly answered defensively, "My feeties were cold."

Jean-Luc rolled over, placed his nose up to his wife's, and said in French, "Cuddle closer." Molly looked skeptical. Nodding toward the Indian sleeping on the far side of the smoking embers, Jean-Luc whispered, "Opechwan is asleep."

The Ottawa warrior said quietly in French, "No, I am awake—now." He turned his head a bit and chided gently, "Lower your voices, and do not do anything to awaken the neighbors."

Now speaking in a whisper, Jean-Luc replied, "Opechwan, we sailed from New York City to attend your wedding. I promised you when we were boys I would be here, did I not?" Jean-Luc grinned broadly and brushed a shock of dark hair away from his forehead. This trip from New York City was feasible only because he had been offered a profitable shipping delivery to Fort Detroit and because Jean-Luc's father wanted to spend time with his grandchildren. Jean-Luc said, "We are happy that you found someone to love."

Opechwan smiled. Jean-Luc continued, "You would like our little girl and her two brothers; they are full of curiosity. But when we stopped in Montréal we left them with my father. They couldn't make the journey. Plus, my father really wanted time with his grandchildren." Jean-Luc paused, and then said, "By the way, my father told me to say, 'Bonjour,' and that he hoped you are well. He, too, is happy you have found someone." Opechwan beamed at the memory of Jean-Luc's welcoming family. Jean-Luc continued, "I actually enjoyed the walk. The twenty-five miles passed quickly."

Opechwan was used to Jean-Luc's teasing. He stood and began rolling his bedding. This remarkable friendship between a New York businessman and an Ottawa warrior had weathered encounters with dangerous animals, war, time, and now miles of separation. Two years earlier, Opechwan's first wife had died from a fever. Referencing their late in the night arrival at the tribe's location, Jean-Luc said, "I am sorry we missed Kateri. We are looking forward to getting to know her. Is that not so, Molly?"

"We are," Molly said as she stood. She began to roll the blankets

Opechwan said, "After the death of my brother Pontiac, the tribal council decided to move the village to the location we inhabited before the Ottawa moved to Montréal. This responsibility to move my people fell to me. Pontiac and I were born here."

Jean-Luc started to say something teasing but sensed that Opechwan's role as sachem required his friend to behave with dignity. Opechwan continued, "I have a cousin attending from another tribe. My mother was from a tribe a four days walk to the north. Normally, a couple lives in the wife's lodging, but my mother and father lived with the Ottawas. He added, "We were at war with the Chippewas then, and they would have killed my father. I met this cousin when our tribes united and took to the warpath."

With this reference to the rebellion, Molly and Jean-Luc noticed that Opechwan had added four honor feathers to his headband. When Opechwan saw his guests' eyes on them, he explained, "These are for the braves of the Peoria tribe—not whites. I avenged my brother's murder by the Peorias. The Ottawas made a treacherous band pay with their blood."

Molly glanced at Jean-Luc for comfort. Afraid of offending his friend, Jean-Luc acted as though nothing about the conversation troubled him. Molly threw off the covers, walked to the teepee's opening, and peered out uneasily. While looking around, she asked in French, "Opechwan, is it safe to go to the river to fetch water?" Jean-Luc frowned at his wife's apprehension.

Opechwan said in a matter-of-fact voice, "I have spoken to my villagers; they understand my friendship with Jean-Luc. He fought by our side in Canada." Not accounting for wedding guests from regional tribes, Opechwan described an overly optimistic report of the Indians' openness to the St. Alemberts' presence. Relations between the red men and the white settlers streaming into the southern areas below the great lakes were quiet but far from harmonious. After all, Opechwan and his kinsmen fought ferociously during Pontiac's Rebellion and died in large numbers. Many of these adjacent lodges displayed mourning totems (planks with carved otters pointed downward) from those dark times.

Knowing that Opechwan had taken part in his brother Pontiac's uprising, Molly worried about Opechwan's attitude towards her and Jean-Luc. Ten years had passed since the rebellion, and twenty years had passed since the boyhood event that had bonded Jean-Luc and Opechwan, Molly wondered whether she and Jean-Luc could rely on Opechwan's protection if trouble began.

Molly stood, tied her auburn hair back, pulled a shawl around her shoulders, picked up a leather bucket, and stepped into her moccasins. She picked up a small log and used it to poke the embers. Then, she softly placed the log onto the glowing coals. Jean-Luc rolled back and closed his eyes. Opechwan also began stoking the fire to knock off the morning chill in his lodge.

Molly said, "I think I'll go to the river." She then pushed open the teepee flap and peered out warily. Seeing that there was enough light to make her way, she stepped outside. The freshness of the breeze instantly struck her as wonderfully sweet. A dog in the next teepee growled softly, and Molly heard its owner scolding it. The sun was moments from peeking over the horizon, but the sky had begun to turn orange and she had enough light to see the path.

Molly scrutinized the village from her lodging's central location and stood in awe at the vista of seventy-five teepees sited around a wooden totem venerating the otter. The embedded totem, as well as Opechwan's teepee, was centrally located. Light gray smoke wafted through the openings of the lodgings. Not seeing anyone astir, Molly believed that a quick trip to fetch water would be harmless. At that moment, a man wearing white pants and the scarlet tunic of the British Army emerged from an adjacent teepee with a looking glass, soap, and razor in his hands.

Startled at the sight of a white woman, he said, "Oh my!"

Molly said in a low voice in English, "Good morning, sir." She estimated his height at six feet and noticed his bright red hair, which he tied back (much as Molly did). She estimated his age at twenty-five.

The man said, "It appears that we are heading to the same place."

Molly nodded and the two walked the short distance to the village perimeter and started down the path to the nearby river. After walking a short way, Molly said in English, "I am Molly St. Alembert. You are a captain in the regulars, are you not?"

Introducing oneself is not an Englishman's forte. It actually makes them quite uncomfortable. The officer didn't answer, and an awkward silence ensued. Finally, he said, "Captain Archer of the 37th Foot, at your service." He managed an uncomfortable smile. "I am here to attend a wedding." After walking a short distance, he asked, "Your name is French; are you from the continent?" He hoped that she was. "I would enjoy hearing news from Europe."

"Actually, my husband and I are New Yorkers." Disappointed, Captain Archer pursed his lip. Molly asked, "Do you feel safe here?"

"The Ottawas are not on the warpath. I feel that it is perfectly safe," he said, concealing his true opinion. "I am attached to Colonel

Johnson of Fort Detroit. He sent me to represent him at the wedding—to 'wave the flag.'"

Molly said, "That is why my husband and I are here, too. I mean, we are here for the wedding—no flag waving." She sensed his discomfort, she became somewhat anxious herself.

"I am glad to hear that you are not settlers."

"Why is that, Captain?"

"His majesty, in the Proclamation of '63, promised the Indians to prevent colonials from crossing the mountains. So, I am not altogether pleased to encounter a colonial in this territory."

"We aren't settlers; as I said, we live in New York—on the coast." Molly struggled to control her emotions. This conversation wasn't helping her disposition. She continued, "I thought that the recent treaties had smoothed over Indian fears of colonial intrusions." It was Molly's turn to be disingenuous. "They have, haven't they?"

"Perhaps, at least we hope so." Attempting to change the subject, he asked, "How do you know the groom?"

"My husband is friends with Opechwan. They were inseparable as boys. Although during the last eight years they lost contact. Men who are friends as children hold a special bond. My husband, Jean-Luc, is dedicated to his companion. He was determined to come."

"I am told that the groom is the brother of Pontiac." That name needed no elaboration. Molly knew that Chief Pontiac had been a young sachem allied with the Marquis de Montcalm at Quebec; she also was aware that Pontiac had led a rebellion ten years earlier that temporarily united a large number of tribes. The Indian rebellion attempted to push the colonial settlers back across the mountains.

Molly said, "That is true."

Captain Archer nodded and asked, "If I may inquire, how did your husband become friends with this Indian."

"As children they lived near each other and were playmates—they grew up hunting, swimming, and fishing together. During the '50s, the tribe was lodged outside Montréal where my husband's family lived. One day as they were playing, a bear attacked, and Jean-Luc saved

Opechwan's life by killing the beast. By placing himself between the beast and his friend, he made it possible for Opechwan to escape. According to tribal custom, Opechwan pledged to return the act twofold. I think the two of them have been through enough scrapes to qualify as all even, and I honestly think at this point, they like their relationship just the way it is. I know that my husband still retains a fierce fealty to his friend. And until the moment Jean-Luc married me and we moved to New York, the two rarely were apart."

"I see," said Captain Archer. "That explains your being here." Molly's expression didn't change, but she didn't appreciate the comment. Captain Archer asked, "Are you returning after the wedding?"

Molly said wryly, "Our business will not run itself."

Captain Archer, noticing that his question had offended, forced a smile and said, "Of course."

A moment later, they arrived at the water's edge. Captain Archer knelt and began to lather his shaving brush.

Molly, too, knelt and splashed water on her face. "Ooh, now that feels wonderful!" She wiped her face and dipped the bucket into the flowing water. It quickly filled, and she stood. Now she forced a smile and said, "It was nice to have met you. Perhaps I'll see you at the wedding." Captain Archer nodded. Molly turned to leave but noticed four native men coming down the path. As they walked past her, the braves gave Molly the once over. They were followed by six Ottawa women. All had come to gather water. The women walked past both groups, chatting quietly among themselves.

Molly whispered to Captain Archer, "Those men are not Ottawas."

"How can you tell?" he whispered back.

"Notice the tattoo on their left shoulders? It is a marten," answered Molly softly.

Archer regarded their tattoos and probed. "So?"

"That is not the Ottawa totem. They're Chippewas," she said.

Captain Archer thought a moment and asked, "Chippewas? Here?" Archer sighed and said, "Well, I never understood the native totem. What does it mean?"

Molly said, "Tribes identify with an animal or bird. They consider themselves related to it." She looked down at her filled bucket and mused aloud, "Opechwan did say his mother was Chippewa."

Captain Archer nodded and said, "The Chippewa village is one hundred miles northwest of here. Would they come that distance to attend the wedding?"

"Probably, they would travel that far if the ceremony was important politically."

"Well, the groom *is* a recently elected sachem."

"Opechwan didn't mention that he was the sachem," exclaimed Molly. "That rascal!"

"And that is why I am here," said Archer.

The Chippewas calmly regarded Captain Archer, whom they recognized from visits to Fort Detroit. However, their demeanors turned dark upon seeing Molly, as they knelt to drink from the flowing waters. The tallest brave, a warrior named *Migisi*, glared at Molly. The other men continued to splash water on themselves. After kneeling and drinking from his cupped hands, Migisi [Angry Wolf] said in his native tongue, "That woman should not be here. She must be here for the wedding."

Captain Archer pursed his lips as he swiped his razor over his sudsy lip.

Molly nodded up the slope and said, "I should get back."

The tallest warrior, a Chippewa named Abooksigun, gestured toward Molly. The Ottawa women grew silent, and their faces showed concern.

Captain Archer stood and said with concern in his voice, "I will walk you back."

Molly had felt anxious ever since she stepped out of the teepee, but never more than at this moment.

The eldest among the Ottawa women scolded the Chippewas, "She is a guest!"

Migisi answered indignantly, "Guests do not steal land. That is what her kind do. She is with the land stealers."

The elder woman stood, shook her finger, and said angrily, "She is a guest of the Ottawa—same as you."

Migisi glared at the elder woman but did not respond. The ensuing silence grew tense. Molly glanced over her shoulder and saw the tall warrior wipe his hands angrily on his buckskin leggings. Then he stood, all the while glaring at Molly.

"There's going to be trouble," said Molly.

Captain Archer glanced back. He took Molly by the arm and said, "Return to your lodge."

Molly shouted, "Jean-Luc, come quick."

Six of Opechwan's kinsmen rushed down the path. Having heard their own kinswoman scolding the visitors, they came to intervene. They placed themselves in front of Abooksigun and blocked his way. Migisi and the two others stood and Migisi stepped forward to do the talking. A heated argument broke out between the four Chippewas and their Ottawa hosts. Both sides gestured angrily, and the tone of the dispute was not moving toward appeasement of either party. Thinking that the Ottawas bluffed and wouldn't defend a *Yanqui*, Migisi shoved one of the Ottawas. The brave shoved back. Both groups reached for the weapons in their waistbands.

As Molly and Captain Archer approached the village, they saw Opechwan, Ahmik, and Jean-Luc running toward them.

Jean-Luc stopped and asked Molly, "Are you all right?"

Opechwan and Ahmik did not stop.

Molly said, "Please let Opechwan handle this." Then she, Jean-Luc, and Captain Archer turned and watched the sachems confront the disruption. Opechwan and Ahmik pushed their way to the forefront. Migisi pointed past them (at Molly and her husband) and said, "It is an insult that you invited *Yanquis* to your marriage to our village maiden, Kateri."

Opechwan did not deign to explain his friends' presences in the village. He merely said, "The man is my brother. They are guests *of the Ottawa.*" He emphasized the last words, as any Indian would know the relationship implied protection. "Opechwan understands your unhappiness. You and your kinsmen must choose to be peaceful, or you must choose to depart."

Migisi answered angrily, "You insult the Chippewa. *Yanquis* should not be here. We shall remember your contempt." He looked at Ahmik for support.

Opechwan, too, glanced at Ahmik for his reaction, but the older sachem stood stoically. Only Ahmik's eyes gave a clue to his thoughts. Hinting at the humiliation his kinsmen's behavior caused him to feel, his expression communicated that he had clearly had enough of his braves' disregard of protocol. Opechwan hesitated, as he was not certain what actions Ahmik would take.

Ahmik said, with obvious embarrassment, "Return to the Chippewas."

Migisi felt stunned and did a double take. If he refused, the Chippewas would put to death a warrior who disobeyed his chief in the face of the enemy, and he felt certain the Ottawas would meet that criterion.

Migisi took a step backward. He and his three comrades felt betrayed by their sachem. Finally, after several tense moments standing under Ahmik's glaring visage, he said, "Bah!" and signaled his three allies to follow. They stomped up the path to gather their belongings. Migisi said under his breath to Abooksigun, "Let us take to the warpath," and looked fiercely at any Ottawa villager who looked his way. The Chippewa war chief had been humiliated and felt a keen sense of shame. He realized that his military title would probably be stripped from him when Ahmik reported what had occurred in the Ottawa village. As the implications of their conduct this morning dawned upon the four warriors, a cloud of prideful confusion and regret descended upon them.

Molly watched the four until they were out of sight. Then, Captain Archer tugged on her sleeve. She didn't respond, because she wanted to see whether Opechwan and Ahmik would follow Migisi and his mates to their lodge.

Sullen, the Chippewas quickly and silently took down their teepee, packed it on their travois, and mounted their horses. They departed the Ottawa village on a path leading northwest. As they entered the tree line and disappeared into the shadowy darkness of the forest, Molly sighed audibly. Opechwan sent a small group of his braves to follow from a tactful distance, to ensure that they were actually departing.

An eerie silence fell upon the village. Molly had watched the malcontents as they left. Opechwan walked past her, shaking his head. He angrily threw open the flap to his teepee and went inside. Molly glanced at Captain Archer, who was shaking his head sadly. He didn't appear too shaken (or surprised) by the showdown. Now Molly had seen and heard enough; she wanted to get back to her husband (and to their ship).

"Thank you for walking me back, Captain," said Molly.

Captain Archer nodded. He said, "I will see you tonight at the ceremony." He turned and walked back toward the stream to finish his shave.

Coming down the slope was a striking Indian woman with an erect, proud posture. With her long black hair held by a decorative band around her forehead, she, too, carried a leather bucket. Turning her attention to the woman before her, the squaw said in passable French, "You are St. Alembert's woman." Molly nodded. This striking woman stated, "I am Kateri."

Molly smiled and put the bucket down. She responded in French, "Yes, my name is Molly." Without being obvious, Molly took the woman's measure and determined that Kateri was her height (about five feet six inches), had black straight hair, and clothed in a dress made of a skillfully prepared animal hide. Opechwan's fiancée appeared to be strong and in her prime.

Kateri stepped forward and placed her hands on Molly's shoulders. She slowly placed her cheek against Molly's and then did the same on her other side. She said, "Opechwan is pleased that his friend and woman are here. I am pleased, too."

Molly instantly liked Kateri. Molly knew that reserve was the "Indian way." Thus, Molly understood that what had just occurred was a remarkable show of warmth from Kateri to a person who was not her kinswoman.

Kateri looked past Molly and regarded the British officer; she narrowed her eyes slightly. Molly detected a hint of disapproval of him.

Kateri's Chippewa tribesmen were long-standing rivals of the Ottawas. In the past, relations between the tribes had often been hostile. Yet Pontiac, whose mother was Chippewa, had made a diplomatic breakthrough when he united the Ottawas and the Chippewas under his leadership to battle the encroachers. Now that peace had returned, the two tribes resumed their traditional wariness of one another. Thus, the marital delegation had been welcomed as a diplomatic advance. Kateri and Opechwan hoped that their marriage would seal the alliance.

Kateri said, "Today, we will speak of the ceremony. Come to my lodge when the sun rises to the treetops." She pointed to the tallest maple at the edge of the forest. She said while still pointing north, "I am staying in the eagle and otter teepee in that direction."

Molly nodded and said, *"Au revoir."*

CHAPTER SEVENTEEN

SUNDAY, APRIL 11, 10 A.M.

ENTERING OPECHWAN'S TEEPEE, Molly said, "I met Kateri." Opechwan slowly raised his chin (interested in hearing more). Molly continued, "She is beautiful." Turning to her husband, Molly said, "Wait until you see her, Jean-Luc, she is more than beautiful—she is breathtaking." Opechwan smiled. "*And* I learned that you are the new sachem. The tribe has chosen wisely." Opechwan glanced at Jean-Luc for his reaction.

Molly continued, "I should go to Kateri's. She requested that I come when the sun is at tree level. She wants to discuss tonight's ceremony." Molly nervously peered out the teepee flap. "I think it's time to go." She looked left and then right for the Chippewa warriors (or any other danger). Seeing none, she quickly departed.

Jean-Luc spoke. "I hope her uneasiness is not offending you."

Opechwan shook his head and said, "I understand. Huron killed a baby brother."

"You should have told me that you are the sachem. I think it is wonderful. Do you like being sachem?" asked Jean-Luc.

"It is my duty," said Opechwan. He stoked the fire and rearranged the embers.

"You handled this morning's dust-up well. Did you seek the added responsibility?"

"One does not always choose his path. My people chose me. The only thing that troubles me is that I walk in my brother's shadow." A barely perceptible frown crossed Opechwan's face.

Jean-Luc leaned back and asked, "You inherited the title of sachem?"

Opechwan relaxed a bit and smiled. He sat next to Jean-Luc. "My brother could inspire. I am unsure that I can do the same. When a Peoria traitor killed Pontiac, it fell to me to avenge his murder. It is not that way. No, I planned raids on the Peoria tribe and led the war party against them."

My old friend is a great warrior, eh?"

"No, my friend. I take to the warpath with a reluctant heart. Do you understand that because we spent time together before you left seeking a wife, I had not joined in my tribe's war dance? I only did so in my eighteenth summer?"

"I didn't know that. Is that considered late?"

"Yes, for an Ottawa warrior; it is *late*."

"So, you took to the warpath against the Peorias?" asked Jean-Luc, trying to draw out additional information.

Opechwan picked up his calumet, the tribal peace pipe, and examined it thoughtfully. He said, "We made that decision through a council of elders and older warriors. That is how the Ottawa make a major decision."

"And yet, this morning in dealing with those Chippewas, you told them to return home and not attend the wedding ceremony. There was no council involved."

"With outsiders, I speak for my people."

Jean-Luc asked, "Are the English colonists leaving your tribe alone? Your people appear contented."

"The colonists have many ways to molest us that spreads their unwanted influence here without buying us out."

Jean-Luc felt puzzled and asked, "What do you mean?"

Even a single family of whites living within a day's walk will drive out the 'beasts of the chase.' Even Fort Detroit's soldiers influence what we are able to hunt." Opechwan's explanation of the Indians' dilemma starkly laid out the issues faced by his people. "Before the *Anglais* arrived, we lived in the woods and endured the times of plenty and times of want from the Great Spirit. Our desires were few; if we were thirsty, we drank from the brook; our clothes were animal-skins."

Jean-Luc motioned that he would like to examine the calumet and Opechwan handed it to him. Jean-Luc mused quietly, "And I thought I had heavy responsibilities."

Opechwan nodded toward a leather pouch hanging from a support pole, "Take that and walk with me to the river. I will purify myself for the ceremony at sundown."

Molly stepped outside and looked around the village to get her bearings. Sitting on the ground ten feet away was an elderly woman, smoking a pipe. The woman rested her back against a tall pole (one of many, as each lodge had a pole with a dream-catcher at the top). Each dream catcher had a web of fibers inside a wooden circle, along with some fluttering feathers. Molly estimated that pole extended about four feet above the smoke hole. To Opechwan's people, the dream catcher was a charmed object to protect sleeping people from nightmares. Good dreams could pass through the webbing by sliding down the feathers to the sleeper.

Molly's gaze wandered to the images painted on the sides of the teepees. The one closest to her had images of a buffalo and a warrior on horseback, holding his bow and arrow. A young woman sat on the ground at the base of this wigwam, mending a small area. Beside her stood a girl observing, presumably to learn. On the woman's other side was a cradleboard propped against the dwelling. Nearby stood a drying rack consisting of poles lashed together; running horizontally was a bar holding drying jerky.

Molly would have turned her gaze to another interesting part of the village, but she spotted some movement in the bushes near the jerky. She could see two boys (about the age of six) sneaking closer. Molly half expected the sitting woman to scold the would-be thieves, but at that moment she heard a brave on horseback making a correction to their technique. Molly was observing a tutoring session, where the boys were learning life skills from their uncle. Before becoming an Ottawa warrior, each would one day steal an object from a live enemy as a rite of passage. Molly smiled when she saw the family's dog watching the boys intently, since he, too, wanted to steal some jerky.

Walking toward Kateri's teepee, Molly passed a small rope corral holding two horses. She looked across a meadow and saw six boys, eight or nine years old, practicing their skills with the bow and arrow. On signal, they fired all the arrows from their quiver into the air, with the intent of shooting the last one before the first hit the ground. The howls of laughter coming from the group indicated that they enjoyed the competition and were amused by the results. In the opposite direction near the woods, Molly watched ten wee ones (about four years of age) challenging each other to foot races. Molly considered the activities and understood that the boys were practicing life skills they would need as adults.

Hearing footsteps outside her teepee, Kateri came out. Seeing Molly, she said, "Our young braves are learning."

Molly said, "They are having much fun doing so, too."

Kateri motioned with her hand, "Come with me." She and Molly approached the group. Kateri said to the nearest boy, "Let me use your bow." The young man handed her the bow with a big grin. Kateri said with a chuckle, "And an arrow." Sheepishly the boy drew one from his quiver and handed it over. Kateri said, "Now, when I shoot this into the sky, the rest of you judge the arrow's trajectory; the one whose arrow follows my arrow's path nearest—wins.

Closely observing Kateri with the bow and arrow, Molly stood back. Kateri drew the bowstring back and pointed the arrow nearly vertical. She closed one eye as though she had a target and released the bowstring from her fingertips. Immediately, the boys followed. Molly watched the arrows climb toward the clouds, stop at the apex, and begin their descent to the empty nearby field. Kateri and Molly strolled over to where the arrows had fallen and were sticking into the ground. The winning arrow was easy to detect, as it was mere inches from Kateri's shaft.

The youngster who had won pulled his and Kateri's arrow from the ground came running up to Kateri to return her arrow, and was rewarded by the beautiful maiden affectionately tussling his hair. Molly then followed Kateri the short distance to her teepee. Two little girls and three older women immediately surrounded her. The wedding attendants began to labor, preparing the bride and her accoutrements for the ceremony. The eldest woman gently nudged Kateri to remind her that her visitor needed to be introduced. The two eight-year-old girls immediately stopped giggling and turned their attention to the newcomer.

Kateri said, "This is my betrothed's friend's wife. Her name is Molly." The women nodded but did not smile nor come any nearer.

The girls, who appeared to Molly to be around eight years old, were waiting to comb Kateri's long, black hair. They, too, nodded towards Molly but could not remain stoic and began giggling once more. They came forward and began combing Kateri's hair. After what Molly thought was five minutes or so, the eldest woman scooted the eight-year-olds out of the teepee. They departed looking disappointed. Then two women carefully folded a white blanket with red symbols embroidered in the center. When finished they lovingly placed it on Kateri's sleeping area. The old woman supervised them closely, and her eyes seemed to Molly to twinkle with approval for the attendants' preparations. She leaned over to Kateri, whispered a final message, and quietly departed.

Molly nervously asked in French, "Are you ready for the big night?"

Kateri said, "The firewood is stacked, my blue blanket is folded, and I completed my white blanket only *last night*." Kateri allowed a sigh of relief for she had been apprehensive about whether she could complete the white blanket before the wedding. Our people will cook all day, and the feast will be an honor for my husband." She patted a leather-covered stool beside her and said, "Sit next to me so that we can talk."

Molly sat down, glanced at the teepee flap, and forced a smile. "What can I do to help with tonight's ceremony?"

"The sachem speaks words of honor of your man. He is pleased that your man came. In case the sachem does not convey that to your man, I wanted you to know that." Kateri looked down and away. She said softly, "I have not seen him this happy."

"I think it is wonderful that they have a close friendship. My husband was determined to come." Realizing that this made it sound as if she were unenthusiastic about coming to the wedding, Molly added, "I am glad I came, too."

"I sense that you are afraid of being among us."

Ashamed it had become obvious Molly looked down at the ground.

Carefully avoiding her private name for her betrothed, Kateri said, "Do not be afraid. To the sachem, your man is our kinsman—and you also. Every Ottawa is your friend. No harm will come to you while you stay among us."

Molly felt herself relax for the first time in days; Kateri's assurances convinced her.

Kateri said, "Your man brought the sachem gifts. That is what friends do. That is the way of the Ottawa. All my tribe can see that you are friends of the Ottawa."

Molly smiled and gently patted Kateri's arm. She said, "My husband feels a strong bond with the Ottawa's sachem." Molly had quickly picked up the respect inferred when not using the subject's name. "With my people, other gifts are brought to the wedding." Now Molly smiled broadly for the first time since arriving in Ottawa territory. "We have very special gifts for the sachem and his bride to be."

Kateri smiled, for Molly's words honored her. Kateri and Molly began to feel comfortable in one another's presence. Kateri put her arm around Molly's shoulder and said, "We will be like our men—good friends."

"Yes, I would like that. Now, tell me what I'm to do during the ceremony. I am excited for you and cannot wait to see the relevance of the blankets and the woodpile.

Unbeknownst to Opechwan's villagers, the Chippewas had doubled back and were lying in wait, hidden in the forest outside the village. They observed the wedding preparations from their hiding place. Watching the busy villagers completing last-minute decorations and preparations for the wedding feast, Migisi turned to his kinsmen and said, "I want to capture the *Anglais* alive." His companions nodded. After an hour, they withdrew up the trail three miles to find food and wait.

CHAPTER EIGHTEEN

SUNDAY, APRIL 11, 8 P.M.

ON THE SIGNAL from the village's eldest woman, a solitary drummer began a steady, rhythmic beat. After several moments, a lone singer began chanting.

Inside Kateri's dwelling, Molly glanced at the bride, who had noticeably stiffened upon hearing the music. Molly bent over and picked up the blue blanket that lay folded on her bedding. Kateri stood erect and turned and faced the teepee's entrance. Molly carefully draped the blanket on Kateri's head and shoulders.

Molly said, "I think that it is romantic that this blanket represents your sadness in living alone. Well, in a short while, you'll never be alone again." Kateri smiled and breathed deeply. "Well, let's find you a husband."

Kateri beamed, knowing that she had soothed Molly's anxieties about being among the Ottawas. Now, both women were primed for the ritual. With her shoulders back and head erect, Kateri stepped outside with Molly. They entered the villagers' circle together.

Outside the circle lay many blankets spread with baskets of food for the villagers. A short distance from the center of the village, a circle of stones had been placed, enclosing a large, unlit stack of wood. Two small fires had been lit on opposing sides of the circle and flickered warmly in the twilight. The villagers encircled the stones. Just inside the villagers' circle stood Opechwan, also wrapped in a blanket of blue. Jean-Luc stood to his left. Kateri began her walk toward the circle. As she did, Opechwan did the same. Molly and Jean-Luc remained where they were. Meeting at the outer edge of the stones, but on opposing sides, each stood in front of one of the small fires, Kateri and Opechwan faced one another looking over the large unlit stack of wood. The drummer and singer had picked up their tempo. The villagers began a song of celebration.

With the bride on one side and the groom on the other, each stood behind the symbolic small fires that represented their individuality. Moments passed as the villagers' singing became more intense and the drummer gradually raised his tempo to a rapid pace.

Unaccustomed to Ottawa rituals, Molly glanced uneasily at Jean-Luc for reassurance; but all was well. Jean-Luc's gaze was transfixed upon his friend. But when he sensed Molly's eyes on him, he turned to her, smiled, and mouthed the words, "I love you." Molly silently answered her husband by mouthing, "I love you, too." He took her hand and held it firmly.

Molly looked around and spotted the English officer, Captain Archer. He appeared to be enjoying himself and had been clapping to the music. She returned their attention to the wedding couple and waited breathlessly for the ceremony to begin. When the villagers' chant and drum beats ceased, all present watched for the bride's first step.

Kateri began by taking one step clockwise. With her eyes on her betrothed, she affirmed clearly confidently, "I commit to you in love. I will faithfully keep my promise that my love for you will be eternal."

Likewise, Opechwan took one step clockwise, stopped, and pledged, "And I will love Kateri forever."

Kateri slowly took another step and halted, "I will honor my husband."

After his step, Opechwan said, "Your blood is now my blood." He used the word *blood* to mean kinsmen.

Molly took Jean-Luc by the elbow, inched closer, and squeezed. "Isn't this romantic?" Jean-Luc nodded. Molly whispered, "I love weddings."

After Kateri's third step, she said, "I will submit to my husband." The tribal adults murmured their approval.

Opechwan took his step around the rock perimeter and standing opposite his bride, said, "I will desire Kateri and no one else."

Jean-Luc whispered, "How many steps will they take?"

Her knowledge coming from her afternoon spent assisting Kateri, Molly patiently explained, "Each will take seven paces and with each step declare their intentions." Jean-Luc nodded. Sensing that his wife still looked at him, he turned and smiled.

Kateri's next step was purposefully slower than the others. She turned and faced Opechwan and promised, "I will follow my husband wherever he goes."

Opechwan took a step and vowed, "Our bodies are now one." In approval, the villagers again murmured audibly.

Kateri's eyes flashed a hint of mirth (as did Opechwan's), but she quickly returned to the business at hand. She took another step and said, "In times of plenty and in times of famine, I will be by your side." In the distance a lone wolf howled at the moon, and a village dog barked back, bringing a nervous laugh from the villagers.

Now it was Opechwan's turn, he stepped left and said, "Like this circle, my love for Kateri will have no end."

Kateri stood erect. She knew that the tribe eagerly awaited the fire ceremony that was coming momentarily. After stepping left, she said, "I will be your faithful wife to give and to receive, to speak and to listen, to inspire and to respond."

Opechwan gave the slightest of nods to his bride in silent approval of her promises. He took his next to last step and said, "I will love you more with each passing moon."

Kateri's seventh vow came as the clouds in the night sky parted and revealed a full moon. "I will love my husband forever," she said.

Opechwan felt tempted to rush the final vow—he so wanted to

embrace his true love under the blanket. Silently chiding himself, he deliberately slowed his final promise. "I love what I know of you, and trust in you what I do not yet know. We are now life partners."

Kateri fought to suppress a huge smile, knowing that the tribal elders would deem a smile undignified. She slowly blinked her eyes, signaling to Opechwan her loving acknowledgments of his vows. Kateri looked into her betrothed's eyes.

Having returned to their original stations behind the small fires burning at their feet, they knelt. From opposing sides of the circle, Opechwan and Kateri slowly pushed the burning embers forward and into the kindling at the base of the wood stack. They remained kneeling until their small fires ignited the stack. As the flames grew higher, the symbolism was lost on no one — individuals no more, Opechwan and Kateri were now man and wife; and they would accomplish more as a loving couple than as individuals. Slowly, the loving couple stood and moved towards one another around the perimeter of the rock circle. When they met, Opechwan held out his hands and took Kateri's in his; he gently stroked the backs of her hands with his thumbs in a show of tenderness.

As the fire crackled (the only noise to be heard in the village or forest), three aged women came forward with the white bridal blanket and draped it over the heads of the newlyweds. Under the blanket, Opechwan pulled Kateri to him and kissed her lips softly. Afterwards, Kateri placed her face against Opechwan's chest. He gently lifted the white blanket up and then wrapped it around his and Kateri's shoulders.

Seeing their friends blissful, the St. Alemberts smiled at one another. Molly took her husband's hand and squeezed it affectionately. She whispered, "We'll have the teepee to ourselves tonight." Jean-Luc nodded and kissed his wife's forehead.

When the villagers saw their sachem placing the white blanket about his and Kateri's shoulders, they began slowly inching their circle outwards. At first a few individuals but then almost everyone began singing in honor of the newlyweds. Tribal drummers began a rhythmic cadence that directed the village men to form a circular dance.

After the warrior's dance ended, but before the villagers became consumed by their delight for the couple, Opechwan held up his hands to quiet the people and said, "Thank you all for coming to our wedding. We hope you will enjoy the music and dance. There is much food here for you to enjoy." Kateri stood by her husband's side and smiled modestly. The happy couple walked to an area outside the circle to accept congratulations and chat with kinsmen.

The dancing, feasting, and celebrating continued for several more hours. When the tribal elders realized that the married couple had slipped away to Kateri's teepee, they signaled that the celebration had ended and encouraged the people to return to their lodges in a show of respect for the new couple.

The following morning, Molly awakened and looked at her sleeping husband. She leaned over and kissed his forehead. Jean-Luc opened his eyes.

Jean-Luc said, smiling, "I like to be awakened by a kiss."

"Come, husband, we should return to the boat. Let's get dressed. After breakfast, we will call on the wedding couple to express our thanks for their wonderful hospitality," said Molly.

An hour later, Molly and Jean-Luc walked across the grounds among the Ottawa lodges, making their way to Kateri's teepee. They encountered Captain Archer, who was packing his saddlebags. After shoving in the last article, he secured the flap.

"Quite the ceremony, wasn't it?" asked Molly.

Captain Archer said. "I doubt that I shall ever forget it. It was quite moving, actually."

Molly said, "We thought it was lovely."

Captain Archer said, "My follow-on assignment is to be in Philadelphia. Do you ever sail there?"

Jean-Luc said, "We deliver supplies there."

"I hope our paths cross again in Philadelphia," said Captain Archer.

"Are you returning to Fort Detroit alone?" asked Molly.

"Yes. I rode down unaccompanied. The local tribes are peaceful, so I am not expecting trouble. This marriage should ensure that the Ottawas and Chippewas remain peaceful."

"I did not realize there was bad blood between the tribes," said Jean-Luc.

"Oh, yes, this marriage is like Romeo and Juliet. That makes this union all the more remarkable," said Captain Archer.

CHAPTER NINETEEN

MOLLY AND JEAN-LUC watched Captain Archer and Chief Ahmik ride into the forest. A cloud of anxiety hovered over Molly, because she knew they had a hike through the forest to reach the boat. Plus being around Indians for the past two days had kept her on edge. Then there was the run-in with the Chippewas. Molly instinctively gripped her pistol and checked its frizzen. Satisfied, it was ready for action, they began their trek to the lake.

After walking several miles, Jean-Luc said, "Let us stop for water and rest."

After resuming, a sense of unease came into Molly's mind. On several occasions, when the birds had stopped chirping, that nagging feeling of being watched returned. This feeling of angst was no stranger, and Molly had learned through experience to trust her instincts.

Jean-Luc indicated they should get moving again. As Molly stood and knocked leaves off her clothing, Jean-Luc whispered, "We are not alone."

"What?"

"There are four Indians on horseback over there. They are watching us." Molly started to look, but Jean-Luc said in a hiss, "Do not look at them! If they start to approach, I will deal with them. Let us walk quickly—no running and do not show fear."

Molly nodded.

For the next three hours, Molly and Jean-Luc walked with a quickened pace, but neither mentioned stopping to rest. Jean-Luc kept an eye on the mounted braves without being obvious. The cat and mouse contest continued.

Migisi halted his group. When they had circled around him he said, "There is enough distance that no one will hear a gun. I want the woman alive."

Molly looked over her shoulder and her heart sank, because it looked as though the Indians were closing in. "They're coming closer, husband."

Jean-Luc said, "Run!"

Molly and Jean-Luc sprinted between the tree trunks of the shadow-filled forest. The Chippewas tried to close the gap but were as yet unsuccessful.

"The river is not that far ahead," said Molly.

Tired from running with the musket, Jean-Luc stopped and turned to face their pursuers. "If I am to die today," he said gulping air, "I plan to sell my life at a dear price."

Migisi could see his enemy stopping to fire his musket. The Chippewas instinctively ducked behind trees to take cover, and awaited the musket shot.

Molly, too, stopped and turned toward the Chippewas. Crouching, she aimed her pistol at the nearest pursuer but held her fire.

Migisi and his warriors had trapped Molly and Jean-Luc with their backs to the Maumee River. Molly and Jean-Luc hunkered side by side, taking cover behind a large tree. Migisi paused to assess the chances of killing or capturing the two colonials without injury to himself or his warriors. He waved his men to move far enough apart that a single musket ball couldn't drop two of them, yet near enough to support one another should the couple attempt to run for the river. Jean-Luc, also gasping for air, thought for a moment. Then, he noticed one of the Indians exposed behind a tree that was too thin to provide adequate cover. He said, "I believe that I can drop one of them."

Molly said, "That leaves us with one shot and outnumbered."

"True, but they know that we have a pistol. That may buy time for us to reload."

"You mustn't miss," she said.

Jean-Luc looked down at his musket and slowly yet firmly pulled the flintlock back until he heard two clicks. "The odds are good enough to chance it." He rested his elbow on his left knee and squinted down the barrel. "I need a branch or something to better my chance."

Molly said, "Here—use my shoulder." She fell to both knees, and Jean-Luc rested the barrel on her shoulder. The Chippewas remained behind their trees.

Jean-Luc said softly, "Steady." Molly closed her eyes and prepared for the blast. Jean-Luc slowly squeezed the trigger. The flintlock sparked, and the musket belched gray smoke. The lead musket ball whistled toward its mark. It went through the Indian's buttock and spun him half around. Though the wound was not mortal, he would not participate further in the chase.

Molly did not bother to congratulate her husband for his marksmanship. Instead, she said, "Take my pistol and shoot any of them who comes near." Jean-Luc nodded, knowing that Molly would reload the musket; they exchanged weapons.

Seeing his kinsman bleeding profusely and lying on the forest floor, Migisi let forth a blood curdling war whoop. The others echoed his savage cry.

Molly feverishly began the reload steps. "This is our last ball, and there is not enough powder for a full charge."

Jean-Luc nodded grimly and kept watching the Indians. "They are moving in," said Jean-Luc. He felt that the Indians' attack would come at any moment. "Is that musket ready yet?" he asked.

"It is," answered Molly, as she returned the ramrod to its slot under the barrel.

"We need to drive them back somehow," whispered Jean-Luc.

Molly said softly, "Let's trade ground for time. Maybe, you can hit another one to better our odds."

Jean-Luc nodded, and then added, "Run several steps and stop. If they shoot, that may make them miss."

Molly and Jean-Luc turned and sprinted toward the river. When she saw her husband dive to the ground, she followed. In that instant, three shots rang out and the balls zipped through the forest trees inches above their heads. Immediately, they leapt to their feet and renewed their dash toward the river.

While Migisi and Kiwidinok knelt to reload, Ominotago ran after the St. Alemberts. He swiftly closed the gap and leapt for Jean-Luc. Jean-Luc saw his assailant and raised his musket with both hands to block the downward blow. Ominotago's attack knocked Jean-Luc's musket from his hands, but the tomahawk's handle splintered, rendering it useless.

Jean-Luc grabbed Ominotago in a headlock and punched his face repeatedly. Having been knocked to the ground, Molly saw the Indian reaching for the knife in his belt. "Look out, he almost has his knife," said Molly. Wrestling on the ground, each one tried to get the upper hand, but Ominotago couldn't reach his knife. Molly leaped upon Ominotago's back and held his arms. Jean-Luc then bit down on Ominotago's thumb and held it tight. The Chippewas behind the trees heard their friend's scream.

Migisi said, "Kiwidinok, help your friend. I will seize the woman."

In excruciating pain, Ominotago jerked his hand free, but that move also freed Jean-Luc's hand. Jean-Luc grasped the knife and pulled it from Ominotago's sheath. He thrust it into his side. His enemy fell to the ground writhing in pain, and began to crawl toward the river.

Kiwidinok sprinted forward and tackled Jean-Luc. Molly leaped to her feet and pointed her pistol at the Indian.

Jean-Luc yelled, "Save your last shot. Save it!" Holding onto his assailant's wrists, the pair rolled on the ground and plunged over the riverbank into the water.

Realizing that she and her husband would be defenseless once she fired the final ball, Molly decided, nevertheless, to shoot the Chippewa if it became necessary. Molly spun around looking for the last attacker.

Though fatigued from his previous brawl, Jean-Luc fought ferociously. The Chippewa, though not large, was fresh and determined. With all his might, Jean-Luc held his enemy's wrists to prevent the tomahawk coup-de-grace. He was able to pull his right wrist from the Indian's grasp and he punched him in the jaw. The blow snapped Kiwidinok's head back, and the momentum caused Jean-Luc to lose his grasp of the hand holding the tomahawk. The blow dazed the Indian, temporarily preventing him from pressing his advantage. However, the cool water revived him. By the time his head cleared, Jean-Luc had moved to waist-deep water.

Though armed, Migisi wanted to capture both the man and the woman alive. He crept to within fifty feet of Molly and readied to rush her. Migisi lifted his head to see what was happening with the fight in the river. Molly pointed her pistol at him, but before she could pull the trigger, he ducked out of sight.

In the river, Kiwidinok waded toward Jean-Luc with his tomahawk poised to strike an incapacitating blow. Jean-Luc knew Molly could easily shoot Kiwidinok now, but that would leave her defenseless. He yelled, "Save yourself! Run down the riverbank, swim if you have to, but find the paladins!" Jean-Luc grasped his enemy's wrist again and their life and death struggle recommenced.

"I'm not leaving you behind," screamed Molly.

Responding to his wife's words, Jean-Luc became possessed with superhuman strength. He unrelentingly forced the Chippewa's wrist backward, causing him to loosen his grip on his tomahawk.

Migisi moved ever closer and drew within striking distance to Molly. She sensed his proximity and knew that he had sneaked in during moments when her attention had been on the struggle in the river.

"I am losing my grip on his wrist," shouted Jean-Luc. "Save yourself!"

Ripping his wrist from Jean-Luc's grasp, Kiwidinok raised his tomahawk.

Molly turned from Migisi, and saw her exhausted husband about to be killed. Jean-Luc's chest heaved spasmodically as he gasped for air. He held up his hand in a pitiful defensive gesture. About to see her husband tomahawked, Molly did not consider the horrifying dilemmas of rape and tribal adoption. She did not dwell on these unspeakable outcomes for a moment. At this point, she made the most selfless decision of her life.

CHAPTER TWENTY

SUNDAY, APRIL 12, LATE MORNING

MOLLY TURNED TOWARD the fight in the river. The hand-to-hand struggle brought the men near the bank. Without a second to lose, she pointed the cocked pistol and pulled the trigger without siting. Her shot struck the warrior in the chest. He flung backward and began to sink.

In a pitiful voice, Jean-Luc shouted, "Run, Molly!" He snatched the dead Chippewa's tomahawk before the corpse disappeared beneath the river's surface. He thrashed through the waist-deep water to pull himself onto the bank, where he could join his wife in her struggle against their remaining enemy.

However, Migisi had seen his kinsman shot and was too combat savvy to move any closer to such a skillful enemy. And he held a loaded musket, so he held the winning hand. He stepped from the underbrush and stood ten feet from Molly as a dripping wet and dog-tired Jean-Luc staggered to her side.

Jean-Luc raised the tomahawk. Functioning on adrenaline only, he stood ready to die fighting. Molly turned the pistol in her hand and held it as a club. Without taking his eyes off the Chippewa, he scolded Molly under his winded breath, "I wanted you to run. Now, we are *both* going to die."

"I could not abandon you."

"Yes, and what have you accomplished?" Jean-Luc asked with angry sarcasm.

"Let's not quarrel, husband. Not at the end." Even with mere seconds to live, Molly would not let her husband get in the last word. She added, "What I accomplished was saving your life. A 'thank you' would be nice."

His wife's ludicrous comment (given the situation) brought an involuntary smile.

Migisi motioned with his musket barrel for Jean-Luc to drop the tomahawk. Jean-Luc defiantly shook his head. Migisi motioned again. Jean-Luc raised the tomahawk in a motion suggesting that he was going to throw it. His motion caused the Chippewa to flinch. Knowing that cruel deaths awaited them, the St. Alemberts preferred death to the agonizing alternative.

Molly whispered bitterly, "He will not allow us to cheat him out of his fun. Do you think you can make him miss?"

Jean-Luc nodded, though he didn't really believe the idea was feasible. Assuming that Migisi would fire at him and then deal with his wife, Jean-Luc decided to try feigning throwing the tomahawk a second time in hopes of throwing off the Indian's shot. Jean-Luc whispered, "If he misses, let us charge him and gang up on him." Molly and Jean-Luc slowly moved sideways toward a nearby tree.

Migisi raised his musket and aimed at Jean-Luc's legs.

Correctly reading his intention, Jean-Luc said, "He intends to take me out of the fight. If that happens, get ready to swim for your life." The Chippewa raised his barrel and aimed it at Jean-Luc's leg. Jean-Luc observed Migisi's eyes closely, looking for a clue that he was about to pull the trigger.

Then, Migisi lowered his barrel a bit. His expression altered from confident sneer—to shock—and then to agony. Molly glanced at Jean-Luc for his reaction, and then back at the Indian. When she looked back, the warriors' musket slipped from his grasp. Then, Migisi sank to his knees, his eyes turned lifeless, and he slumped face first onto the earth.

Molly pointed and said, "Look!" Migisi had two arrow shafts in his back. She and Jean-Luc took a cautious step toward the body. She tapped Jean-Luc on the shoulder and pointed to the shafts' feathering. "One has red fletching and the other white."

Recognizing his wedding gifts, Jean-Luc knew that Opechwan and Kateri were close by, Jean-Luc scanned the trees for his friend. He shouted, "Opie." There was no answer. He tried again, "Opie."

Next, Molly shouted, "Kateri."

Jean-Luc took Molly by her wrist and said softly, "They can hear us, Molly. They choose not to answer."

Molly regarded the body and said, "Killing this man must have been difficult. After all, he was Kateri's kinsmen."

Jean-Luc whispered, "And killing him could prompt retribution from the Chippewas."

Molly asked in a low voice, "We should thank them, shouldn't we?"

"Under the circumstances, I do not believe they want that," said Jean-Luc. "Try to understand how conflicted they must be. Let it go." He then placed his right hand over his heart and slowly raised his left hand into the air. Molly instinctively followed his example. Jean-Luc turned and said with sadness, "By saving my life, Opie has squared the debt. I shall miss him."

Molly nodded and said, "And he upheld the Ottawa's tradition of protecting friends."

Jean-Luc knelt to take the dead warriors' tomahawks and said, "But it may come at a cost for the new chief."

Molly said, "We should get back to the boat."

←—◆—→

SUNDAY, APRIL 12, NOON

Belfort adjusted his chapeau as he leaned against the cabin bulkhead. He had a fishing pole in his hand. Every so often, he would move the pole slightly to entice a fish onto his baited hook. Belfort considered fishing to be a pastime of the lower classes, and he was not enjoying himself. He glanced at Charnay, who was sharpening his knife near the bow. Both paladins had no idea that the St. Alemberts were fighting for their lives at that moment. Belfort turned to his partner and said, "Geoff, I am tired of fishing. What would you say to some knife-fighting training?"

"Keeping your skills sharp is always a good idea, Rici. Come up here."

Belfort put his pole down and went to the bow.

Charnay said, "The lake is calm, Rici, but let us take care to move slowly and deliberately so that neither of us falls overboard or gets cut." Belfort nodded and took his knife from its sheath. Charnay held his knife by his leg and said, "First, avoid knife fights, Rici. Avoid them if at all possible, because you *will* get cut."

Belfort nodded and smiled weakly. He asked, "What is really the first thing to do in a fight, Geoff?"

Charnay said, "All right, if you must defend your life with a blade, the first thing you do is take a step backward. Get out of striking range. Then, quickly evaluate your environment. Are you in an open or confined space? That being done, immediately begin evading. Your goal is to have an opportunity for a quick counterattack that ends the fight."

"Hopefully, you have more to teach me than that," said Belfort with a hint of disappointment.

"We are just getting started, Rici. Have patience. Now, if they are inexperienced, their first move will be an uncontrolled slash at your head. That is your opportunity for a swift counterattack." Rici nodded. "Slowly now, act like you are slashing high." Belfort brought his knife in a slow arc, and Charnay took a step back and to the side. Charnay then brought his blade over Rici's forearm with its point down. He said, "I would then slash *up* with my knife at your *forearm* and try to force you to drop your knife." Belfort nodded. "Now you try it on me."

They practiced the move several times. Belfort asked, "What if the attack comes from below?"

"As before, take a step back and to the side and bring your knife over their forearm, and slash *down* at the *wrist*." Understand?" Belfort nodded. "Try it on me."

Several iterations later, Belfort commented, "I think I understand. Is there more?"

"Oh, yes. There is more. The inexperienced will use their other arm as a shield. I know it is counterintuitive, but do not do that. It only takes one or two slashes from your enemy's knife and you will find yourself injured, losing blood, and possibly unable to defend yourself."

"So what do I do with my left arm?"

"Hold both the knife and open hand close to your face. Keep moving, and never stand flat-footed."

Belfort asked, "I get the feeling that there is much more."

Charnay said, "Look, Rici, if you look like you know how to handle yourself, you might be able to discourage your enemy and back away to safety. If that does not work, issue a warning. This once worked for me. I said, 'My knife instructor gave me this knife as a present, and I sharpen it every night. You do not wish to come any closer. Let us go our separate ways, shall we?'"

"That actually worked, Geoff?

Charnay nodded and said, "It did for me on one occasion." Becoming serious again, he said, "Another thing, employ your knife as a distraction while you use your fist, elbows, and knees as weapons."

"Is there more?" asked Belfort.

Charnay placed his hand on Belfort's shoulder and admonished, "Do not throw your knife at your enemy—ever. By doing so, you disarm yourself."

Belfort said, "Thank you, Geoff. You have given me a lot of information rather quickly."

While the paladins discussed hand-to-hand tactics on deck, the Miami neophytes were trekking through the forest two miles up the lakeshore. When they arrived at a clearing, Lone Eagle signaled to halt and make camp.

Presently, the Miami youths had their campfire roaring to cook that morning's catch of three ducks and five rabbits. Soon the rabbits were skinned, cut into parts, and placed on sticks to cook. Hopping Bird showed the boys the preferred way to cook fowl. He led them to the lakeshore (an arrow flight's distance from camp) and instructed them to thoroughly wet the duck's feathers. With that task complete, Hopping Bird and his teenagers returned to camp. He then showed them his method for digging under the fire. With their attention glued to his demonstration, he placed the ducks in the sand under the coals. Hopping Bird stood, slapped his hands together to shake off the sand, and said, "When they are cooked through, the feathers and skin will fall away. This way, the meat will stay juicy and will fall off the bones."

As had become their routine, the young Miami hunters eagerly anticipated a story from one of their mentors. They sat in a large circle in anticipation of a breath-taking tale. It would take an hour for the ducks to cook, giving Lone Eagle plenty of time. Setting the tone, Lone Eagle said, "Once I was lost in the Forest of the Bears."

One boy interrupted him to ask, "You have been lost, too?"

Lone Eagle nodded and said, "We are here to learn the ways of the forest, so that it does not happen again to any of *us*." Rubbing his neck, he asked, "Now, where was I? Oh, yes, I was lost. As I pondered my options, I observed a mouse out gathering wild beans for the winter. I also saw his neighbor, the buffalo, who had come down to graze in the meadow. This, Mouse did not like, for he knew that Buffalo would trample down much of the long grass, and there would be no place for Mouse to hide. Mouse squeaked at Buffalo, but the large beast paid him no mind. So Mouse decided to offer battle like a warrior."

Lone Eagle looked at their faces to see which of the boys realized that his hunting tale had evolved into a fable. Lone Eagle continued, "'Ho, friend buffalo, I challenge you to a fight!' the mouse exclaimed in his small voice. Buffalo paid him no attention, thinking it a joke. Mouse angrily repeated the challenge, but his enemy went on quietly grazing. Then little mouse laughed with contempt as he offered his defiance. Buffalo at last looked at him and replied carelessly: 'You had better keep still, little one, or I shall come over there and step on you, and there will be nothing left!' 'You can't do it!' replied Mouse. 'I tell you to keep still' insisted the Buffalo, who was getting angry. 'If you speak to me again, I shall certainly come and put an end to you!' To provoke him, the mouse said, 'I dare you!'

"What happened?" gasped one young hunter.

Lone Eagle felt gratified. He was so concentrated on entertaining the boys that he did not notice Chava and Miakoda leave the circle. Neither he nor Hopping Bird paid the pair any attention assuming that they had left because they needed to relieve themselves. Lone Eagle continued his dramatic fable and said, "At that baiting, buffalo rushed the mouse and trampled the grass clumsily and tore up the earth with his front hooves."

"Did mouse die?" asked another.

Lone Eagle glanced at him but didn't stop his story to answer. He said, "When he had tired, he looked for the mouse's lifeless body, but he could not see him anywhere. Buffalo said, 'I told you I would step on you!'

The audience scooted closer. Lone Eagle smiled to himself. Milking the suspense, he said, "Then, buffalo felt a scratching inside his right ear. He shook his head as hard as he could and twitched his ears back and forth. The gnawing in his ear went deeper and deeper until he became wild from pain. He pawed violently and tore up the sod with his horns. Bellowing madly, he ran as fast as he could, first straight forward and then in circles: but when he was out of breath, he could do nothing but shudder. Then Mouse jumped out of his ear, and said: 'Well, now you know that I am master?' 'No!' bellowed Buffalo, and again he started toward Mouse, as if to trample him under his feet. The little fellow was nowhere to be seen, but in a minute Buffalo felt him in the other ear. Once more Mouse gnawed his inner ear until Buffalo could stand it no more. He ran in wild circles around the prairie. Mouse did not stop his torment, until Buffalo fell to the ground dead. Mouse came out of his ear, and stood proudly upon Buffalo's body. 'Look at me, everyone!' said he, 'I have killed the greatest of beasts. This shows that I am master!' Standing upon the body of the dead buffalo, Mouse called loudly for a knife with which to dress the carcass."

Lone Eagle sat back with a self-satisfied feeling. Knowing that the young hunters thought that he was finished, he waited a few moments to allow them to digest the point of the fable. He watched their eyes carefully to see which teens understood and which ones did not. Not sensing anything amiss, Lone Eagle continued his fable and said, "In another part of the meadow, Red Fox, very hungry, was hunting mice for his breakfast. He saw one and jumped upon him with all four feet, but the little mouse escaped, and Red Fox was terribly disappointed. But then he heard a noise in the distance and cocked his ear: He heard a tiny, squeaky voice! 'Bring a knife! Bring a knife!' When the second call came, Red Fox started in the direction of the sound. At the first knoll he stopped and listened, but hearing nothing more, he was about to return to his hunting spot. Then he heard the tiny, squeaky voice plainly. 'Bring a knife!' Red Fox immediately set out again and ran as fast as he could. By and by he came upon the huge body of Buffalo lying upon the ground. Mouse was still standing upon the body. Then Mouse saw Red Fox, but felt sure of himself due to his conquest Mouse said to Red Fox, 'I want you to dress this carcass for me and I will share with you the meat,' said Mouse (but in an haughty tone). Red Fox said with extreme politeness, 'Thank you, my friend, you are very generous with your conquest.' After Mouse stepped down and walked to a near-by mound, Red Fox dressed the carcass. Mouse looked on and super-vised with haughty instructions. 'You must cut the meat into small pieces,' he said to Red Fox. When Red Fox had finished, Mouse paid him with a small piece of liver. Red Fox swallowed it quickly and smacked his lips. "Please, may I have another piece?' he asked quite humbly. 'Why, I gave you a very large piece! I do not like greedy friends!' exclaimed Mouse. 'You may have the blood clots,' he said with a sneer. Continu-ing to act with deference, Red Fox took the blood clots and even licked off the grass. He was very hungry and asked, 'Please may I have another piece of meat to take home? I have six little kits at home, and there is nothing for them to eat.' 'You can take the four feet. That ought to be enough for all of you!' Red Fox practically groveled as he said, 'Oh! Thank you, thank you! But, Mouse, I have a wife also, and we have had bad luck in hunting. We are almost starved. Can you spare me a little more?'

Lone Eagle had been concentrating on his story, but now a feeling of unease descended and disturbed him. He decided to press on with the story and resolve his uneasiness afterward. He said in his best mouse voice, 'Why, I have already overpaid you for the little work you have done.' With a dismissive wave of his paw, Mouse said, 'I will allow you to take the head, too!' As Red Fox moved forward to accept the head, he pounced upon Mouse, who gave one faint squeak and disappeared down Red Fox's throat."

Realizing that the fable had concluded, the boys poked their friend beside them in the ribs and nodded their appreciation for the story. Hopping Bird asked the group, "What did Mouse teach you?"

Tadewi, sitting beside him, said, "If you act prideful and do not willingly share with your friends—you will lose all in the end."

Lone Eagle nodded and said, "You speak true. That *is* what we might learn from Mouse." Lone Eagle stood and brushed the forest debris from his seat. He silently counted the boys and came up two short. After remembering that two boys had left the circle and not returned, he asked nonchalantly, "Where have Chava and Miakoda gone?" The boys shook their heads and looked around for their friends.

Two miles from Lone Eagle's camp, Chava and Miakoda crept their way west along the lakeshore toward the boat in the distance. The soft sand gave way under their moccasins. These determined Miami learners were not concerned about Lone Eagle, Hopping Bird, or their peers. Focused on the boat ahead and believing that their actions at the boat would earn them the title of warrior, they never stopped to consider how inexperienced in hand-to-hand fighting they were. After all, they reasoned, they wanted to touch the enemy and leave undetected. They assumed that because they had surprise going for them, they could accomplish this feat handily. And as for the chaperones, the boys had a twenty minute head start, and could not be stopped. It was Chava's idea to request forgiveness for leaving the group and suffer Lone Eagle's temporary wrath.

Back at the clearing, Lone Eagle ordered the boys, "Gather your possessions, we are leaving now." His tone implied that he would brook no nonsense. The teens responded enthusiastically. Seeing Chava and Miakoda chastised would please them all.

Hopping Bird walked over and asked, "What is wrong?"

"Chava and Miakoda are not with us. I am certain that they went to the lake."

Hopping Bird nodded. He understood the implication. He left to supervise the boys to speed the process of breaking camp. Lone Eagle gave the hand signal for no talking. The boys nodded and instantly understood that the group had a new purpose.

In short order, the Miamis were in single file and moving toward the lake. With Lone Eagle at the head and Hopping Bird in the rear, the Miamis moved quickly. When several boys began whispering about the two absent young men, Hopping Bird tapped them on the shoulder with his spear, sending the clear message that their lack of noise discipline wouldn't be tolerated.

When the Miami group arrived at the beach, Lone Eagle looked westward in an attempt to spot the two absentees. He didn't see them, but then he hadn't expected to. They would be using the concealment techniques they had recently learned.

At the estuary of the Maumee River, Molly and Jean-Luc stopped at the lakeshore to assess their surroundings. They saw their boat and the one reclining paladin, but not the other. The figure's relaxed posture indicated that nothing was wrong and that the other paladin had gone below. Molly looked eastward. At first, she saw nothing alarming; but as she was about to turn back, she noticed movement on the shore about one hundred yards away. She tapped Jean-Luc on the shoulder and motioned to him to take cover.

After Molly pointed out the Indians to their right, Jean-Luc said in a whisper, "We should shout a warning."

Molly said, "There could be others, and we are defenseless. The paladins are no fools. They won't allow themselves to be caught unaware."

One hundred yards away, Chava and Miakoda crouched in the

bushes. As they observed the boat, Miakoda felt misgivings about this ill-conceived endeavor.

Chava whispered, "Are you ready, Miakoda?"

Miakoda's stomach churned. Feeling tentative, he suggested, "If the men detect us, we will be like ducks on the water. We could dive below the waters, Chava; but even that might not be enough to save us."

Annoyed, Chava knitted his brow, and said, "Do not back away from this opening, Miakoda."

Miakoda's eyes darted from Chava's fuming countenance to the boat and back. He was about to answer that he was willing when Chava turned and crawled from their observation spot across the wet sand and into the lake. His heart pounded; he hated the idea that he wasn't by his friend's side. He wavered a few seconds but then began to crawl reluctantly after his friend. Arriving at the cool, lapping lake water, he silently began what he hoped would be a swim to glory.

About one third of the way, Miakoda scrutinized the man on the boat. Thus far, he and Chava (fifty feet ahead) had apparently successfully gotten this close without being detected. At that moment, movement on the beach caught his attention. He and Chava turned and could see Lone Eagle standing on the lakeshore. His heart felt both relief and apprehension as Lone Eagle signaled for the boys to return.

When Chava resumed his silent approach toward the boat, Lone Eagle turned to Hopping Bird and the other boys and signaled to them to conceal themselves. He quietly entered the water and began swimming toward his wayward charges.

On board, Charnay crouched behind the cabin's hatch. He whispered to Belfort, "How many now?" He heard three faint taps through the bulkhead. He reached over and gripped a second musket.

Belfort had feigned taking a nap on deck from the time he detected the natives on the lakeshore. He kept his flintlock beside him but flush with the deck and out of view of those on land. He cracked his eyelids and observed the two youths approaching the boat. The oldest of the three appeared to be trying to get the younger ones to return to the shore. Belfort decided to withhold his fire unless he felt threatened.

The arrival of a number of Indians who stayed in the tree line complicated things.

Molly and Jean-Luc continued discussing their options. Molly said, "Foremost is the safety of the boat, because without it we are in major trouble. Next, we are an arrow's flight away from a dozen or so Indians, and we have no defense except concealment."

Jean-Luc nodded. Feeling helpless against the dilemmas they faced (and exhausted from the fight against the Chippewas), he lowered his head and mumbled an expletive.

Hopping Bird signaled the boys to draw an arrow and have it at the ready. Should their tribesmen in the water need it, his group could send volley after volley of arrows toward the boat.

Chava stopped swimming and looked back. Seeing Lone Eagle behind Miakoda, he didn't know how to interpret this at first. He felt initially reassured that Lone Eagle was behind him, but when he saw Lone Eagle motion to him to return to shore, he realized that he was in hot water with his leader. He glanced back at the man sleeping on the boat's deck and thought, "I am close and Lone Eagle is angry with me anyway, I am not stopping." He returned his attention to the reclining figure on the boat and resumed his silent progress through the water.

Belfort's concern grew as he observed the Indians' movements from beneath his hat's visor. He whispered to Charnay, "They have come close enough. It is a bad idea to allow these savages to come any closer."

He grasped his musket, got to his feet, and cocked the firearm. Charnay exited from below and took a defensive stance beside his countryman.

When Miakoda saw this, he turned and swam as fast as possible for the shore. Abruptly stopping, Chava began treading water. Though utterly defenseless, he chose to defy the musket-wielding men.

He screamed in his Miami language, "I am not afraid of you. I am Chava of the Miamis."

Lone Eagle yelled to Chava, "Swim for the shore. Do not tempt death."

Hopping Bird faced a dilemma. If they fired their arrows, the hostile act could get his tribesmen killed. But if he waited until the white men fired their muskets killing one or both, it would be too late for effective action. He said to his followers, "Draw back your bows, but do not send an arrow without my order."

Concealed, the Miami youth assumed good firing positions. As one, they nocked an arrow, drew back their bowstrings, and aimed. At Hopping Bird's command, fourteen arrows would scream over the lake's waters toward the boat.

Molly and Jean-Luc crouched behind vegetation and watched the drama unfold. Straining to see the Indians on her right, Molly held her breath and hoped that neither Frenchmen would start a fight.

Lone Eagle did not acknowledge Miakoda as he passed. Lone Eagle kept an eye on the men on the boat, as he waited for Chava to reach him.

As Chava swam up to Lone Eagle, he said, "I am not afraid of them."

Lone Eagle did not respond or even look at Chava. He motioned with his head for Chava to swim ashore. Chava nodded and began his swim with the sickening knowledge he had crossed one of the tribal elders. He understood that he had made a life-altering mistake.

Hopping Bird kept his hand raised, as a sign to withhold firing their arrows at the boat. The boys understood. Hopping Bird kept his gaze on the two men on the boat. He thought that if they aimed at any of his tribesmen, he would unleash a volley of missiles sure to send the men scurrying below deck. His boys could keep it up until all three Miamis were safely ashore.

Charnay said in a low voice, "Rici, it would appear that our adversaries have chosen the wiser course of action. Do not point your weapon at them; I believe that that would surely provoke an unwelcome response. Our show of strength has discouraged them."

Belfort nodded but did not take his eyes off the American natives. "You do realize, Geoff, that I was selected as a paladin for my good judgment?" Belfort laughed softly but then added, "I do not want to die here when there is so much to live for back in France."

Molly and Jean-Luc observed the drama from close range. Their current problem was to remain undetected.

Molly whispered, "Pray that they head east."

Jean-Luc's response was to take her hand and squeeze it gently; he motioned for her to lie flat. Molly did as he wanted.

When Lone Eagle felt the bottom of the lake, he waded ashore where Chava and Miakoda waited. His expression was solemn (more disappointment than anger). Without looking back at the boat, he and the boys walked into the tree line.

Hopping Bird exhaled in relief. He motioned to his young warriors to return their arrows to their quivers. As Lone Eagle walked out of the lake, he glanced at Hopping Bird and nodded a silent understanding that a tragedy had been averted.

After the Miami hunting party walked into the forest, Lone Eagle stopped the group. He motioned for Chava and Miakoda to come forward. The two teens approached Lone Eagle and stopped. The other boys came forward and formed a semicircle.

Lone Eagle said, "A great wrong just happened, Chava and Miakoda." The two teens felt searing shame, and their heads instinctively lowered their chins to their chests. "You two placed the rest of us in the position of breaking the peace and bringing the white man's soldiers down upon our villages. For what reason? To save the lives of their selfish kinsmen." Slowly, the group of teens inched closer to their wayward peers. "We then will resolve this issue before our hunting party returns to our lodges, and speak of it no more. Understand?" Chava and Miakoda nodded sullenly. Lone Eagle turned and faced the other thirteen hunters. He said, "Form two lines. Then be ready with your bows."

The young hunters did as instructed. All of them knew what would happen next. To the thirteen, the challenge was to strike painful blows on the two being punished without breaking their precious bow (for to do so would require much labor to manufacture a new one). Chava and Miakoda began their punishment stoically, but as the stinging blows rained in, they were beaten to the ground and crossed the endpoint on their knees. The memory of the beatings from their peers would remain with them forever.

Lone Eagle pondered what his words to the tribal elders would be. Deciding to think on this more when he was rested and no longer angry, he turned his attention to the trail home.

Jean-Luc watched the Indians depart (and ensured that they had truly gone) before he signaled the paladins. Then he and Molly swam to the boat.

← ● →

TUESDAY, APRIL 14, NOON

Chief Opechwan stopped his contingent on the outskirts of the Chippewa village and dismounted. Kateri slid off her Palomino and joined him. Each took the reins of a pack horse carrying a Chippewa corpse and began their walk into her former village. Remaining outside the boundary were twenty Ottawa braves ready to come to their rescue if this diplomatic visit turned dreadful.

As they walked toward the village totem, Chippewas came out of their wigwams and stared at them. To Kateri's great relief, she spotted her father, Ahmik, exit his wigwam and walk in their direction.

The three met at the eagle totem. Ahmik took the reins of the horses. He asked, "What happened?" His face revealed his discomfort. These four dead Chippewas represented shame and treachery. They had embarrassed the sachem in the village of the Ottawa.

"They tried to kill our friends," said Opechwan.

Ahmik nodded.

Kateri asked, "Father, will there be more killing?" Her question was to learn whether the Chippewas intended to retaliate.

Ahmik shook his head and said, "I have spoken with the council concerning the delegation's conduct. It is our desire to remain at peace with our Ottawa brothers and sisters."

Opechwan held out his hand. Ahmik grasped it, and the two men had an accord.

PART III

Code Duello

CHAPTER TWENTY-ONE

MONTRÉAL, MARCH 15, 1773, 10:30 A.M.

UNKNOWN TO THE arrivals from Fort Detroit, the man who had secretly summoned the St. Alemberts to Montréal was sitting, along with his messenger, in the tavern across the street, inside the fort's log walls. This man and his messenger had begun coming to that establishment only seven days earlier, in anticipation of Jean-Luc's return. After missing his first opportunity, he wasn't about to allow himself to fail in his last opportunity to confront his rival. The man was a former suitor and shipmate of Molly's from her war days aboard the *H.M.S. Pembroke*. His name was Rhisiart Nance. He had been smitten with Molly from the moment they first met. Nance could never forget the day Molly told him they were "just friends." Ever since Molly declared her love for Jean-Luc, Nance wanted to kill his French-Canadian rival.

Thirty-two-year-old Nance had arrived in North America from Wales in March of 1759. Only months later, he narrowly escaped death from a Huron ambush on his Mohawk River encampment. The attack did claim the life of his trapping partner. To combat the French and Indian threat he enlisted onto the English frigate, *H.M.S. Pembroke*, with Molly and her father, Peter. There, he fought alongside the Lakes and indulged an infatuation with Molly that, unfortunately, was one sided. When he discovered she loved a French Canadian, he never overcame his emotional devastation. People had said "time heals all wounds," but he knew that it wasn't necessarily so. Since then, he had had numerous Indian girlfriends but had never gotten over Molly. In the years since the war, Nance had grown rich in his Great Lakes peltry business by working himself and his employees relentlessly. Now, he employed forty-eight people.

Nance waited patiently for his employee, the man with the teardrop tattoo, to identify the quarry. As ships arrived at the Montreal dock, he sent the messenger to scope out the debarking crewmembers.

As the *Marie* docked, Nance's employee walked toward the vessel to take his position leaning against the gate post. As soon as he spotted Jean-Luc, he did an about face and nodded to Nance. Nance stood and motioned for his man to skedaddle.

No sooner had the crew secured the ship, Jean-Luc debarked to have his ship's papers stamped by the harbormaster and pay the docking fee.

Nance had positioned two of his recently returned trappers to keep an eye on the house of Rafael St. Alembert. He expected Jean-Luc and his party to proceed straight to the old man's residence. Before he went there himself, he saw another two men exit the ship and join the St. Alemberts on the pier. Nance frowned at this unexpected complication; but his plan had worked thus far, and he long believed in planning the work and working the plan. This development would not force him to alter it. He wanted to arrive first and began walking toward the St. Alembert house.

Meanwhile, Rhis Nance had proceeded north on rue de Calliàre and then took a left onto rue du Saint-Sacrement. Confident he would arrive before the St. Alembert group, he met his two employees standing on the corner of Rue St. Alexis and Rue du Saint-Sacrement.

One of the men asked, "Mister Nance, you sure you want to go through with this?"

Nance said, "I went to a great deal of trouble to organize and implement this. Yes, I want to go through with it. *I have to.*"

"Why do you have to?" asked one.

"Because broken hearts never heal. This man stole the woman I was meant to marry."

As they turned and started up the street, they discovered a dwarf standing in the middle of the road blocking their path. He wore a red coat, a comical hat shaped like a droopy cone, and leather breeches. Holding a wooden stick, the red-bearded dwarf said, "*En garde, Frenchman,*" and struck an exaggerated fencing pose.

Irritated, Nance said, "Get out of my way."

One of Nance's employees asked, "Where did he come from?"

The other man added, "I do not know where he came from."

Nance attempted to brush past the red dwarf, but the little guy poked him in his thigh with the stick.

"Ouch, that hurt!" Nance snatched the stick from the dwarf and broke it over his knee. "Now, get out of here before I lose my temper."

As the three men laughed and strode past the dwarf, the little man stood aside with his arms folded and his eyes narrowed in hatred. The dwarf stomped into the alley and disappeared.

Charnay gently elbowed Belfort and nodded toward the three approaching strangers. The men clearly were intending to speak with Jean-Luc. "Jean-Luc St. Alembert!"

Jean-Luc answered matter-of-factly, "I am Jean-Luc St. Alembert. May I know your name, sir?"

"My name is Rhis Nance. And it was I who summoned you to Montréal."

"Why would you do that?" asked a befuddled Jean-Luc.

Molly asked, "Rhis? What is this about?"

Nance ignored Molly's question but did say in acknowledgment, "Good morning, Molly." He then turned his scrutiny back onto Jean-Luc, removed one of his gloves, and threw it on the ground at Jean-Luc's feet.

"What are you doing?" asked Molly.

Jean-Luc regarded the glove and asked, "What is your meaning, sir?"

Belfort said wryly, "It would appear that he is challenging you to a duel, Jean-Luc."

Flabbergasted, Jean-Luc looked at Nance to ascertain his earnestness.

Molly pushed through the paladins to confront Nance. She asked, "Is this about me, Rhis?"

Nance didn't look at her but focused intently on Jean-Luc. "What about it, St. Alembert? You accept or not?"

Molly shook her finger in Nance's face and said in English, "Pick up your stupid glove, Rhis. There isn't going to be any duel."

Jean-Luc glanced nervously, first at the paladins and then at his father. Not discerning guidance in their expressions, he said hesitantly, "I accept your challenge."

Surprised, Molly whirled about and asked, "Husband, have you lost your mind?"

Rafael stepped outside and said, "Molly, We will handle this."

"Yes, Papa. Please talk some sense into these beetle-heads." She stepped away and trounced up the steps. She glanced angrily at Jean-Luc and stopped when she reached the open front door. She turned around to listen.

Rafael asked, "We need a meeting to discuss the details. Who will represent you?"

Nance said, "My representative is 'Big Ben' here." He slapped his associate on the shoulder affectionately. "His name is Ben Chartrand. You will find him in front of the cathedral at six p.m. Until then." Rafael nodded. Nance and his two companions walked down the rue de Notre Dame, leaving the St. Alembert contingent in an agitated state.

Charnay said, "Let us move inside, where we may speak plainly and without being overheard."

Inside, Jean-Luc struggled to regain his composure. He felt as if someone had drugged him. Distracted by this frightening challenge that seemingly came out of nowhere, he stood there speechless.

Rafael said, "Yes, let us go inside."

Jean-Luc's father and the two paladins looked at Jean-Luc for direction. Jean-Luc said, "We will discuss this in father's study. The meeting is only for the men."

Molly would not embarrass her husband nor make a scene, but she would give Jean-Luc her full ire when she got him alone. She said, "Come with me, children." Molly and the children walked upstairs, and she closed the bedroom door behind them.

Rafael held his arm out to direct the men to his study. "Let us speak in here."

Upstairs, Molly said, "Unpack and place your clothes in the dresser. I will return shortly." Nancy took charge of her younger brothers, Molly tiptoed down the stairs and placed her ear against the study door to listen to their discussion.

Belfort said, "Jean-Luc, I will represent you in the meeting, if you like."

Charnay attempted to get Belfort's attention. He shook his head slowly. He was concerned that his rash partner was jeopardizing the mission.

Sieur St. Alembert quickly said, "No, no, I will represent my son."

Molly whispered to herself, "Papa, you must talk Jean-Luc out of this nonsense!"

Inside the study, Belfort suggested, "Perhaps, then, you will allow me to accompany you. These backwoodsmen have blood in their eyes, and you could be in danger."

Rafael said, "I accept your offer. Since we have only a few hours before the meeting, Monsieur le comte, please describe the steps to be followed."

Jean-Luc said, "That would be helpful. I have never dueled."

Belfort said, "At tonight's meeting, you can try to avoid this unpleasantness by apologizing."

Jean-Luc asked innocently, "What reason have I to apologize? I have done nothing to this man."

Belfort said glibly, "You mean other than sweeping his true love off her feet."

Sieur St. Alembert glanced at the silent passenger. He thought Charnay was growing annoyed with his friend.

Under the circumstances, Jean-Luc did not smile at Belfort's canard. He said, "Molly and I, we—I never saw that man *until* the day Molly and I escaped with our lives at the farmhouse [in Charlesbourg]. Certainly, Molly never mentions him. This man threatened my life that day. He would have killed me, too, but Molly moved between us. She is the reason I am alive."

Rafael smiled grimly at his son. He said, "Jean-Luc, what your friend is suggesting is an apology to satisfy your challenger's ego. I should try to defuse the situation." He then turned to Belfort and asked, "Monsieur, what issues must be settled at tonight's meeting?"

Belfort stood, walked to the window, and looked out. He said, "First, dueling is not like brawling. A duel is a controlled affair between gentlemen of honor."

Charnay said, "Stop right there. This backwoodsman is no gentleman of honor. It is true that he does not want to shoot Jean-Luc in the back, so he is merely thinking that a duel is a just way to proceed." He turned to Jean-Luc and asked, "Do you realize that if you are apprehended by the authorities, dueling is illegal and you will go to jail, or worse?"

Jean-Luc nodded solemnly.

Belfort said impatiently, "Let us get back to tonight's meeting. Jean-Luc, you will decide the weapons—it is your choice; you will also select the time and place."

Jean-Luc said softly, "Father, where do you suggest that we can duel and be unmolested?"

"The river island, Île des Soeurs, is inhabited only by nuns, and they have cultivated only the eastern half. The western tip should put us out of earshot of the authorities." He and Jean-Luc turned their attention back to Belfort.

Belfort said, "Jean-Luc, you also decide when the duel is completed. For example, after one shot, two shots—three, even."

"One is quite enough," said Jean-Luc, shaking his head.

Rafael nodded in understanding. In the hallway, Molly pressed her ear against the door.

Belfort said, "Before the duel begins, it is important to keep the participants separated. In addition, the loading of Jean-Luc's pistol is to be done in the presence of Monsieur Nance's second and vice versa. Nance's second will ensure there is no double-shot, and we will ensure they do not double-shot. *Code Duello* also requires that the pistols be smooth-bore. In the end, a duel is about honor, not slaughter."

Charnay said, "During the duel, if there is any cheating, you, as Jean-Luc's second, are to protect him and dispatch the cheater. Therefore, you and Nance's second will also be armed. Any questions?"

Rafael shook his head.

Belfort said, "To ensure that nothing is overlooked, I will accompany you to the meeting. Nance's second will probably have that third individual with him, anyway."

Charnay said, "And to keep a lid on this boiling teapot, I will accompany you both."

Rafael said, "Thank you, gentlemen. I appreciate the gestures."

Charnay pulled Belfort aside and said, "Rici, this duel is threatening our purpose here. Are you not getting carried away with this role as duel advisor? Years of work earning Jean-Luc's trust will be lost if he is killed."

Belfort nodded solemnly. He had not considered how angry the king would become should that occur.

Molly, upon hearing that the meeting was concluding, tiptoed back upstairs. Moments later, Rafael opened the study door and everyone walked out.

Jean-Luc said, "I am going upstairs to spend time with my family."

Rafael closed the door and said, "Our meeting is in a few hours. Until then, may I offer you something to eat and drink?"

CHAPTER TWENTY-TWO

MARCH 15, 1:00 P.M.

JEAN-LUC ENTERED the upstairs bedroom and softly pulled the door shut behind him. Molly sat on a bed, staring out the window. Nancy looked at her father with a worried expression. The two young boys, oblivious to the tension, played with tin soldiers on the floor.

Jean-Luc tried to sound upbeat but failed, as he said, "Nancy, take your brothers downstairs for a while. I would like a word with your mother."

Nancy gave her father a nervous smile and nodded. She stole a quick glance at her mother, who was still staring blankly out the window. She said, "Come on, we're going downstairs so that Papa and Mama can talk."

"May we play in back of the house?" asked Peter, innocently.

Before Nancy could answer, Molly turned and said crossly, "No, stay indoors."

"Ah, shucks," said Rafe.

Jean-Luc said, "Go on, children."

After the kids filed out, bounded down the stairs, and scampered across the foyer, Jean-Luc crossed the room and sat on the bed beside Molly.

Molly turned and asked, "What now, Jean-Luc? What did you *men* decide?" Her sarcastic emphasis provided Jean-Luc his sign that this discussion was not going to be easy.

"Please do not be angry, darling. This is not easy for me either."

"If dueling wasn't so utterly pointless, I might understand your willingness to throw away everything we've worked for. For all I know, I will be a widow tomorrow and our children fatherless."

"I have no choice."

Though fuming, Molly held her tongue and did not interrupt.

"I cannot shrink from Nance's challenge; it would have far-reaching consequences. My father is French nobility. Our traveling companions are nobility. To display cowardice in front of them—in front of my father, I could not live with myself. In short time, all Montréal would know of my loss of honor. When the news reached New York, I would become an outcast."

"These consequences are not worse than death. They are not worse than children being fatherless, the shipping business without its founder, or me being without my husband."

"If I had not accepted the challenge—I could be excommunicated by the church."

"I don't believe it," said Molly.

Jean-Luc said, "It is true. Even my father could be excommunicated. Under any circumstances, he would be affected. He could not continue living in Montréal if his friends and neighbors knew that his son was a coward. Loss of honor has serious consequences to a gentlemen."

"Jean-Luc, we live in New York, not in France, not Montréal. We could set sail today."

"Molly, this is not an abstract concept. I *must* defend my honor."

Molly saw in her husband's expression that his foreign way of thinking gave him no way out. She crossed her arms and turned away. "Don't think I'm going to nurse your wounds."

"In that case, I had better shoot first and hit my target." Jean-Luc smiled, but Molly was in no mood for gallows humor and did not smile. Becoming serious, Jean-Luc said, "My father and the paladins are meeting with Nance's representatives this evening. They will work out the details. As the challenged party, I get several options. We spoke at length, and I am comfortable with pistols."

"You don't ever practice with a pistol," said Molly.

"I am usually too busy, but still, I am comfortable with firearms and I am a good shot," he stressed. "I feel positive about my chances."

Still not convinced, Molly said, "Rhis will have been practicing."

"He did not know which weapon I would choose. He would have had to split his time practicing with the sword and knife." Jean-Luc held out his palms beseechingly. "Besides, it is not ordained that anyone is going to die. Sometimes, just wounding the other person is enough."

Molly asked, "Enough for what? To satisfy *the code*? What if you end up paralyzed? What if you are incapacitated? You haven't given me one reason to accept this idiotic behavior."

"Molly, is it not enough to know that a gentleman has no choice but to defend his honor?

Molly snorted. After an awkward moment of silence, she said, "I have to go out for a while. It would be a wonderful idea for you to spend some time with the children." Jean-Luc took a step toward his wife, but she abruptly turned and opened the door.

"Where are you going?" he asked.

Without answering, Molly closed the door behind her and walked downstairs. She found Rafael in the foyer and asked, "Papa, may I borrow one of your pistols?"

"Of course, my dear." Rafael walked into his study, opened a drawer, and picked up a pistol. "I will accompany you," he said.

"I have much to ponder, Papa. I will not be gone long; however, I am not that familiar with Montréal, and just knowing that I can defend myself makes me feel better."

CHAPTER TWENTY-THREE

MOLLY WALKED EAST on the rue Notre Dame. Disliking the chill, she pulled her bonnet strings tight and tied them securely. She stopped a bearded man who appeared to be a voyageur and asked in French, "Sir, can you direct me to the Nance Trading Company store?" The trapper pointed up the street. Molly walked the short distance and stood in the street taking measure of Nance's commercial progress and comparing it to the old days (summer of 1759) when she, then fifteen years-old, knew him as eighteen-year old Welshman new to North America and trapping with a partner.

Molly and Nance had served on the cannon team aboard *H.M.S. Pembroke*. Having fought by his side for four months that summer, Molly had always liked Rhis Nance a great deal, but she never had the romantic feelings that he had for her. Although fourteen years had passed, Nance had not moved on emotionally and had never given up hope that Molly would return his love.

Entering the Nance Trading Company door, Molly approached the clerk behind the counter and asked, "Can you tell me where I can find Mr. Nance?"

The clerk eyed Molly curiously. Having no idea who she was or what she meant to the business's owner, he said, "I saw him heading across the street to the tavern. When he is in town, he has dinner there."

Molly turned around and pointed to the tavern across the street and asked with a smile, "That one?"

"That one," answered the clerk, who then returned his attention to his floor sweeping. The clerk watched out of the corner of his eye as Molly departed.

From across the street, the tavern seemed to be a nice, clean establishment. As Molly entered the tavern, she stood in the doorway, waiting for her eyes to adjust to the light.

Nance noticed Molly in the doorway and put down his fork. He continued to slowly chew his mouthful of steak. Seeing that Molly had spotted him and had begun to cross the room, he steepled his fingers and began to drum them slowly. When Molly stopped before his table, he said, "I have been expecting you."

Molly fought her impulse to lash out verbally. She stood silent but felt her body tremble slightly. Molly struggled to suppress her instinct to fight or flee.

Nance said, "Sit down, please." His visitor remained standing. "Would you like something to eat?" he asked. Molly remained silent. Leaning back in his chair, Nance assumed a smug countenance and asked, "Have you come here to plead for your husband's life?"

Molly felt like slapping his face but remained still. After a few seconds, she realized that her former friend had just overplayed his hand, and she smiled slightly. Nance observed her facial expression, but did not know what to make of it. Molly said softly, "Rhis, we served together on the *Pembroke*. We fought alongside one another, and you were present when my family was reunited, but...."

"But, what? That counts for something, I should think."

"It counts for a lot. That is one reason why I have not shot you with the pistol in my bag."

That got Nance's attention! Nance grasped the armrest and sat up. His face blanched slightly. He was angry at himself for betraying this emotion before the woman he thought about every day of his life.

Molly continued with a deliberate voice, "But I have a family now —three beautiful children and a wonderful husband. A man whom I love more than words can express."

Molly's words hit a raw nerve. Nance glowered and slammed his fist on the table. "He is a Frenchman! How could you?" asked Nance. Catching himself, he glanced around the room to see whether his outburst was drawing unwanted attention.

Once more, Molly showed no emotion. She had anticipated Nance's reactions. She said sympathetically, "Perhaps the current situation has come about because I was not clear enough about my feelings. Rhis, we were comrades in arms. That draws people close. We both know that." Molly allowed a slight smile.

Nance said beseechingly, "Please sit down and have some supper with me, Molly. We have so much to talk about."

Molly said, "That night that General Wolfe sent me into Quebec to spy.... "Molly paused to give Nance time to recall the event. (He was there that evening, after all). "The last thing on my mind was falling in love. And yet, that night I met my future husband. And you know something else, Rhis? I knew immediately that he was the one for me."

Nance replied tenderly, "What I recall about that night was being surrounded by French soldiers and their Indian friends. I remember being scared to death. I remember watching you breaking from our group and running to mingle with those terrified French soldiers. I remember being sick to my stomach that I might never see you again."

Unmoved by Nance's tenderness, Molly remained focused on her purpose in coming. She said, "Rhis, I don't wish to see you die. Please take your associates and leave town for a few days. My husband and I will depart as well. We can all forget about this misguided challenge."

Rhis said, "I'm not leaving Montréal. I have built a business that spans hundreds of miles and all points of the compass. You *have* noticed that I am rich now." Again, Molly did not change expressions. "I want to shower you with gifts and provide you with anything your heart desires. We can travel. We do not have to live on the frontier."

"I have noticed, and that is my point exactly. The head of Nance Trading Company has a great deal to live for. Why throw it all away?" asked Molly.

"I will not lose the duel. Your husband will."

Struggling to remain calm, because her pleas were not fazing Rhis, Molly said, "In that case, perhaps you would like to meet my children. I meant, of course, your future children, since you mean to wed me after killing Jean-Luc—their father." Nance glared fiercely. Seeing her meaning sinking in, Molly waited for Nance's response.

Nance said, "The heart wants what the heart wants. There is no denying that."

"I'm not asking anything to be denied. I came here to ask an old shipmate not to destroy my family," said Molly with a deliberately detached expression.

Nance said, "Not a family, Molly. Perhaps a husband, but not a family. Too much is at stake now. There are reputations at stake. There is no turning back." For the first time, Molly's expression cracked, and she knitted her brow. Rhis continued, "As we speak, my men are meeting with your husband's representative."

"I see," said Molly, seething with anger but remaining outwardly serene. She slowly turned and walked toward the door.

Nance called out, "By the way, who are those men who are accompanying your husband?"

Molly stopped and turned around. She said, "Should they feel it necessary that you know, they will tell you themselves."

Nance thoughtfully pinched his lip and watched her every step. After Molly had departed the tavern, he banged his fist on the table. She will protect her family and always has, he remembered. And if I kill her husband, *she* will kill me. Nance looked at his now-cold steak and pushed the unappetizing object to an arm's length.

Sieur Rafael St. Alembert and the Comte de Belfort sat by the fire in St. Alembert's parlor. Having chatted amiably for five minutes, they were waiting for Charnay to return from a comfort break.

Shivering, Charnay walked in rubbing his arms. He said, "Brrrrr. That privy is cold."

Rafael smiled and said, "I apologize for the primitive conditions. But, it is well that you have finished, because it is time for us to leave."

As Belfort stood, Charnay said, "Let us go, then." He then took Belfort gently by the arm and said, "Remember, our purpose is to defuse the situation. We do not want this duel to take place. We must be on our most conciliatory behavior." Belfort frowned slightly. Noticing his ally's reaction, he added, "Rici, there is much to lose and nothing to gain by this quarrel."

"Oh, I know that. It is just that I cannot tolerate backwoodsmen challenging the honor of gentlemen," said Belfort.

As he opened the front door, Rafael said, "I do not like it either, but I have dealt with these *coureurs-de-bois* longer than you two have been alive. Certainly, they test your patience, but Sir Geoffrey is correct. We must dissuade them from this deadly contest. As to their loutish behavior, I that think much can be attributed to them living among the savages." The paladins nodded.

Jean-Luc, upstairs with the children, heard the front door close. He had stopped pacing long enough to walk to the window. He parted the curtains to watch his father and the two paladins walk up the rue Notre Dame. He felt a lump in his throat as he realized that they held his family's future in their hands.

Little Nancy said, "You look upset, Papa."

Jean-Luc turned to his daughter and two sons. "No, no, I am fine." He somberly turned back to the window.

Nancy said, "But, Papa, you have been pacing. You never pace — unless you are worried."

Jean-Luc said, "Come here, children." The boys put down their toys and stood and walked to the window where their father stood. Jean-Luc knelt and drew his children close. He bear-hugged all three at the same time. The children loved it when their papa did what he laughingly called the "tous ensemble." But it caused his little girl to think he *was* worried about something. Since turning ten, Nancy had increasingly been able to read her father's moods. As in a reversal of roles, Nancy patted her father's cheek and said, "Everything will be all right, Papa."

Benjamin Chartrand and Elijah Laval, who were Nance's employees and were to act as Nance's seconds, stood on the corner of the rue Notre Dame and watched several nearby soldiers pass on the far side of the street. Chartrand and Laval were as different from each other as night and day. Chartrand was physically imposing, loyal, and prone to live for the moment. Laval was of only moderate height, loyal only as long as the money flowed in his direction, and capable of thinking on his feet. However, these two men had one thing in common: both aspired to assume the role of next-in-command to Nance in Nance's trading empire.

Jean-Luc's father and the paladins walked toward Chartrand and Laval and then stopped short. The two sides offered neither greetings nor handshakes. Noticing that the sun was setting, Belfort said, "It is quite cold out. If it is it agreeable to all, I suggest that we move our meeting inside the tavern across the street. There, we can discuss the arrangements over drinks." Chartrand turned toward the tavern and then glanced at Laval, who nodded imperceptibly. Chartrand then slowly returned his gaze to St. Alembert's agents and nodded. Laval gazed only at Chartrand; and seeing that the tavern had been agreed to, Laval obliged his older confederate and dutifully began walking across the road.

Charnay closely scrutinized this communication between Nance's subordinates. He could see that Chartrand was a few years older, but that the smaller trapper, Laval, appeared to be the more mentally agile.

The five men crossed the dirt street and entered the tavern. Molly saw them as she was walking down the rue Notre Dame after speaking with Nance. She glanced around the street and adjacent square, and then she ducked into the rooming house half of the tavern. Inside the lobby, her mind raced to find some way to eavesdrop. Her gaze settled on an empty drinking glass. Looking about, Molly could see that the desk clerk was paying no attention. Molly took the glass and pressed its open end against the wall. As the five men pulled out their chairs, Molly could hear her father-in-law Rafael's voice clearly.

After everyone was seated, Laval used the awkward silence to study the negotiators. While Chartrand squirmed in his seat, he looked across the room for the bar maid. Finally, Laval began by saying in a soothing voice, "We are here to negotiate the particulars for the contest."

Charnay noted that the trapper didn't say the word "duel." Charnay glanced at Belfort, who was also looking about the room; Charnay also glanced at Sieur St. Alembert, who was staring at Laval. Sieur St. Alembert showed remarkable restraint, thought Charnay.

Laval lowered his voice and asked, "What will be your choice of weapon?"

Sieur St. Alembert said matter-of-factly, "Our gentleman chooses pistols. Are you able to supply dueling pistols?"

Chartrand snorted and said, "Why, we have them aplenty. What pace of distance do you want? Five, six, ten, what? Does the gentleman want as far back as possible?"

"Ten is sufficient. I have answered the question," emphasized the white-haired father. He looked first at Laval and then turned and gave Chartrand a stern look.

Laval said, "Pistols it is. That was easy. We shall provide them, and they will be loaded in the presence of the seconds. The challenger will choose his pistol first? Fair enough?" Laval looked about the table. The three men representing Jean-Luc nodded.

A barmaid approached the table and asked, "You five look thirsty. What can I bring you?"

Sieur St. Alembert said for the group, "Nothing for me, thank you." The paladins shook their heads slowly, not really looking up at the maiden.

Seemingly to irritate his opponent's father, Chartrand said, "Bring me a spruce ale." Laval shook his head.

The barmaid walked away, but the five men sat silent as they awaited her return with Chartrand's drink. After she arrived with his ale, Chartrand immediately knocked back his beverage in three gulps and then banged the pewter mug on the table. The aristocrats raised their eyebrows in mock admiration for the man who could dispatch an ale so rapidly. The barmaid asked, "Want another one, hon? You seem parched."

"Why, yes. I would. No one else is drinking with me?" asked Chartrand.

Sieur St. Alembert said nothing as he waited for the barmaid to depart. As she walked away, he said in a neutral tone, "We have not come to socialize."

Chartrand said, "No, but you have come to arrange the death of your son."

Charnay and Belfort looked back and forth between the elder St. Alembert and Laval's reaction to Chartrand's continual provocations. He noted that the smaller agent did not admonish his ally but did seem irritated. And he also noted that his host's face flushed with anger with each insult to his son's honor.

"We must now choose a site. As a resident of Montréal, do you know a secluded area?" asked Laval of Sieur St. Alembert.

The paladins turned to look at Jean-Luc's father. Sieur St. Alembert said, "I do. I recommend a secluded glen on the southern half of Île des Soeurs. Do you know it?" Laval nodded. "On the northern half, there is a convent; but the other side of the island holds a forest and a small lake. We can meet at nine tomorrow morning at the clearing south of the lake."

Laval reiterated the site, "South half of the island, south of the lake, forest clearing, at nine. Got it."

Sieur St. Alembert said, "Take precautions not to alert the convent sisters. We should be able to have the contest and depart without the convent's occupants knowing that we were there."

Standing with her ear to the wall, Molly could overhear the

discussion. Molly stepped away from the wall since she did not want to be observed eavesdropping, but also to mull over her options in deciding a plan of action. Glancing about the room for any hotel guests who might have been observing her odd behavior, she decided to return to her father-in-law's home.

Chartrand, sensing that the meeting was about to adjourn and wanting to get in one last insult, said, "We will be there, so make sure that your son is there. I am going to enjoy this."

Sieur St. Alembert's back stiffened. He said, stiffly, "My son is eagerly awaiting this contest and is an excellent marksman. You did not just insinuate my son a coward, did you?"

Chartrand shrugged his shoulders as he stood and said, "He did give me that impression this afternoon. I suppose I am."

Laval closed his eyes and put his hands over his face. Chartrand glanced at his ally and looked surprised. The paladins looked at one another, and then at Jean-Luc's father. Not knowing this man well, they did not know what to expect next.

Sieur St. Alembert said, "Perhaps, it is you who is a coward. I noticed that you had to imbibe some liquid courage to loosen your tongue. I view it as particularly cowardly to denigrate my son's reputation while he is not here."

"Perhaps we should be going, now that our business is complete," said Laval.

Laval pushed his chair back and started to stand. Chartrand put his large hand on Laval's shoulder and shoved him back into his chair. "Wait a minute. Are you now calling me a coward?" asked Chartrand with a malevolent sneer. Sieur St. Alembert said nothing but raised his eyebrows as if to ask "is my meaning unclear?" Chartrand sat back down and said in a hiss, "You and I can settle this, just like the boss and your spineless son."

"Accepted," said Sieur St. Alembert. He turned to Belfort and asked, "Please advise us how to conduct a *second* contest."

Belfort said, "It is identical. Since you are the challenged, the choice of weapons is yours."

Laval sank onto his chair as he watched events spinning out of control. He realized that as soon as Chartrand challenged the old man, that he, Laval, would be the solo second and outnumbered. Chartrand leaned forward in his chair and glared at St. Alembert, who returned his fierce gaze with barely controlled fury.

Sieur St. Alembert answered while maintaining his intense gaze on Chartrand. "Pistols."

With Laval drained emotionally, Belfort spoke up. "The second contest is conducted *concurrently,* but at right angles to the first."

Laval squirmed but finally uttered, "Makes sense." Under his breath, Laval said in a hiss, "The boss isn't going to like this."

Belfort leaned over and whispered, "Actually, the seconds often end up dueling, too. It happens more often than you would think." Laval swallowed hard because he knew that he would be outnumbered. He did not know what to expect from these two strangers tomorrow morning, since he knew nothing about them.

Laval and Chartrand stood up. Chartrand said in a self-assured tone, "Tomorrow at nine." Then, without the usual social pleasantries, Chartrand walked out.

At the moment, the barmaid approached the table with Chartrand's drink. She asked, "Where is he going? Is he coming back?"

Belfort said, "I am afraid not. Here, I will take that." He handed her two coins and accepted the tankard.

Molly leaned back from the wall in the hotel lobby and repeated to herself, "The fight is at nine. And now Papa is dueling." She looked around and could see several patrons staring at her. Embarrassed, she quickly walked out. Up the street, she could see Nance's men heading to where they would presumably report the details of the meeting. Molly frowned as she imagined Rhis' smirk. She believed that Laval would be proved wrong, and that Nance would welcome the news that Chartrand had goaded the old man into a concurrent duel.

Molly hustled down the street. To keep from tripping, she lifted her dress to her ankles. Exiting from a small trading post, a young, dark-skinned woman wearing a red cape and fur boots stepped into Molly's path. They collided and both women went sprawling. Unhurt, Molly got to her feet and helped the other woman stand.

Molly said, "I am so sorry. This was all my fault." She brushed debris from the woman's buckskin clothing. The slightly younger woman didn't appear to be injured either, and was amused by the mishap. Molly noted the raven hair, and asked in French, "Are you hurt?"

The woman answered in the Gallic tongue, "No, I am fine, really." Then, as if choreographed, both woman began brushing dirt and twigs from their own clothes. Molly and the woman noticed the symmetry of their actions and started laughing. The stranger introduced herself and said, "My name is Anna."

Molly said, "And I am Molly." She shook Anna's hand. "I feel terrible. I was in such a hurry."

Anna said with a wry smile, "Perhaps it was not an accident."

Though Molly felt rushed to return home, she regarded the swarthy foreigner and paused to consider what she had said with conviction and nonchalance. She asked, "Why do you believe our collision was not accidental? I am curious." Molly bent down and picked up her handbag, straightened her bonnet, and looked over her shoulder up the street at her father-in-law's approaching group.

Anna smiled knowingly and said, "There can be only one reason: either you will change my life, or *I will change yours.*"

Her curiosity piqued, Molly asked, "How will we know which one it will be?" Anna smiled knowingly but said nothing. Molly asked, "And how will we know whether our meeting is for good or ill purposes?"

Anna asked, "Are you married?"

Molly nodded.

Anna asked, "Does he treat you well?" Molly blushed and said nothing. Anna asked, "What is wrong? Does he treat you poorly?"

"No, no," Molly insisted. "These are personal questions, and I do not know you. I feel awkward answering."

"Then allow me to earn your trust by reading your palm." Hesitant, Molly bit her lip but then slowly held out her left hand. Anna kneaded the flesh of Molly's hand gently as she studied the lines on Molly's palm. Anna said reassuringly, "I can see that you are married to a good man."

Molly said, "He is very good. I love him very much."

"I also see a warning. You have a line just under the joint of your left pinkie."

Molly's interest was piqued, and she asked, "Let me see." She looked closer at her hand and could see the small line to which Anna referred. "What is the warning?"

"Should you ever remarry, it will be a most unhappy union."

Molly exhaled in relief and said, "Well, there is little chance of that. You had me worried for a moment."

Anna's visage turned serious. She asked, "Do *you* know the future? How can you be so sure?"

Taken aback, Molly remembered the duel in the morning, and said, "Uh-oh." Now intrigued by palmistry (and forgetting the approach of Rafael and the paladins), Molly asked, "Tell me about tomorrow morning."

Anna said in an agitated whisper, "I cannot tell the future."

Disappointed, Molly whispered back, "I wish you could."

Anna smiled knowingly and said, "I can tell you this. The one who encounters Le Nain Rouge *will die*." Though the swarthy palm reader detected Molly's hesitation, she insisted, "If it is you who meets the dwarf, do not mistreat him. Showing kindness may save your life."

"But I thought," said Molly.

Anna quickly said, "That is correct, I cannot tell the future, but the red dwarf is a terrible enemy, or— "

At that moment, Rafael spotted Molly and called out. Startled, Molly turned toward her father-in-law. Seeing him, she waved, but quickly turned back to Anna. "Or what?"

"—or a valuable ally." Anna did not wish to encounter the three approaching men. She said, "I must go."

Confused by this strange forecast, Molly said, "Oh, all right then. It was a pleasure, Anna. I hope we meet again soon."

Anna darted into a nearby alley and disappeared.

Molly felt intrigued by her odd encounter with the swarthy beauty, Anna, and stared down the alley. Molly snapped out of it when a sister from the local convent walked behind her. The familiar-looking nun was wearing a habit and was moving at a rushed pace.

Molly called out, "Sister Angelina? Is that you?"

The nun stopped and turned slowly toward Molly. Surprised, the nun turned and asked, "Molly? I never supposed that I would see you again. Why, the last time was the night you and that Indian boy were captured by Bigot's thugs."

Molly smiled at the memory and stepped toward Sister Angelina, but when the nun stiffened and gave no indication that she welcomed a hug, Molly said in an attempt to thaw the awkward moment, "I remember a certain nun chaperoning me on a picnic in the country when a handsome boy asked to see me." Molly said hesitantly, "I am happy to see you again, Sister Angelina."

Sister Angelina said, "I have thought about you a great deal when I heard you were really English and had been spying on us for the enemy. Actually, I have prayed a great deal over our relationship to discover God's plan in sending you into my life."

"Prayed? Why?" asked Molly.

"Our relationship tested my faith. I was angry with you for betraying my trust. You were not who you said you were. I was hurt, and I resented you for it."

Feeling chastened, Molly could only whisper, "I would feel the same way."

Sister Angelina continued, "But—I then learned the circumstances of your mother's imprisonment, and that Jean-Luc had forgiven you (to say the least)," Angelina allowed a half-smile, "I knew God wanted me to forgive you as Jean-Luc had. There were valid reasons for not presenting yourself honestly."

"Sister Angelina," said Molly, "I don't know how to ask this."

"What is it?"

"May I call on you at the convent tomorrow morning? My reason for asking is an urgent matter." The nun looked taken aback. "I ask that you watch after my three children for an hour, if that is all right? It is only for one hour."

"Why on earth would you come to our island and leave your children for *one hour*?" asked Sister Angelina.

"I cannot say. It is terribly important to both Jean-Luc and me. But now I am behind schedule, and I must bid *adieu*."

"Jean-Luc is in town? Will I be able to see him?"

"Of course, he will be with me when we drop off the children. You can visit with him then. *Au revoir*."

Molly opened the front door of her father-in-law's house and slipped in. Hoping to avoid questions, she had rushed ahead.

When Jean-Luc heard the door; he came out of their bedroom and stood at the top of the stairs. He asked, "Where have you been, darling?"

Ignoring his question, Molly said, "We need to talk, husband."

"I'll be right down."

Molly said, "No, no, I will come up. Are the children asleep?"

"Yes, why?"

Again, Molly didn't answer but hurriedly ascended the steps. When she reached the top, she hugged Jean-Luc in a desperate embrace. "I do not want to lose you," she whispered.

Jean-Luc said nothing for a moment. Then, summoning his gallows humor, he said, "What makes you think I am going to lose?" Feigning indignity, he said, "I happen to be quite confident."

Molly looked into his eyes and said, "Tonight may be our last night."

Jean-Luc said smiling, "Nonsense."

"Rafael is now in this deadly contest."

"What are you talking about?" asked Jean-Luc. He stepped back and held Molly at arm's-length.

Molly said with a tear running down her cheek, "Rhis's representative became angry with Rafael at the meeting and challenged him to duel. There are going to be two duels in the morning—at the same time."

Horrified, Jean-Luc said, "How do you know this?"

Molly lowered her eyes and admitted, "I eavesdropped on their meeting. I wanted to learn the location of your duel, because—"

Jean-Luc released his hold on her arms, stepped away, and put the back of his hand to his forehead in thought. "I should have seen this coming. That man intends to destroy me *and my family.*" Turning back to Molly, he asked, "What did you think you were going to accomplish?"

Molly said unevenly, "I intend to stop these deadly contests. I—have a plan."

Jean-Luc said, "You must not. If you interfere, my reputation would be ruined in New York circles. I would rather die with honor because it is impossible to live in dishonor."

"I do not care about any of that, Jean-Luc," said Molly.

"Socially and financially, our family would become outcasts. A man without honor deserves to be dead. I would not associate with such a man. I certainly do not intend to ever become such a man."

Molly looked into his eyes and said, "I promise not to interfere. But do not shut me out tonight. I wish to be a part of your discussions. Please do not forbid it."

Jean-Luc reluctantly nodded, but then smiled and added, "You will behave yourself?"

The front door opened. Jean-Luc and Molly looked down into the foyer. Rafael and the paladins walked in and hung their coverings on the hall coatrack. Rafael glanced up the stairs and said, "Come down, son, we have to talk."

Jean-Luc nodded and Molly said, "Yes, Papa." She and Jean-Luc started down the stairs.

Rafael held up his hand and said, "No, I wish to speak with Jean-Luc in private."

Molly froze for an instant. She said, "Papa, I—" Molly stopped in mid-sentence and straightened her shoulders and said resolutely, "my family could be destroyed tomorrow. Wild horses cannot keep me away."

"Very well," said Rafael openly unhappy. He did not approve of such brashness in modern women.

Gathering in the parlor, the men took seats while Molly stood behind Jean-Luc's chair. Rafael turned toward Belfort and said, "You know more about this dueling business. Perhaps you could talk us through tomorrow's events."

Belfort said, "Of course." He stood and walked to the center of the room. "At the appointed place," he nodded at Charnay and said, "Geoff and I will represent you two and examine the pistols before they are loaded. We will also observe the loading of the four pistols to ensure that there are no tricks or unfair advantages to be gained."

Charnay added, "The duelists are separated and do not speak to one another. Rici and I will conduct any last-minute negotiations, though I expect nothing of consequence."

"Father and I will select first?" asked Jean-Luc.

Belfort said, "That is correct. Jean-Luc, you and your father will select your pistols before the challengers select theirs."

Thus far, Molly had remained silent, but she interrupted and asked, "Who will be in the first duel?"

Belfort said, "They will be conducted simultaneously."

"How will that work," asked Molly somewhat apprehensively.

Charnay said, "The four men will stand at right angles to one another."

"Since losing is not an option, what can be done to ensure success?" she asked pointedly.

Belfort said in a defensive tone, "Losing, I am afraid, *is* an option. This is an *Affaire d'honneur.* Comportment must be above reproach."

Jean-Luc placed his hand on Molly's and gently squeezed. He asked Belfort, "In the event both are wounded—or both miss, then what?"

Belfort said, "Either way, the duel is concluded. The challenge has ended honorably."

Molly said, "I want to know what can be done to ensure success."

Belfort looked puzzled and asked, "What is your meaning?"

"These two men could practice, could they not?" asked Molly. "I believe in the military it is called drilling." Realizing that this Frenchman had no such intentions, Molly knitted her brows and glared at him. She said, "I want my men to come out of this *affaire d'honneur* alive." Molly's sarcastic tone put off Belfort; however, Charnay enjoyed her taunt.

Charnay stood and said, "I understand her question. There *are* techniques we can work on." Turning to his companion, he said, "Rici, she is right. Though fairness is paramount, Jean-Luc and his father must not lose. Our hopes for Jean-Luc depend on the outcome."

"But, but," sputtered Belfort. "What is to be done the night before?"

Charnay said, "I will show you." He turned to Jean-Luc and said, "I keep two pistols in my valise. Would you retrieve them?"

Jean-Luc walked out of the room and returned moments later. He handed the two pistols to Charnay. Charnay said, "Mistakes happen. Mistakes like firing too quickly, being inaccurate, and mechanical malfunctions."

Molly asked, "Mechanical?"

"If, for example, a pistol misfires, the duelist has five seconds to correct the malfunction."

Jean-Luc said, "That is not much time."

"You are correct, but it is time enough, if the duelist did not fully cock his pistol. The weapon will not fire at half-cock. And that is the usual cause of the malfunction."

Molly said, "So, we want fast, accurate, and fully cocked pistols."

Charnay said, "That is exactly what is required of the St. Alemberts. Fast without accuracy is wasted."

Belfort said, "Ensure that your flintlock clicks twice when you pull it back, sight down the barrel at your opponent's chest, and for heaven's sake squeeze, do not jerk, the trigger."

Jean-Luc said, "I understand. Practice will help. Father, shall we duel?"

Molly said, "First ensure the pistols are not charged and loaded." Both sheepishly verified that their pistol wasn't loaded. "Rehearsal is the best way to control your nerves."

Jean-Luc and Rafael stood. Each gripped a pistol and walked to opposite sides of the room. Belfort said, "When you've turned to face your challengers, your pistol should be waist level pointing slightly downward. Otherwise, your opponent may conclude that you are cheating."

Rafael nodded. Jean-Luc said, "I understand."

Charnay said, "Keep your finger off the trigger until you have raised it to fire. An accidental discharge leaves you helpless."

Molly said, "Let's get started, shall we?"

Off to the side, Belfort stood and raised his handkerchief. He said, "When I drop my arm, you may fire. But first, cock your pistols."

Father and son and son concurrently pulled the flintlocks back until each heard two distinct clicks. As they held the pistols at waist level, the only audible sound was their breathing. When Belfort dropped his arm, Rafael clearly got off the first shot.

Molly grimaced. She said, "More practice. Again."

After two dozen rehearsals, Molly was satisfied. Her men had smooth, fast, and accurate movements. She said, "That is enough practice for tonight. Now, hit the hay. Tomorrow, you must be fresh and alert."

◄—◆—►

At the tavern across from his trading post, Nance, Chartrand, and Laval sat having a drink. Chartrand sat with his chair back facing the table. Laval drummed his fingers nervously. He always fidgeted when the boss was upset, and Nance *was* upset.

Laval said, "I do not understand you, Mr. Nance. We thought that this was what you wanted."

Chartrand glanced up momentarily and then looked sadly at his nearly empty tankard. He raised his eyes to scan the room for the barmaid. "May as well have another," he muttered.

"Go easy, Ben. Tomorrow is serious business," said Nance. He didn't bother looking at his employee; he stared at the table and rubbed it with his finger.

"You heard Mr. Nance, Ben, you have had three already," chipped in Laval.

"Hell, it is not like I am the one that is going to fight St. Alembert." Chartrand looked up quickly and saw his employer glaring at him. He added, "I only meant that I got the easy one."

Nance's temper flared. "So you think I'm going to lose tomorrow?"

Chartrand's mind tried to form the words to placate his boss. It wasn't easy, though. "No, boss. I only meant that killing him is your pleasure. I picked out an easy one. I am going to kill—the graybeard."

Nance asked, "And the old coot is a lord of some kind, is he not? I suppose that that should add to the pleasure of bringing him down."

"You are right, as usual, Mr. Nance." Spotting the barmaid, Chartrand raised his hand to signal that he wanted another tankard.

When the server placed the mug before Chartrand, Nance scolded him, "I said, 'Go easy.'"

Laval saw that his boss was growing exasperated with Chartrand. He said, "I'll buy that ale from you, Ben. Yeah, I will take it off your hands, you know, so that you can be bright eyed for tomorrow's encounter." Laval studiously avoided the word "sober," having been backhanded by Chartrand before over using that word.

"No way in hell am I giving up my drink, you little pipsqueak," said Chartrand, who evidently had enough "liquid courage" in his blood to defy his employer. "I can outfight that old man anytime, anywhere. I have been thinking about where I want to put that musket ball. Do you think tween the eyes is about right, Mr. Nance?"

"Do you think you can outgun the old timer, even hung over?" asked Nance.

"Even hung *over!*" Chartrand growled the last syllable, emphasizing his contempt for the elder St. Alembert.

Nance said, "A gun is an equalizer, Ben. His age won't matter if his aim is true—and yours ain't."

Chartrand banged his fist on the table and drunkenly muttered, "I ain't gonna lose. I'm gonna kill me some 'ristocrat. You are right, boss, a pistol is a *social* equalizer."

In an attempt to soothe the tension at the table, Nance said, "Sure, Ben, sure—easy win tomorrow. I just don't want to lose a good man."

Laval wanted his boss's approbation, too. He asked, "Is there anything special that you want me to do tomorrow?"

"Elijah, you must have our backs. Is that special enough? I don't trust those Frogs that are babysitting Junior. You can't trust *those* people, Elijah. Keep an eye peeled for treachery in both the St. Alemberts and their seconds."

"Yes, sir." Elijah then picked up his tankard and took a sip. He thought, the boss trusts me to have his back. Yeah, that counts for a lot, but I'll be outnumbered tomorrow. Elijah tried to be tactful. He asked in a meandering sentence, "So... Mr. Nance, have you considered... bringing some of the other boys along?"

"Nah. We'll be fine." Suddenly, Nance wanted another drink and held up his hand for the server to bring another round.

Elijah said, "I have everything ready for the duel, Mr. Nance. I got them pistols polished up and shiny. They look like new. Would you care to inspect them and their equipment?"

"You know, I think I would, Elijah."

The two stood. Elijah turned to his friend, "Ben, do you wanna come?"

"Nah, E-li," Chartrand said slurring his drawn-out enunciation. "T'ink I will sit here and contemplate where I'm going to shoot the coot." Chartrand held up his hand with his forefinger extended like a pistol. He pretended to shoot and began giggling. He reiterated, "'Shoot the coot,' now that's funny, ain't it, Eli?"

Laval glanced at Nance, who grimaced in disapproval. He said, "Yeah, Ben, it is funny. See you in the morning. It's going to be early, so turn in soon, all right?"

Chartrand waved him off angrily. Chartrand was tempted to make a disrespectful remark about his two compatriots going to bed early, but he didn't want to be the target of Nance's rage.

Laval and Nance went upstairs. Walking down the dimly lit hall, they entered Laval's room. Nance stood near the door while Laval lit several candles on the table. The two pistol cases were open, and the four pistols were still in them. Nance slowly, almost reverently, picked up one pistol and then one of the others. He admired their workmanship and made a mental note to swap out the pistol he now carried for one of these after the duel. He placed them gently on the table and ran his fingertips over the flintlocks and the trigger housings and then lovingly along the barrels.

"I've waited thirteen years for tomorrow, Elijah. The memory of Molly embracing an enemy soldier—what, after we had fought so hard side by side. I tell you it is as fresh in my mind as if it had happened yesterday. None of this would be necessary if I had shot that Frog dead that day."

"What happened, boss?"

"We moved behind the Army's battle lines on the plains and had made our way undetected to Charlesbourg five miles away. When we arrived, there was fighting. We killed all the French and lost but men. We rescued Molly and her family and young St. Alembert and his Indian pal. For some reason, St. Alembert was being held also; and during her captivity, Molly, well, she took up with him. Her father favored me for sure and couldn't have been none too happy to see his daughter smitten with one of the enemy."

"Why didn't you kill him then and there, boss?"

"My girl stood between me, my muzzle, and the coward." Nance picked up a pistol and hefted it; he cocked the flint and aimed at an imaginary target. When he squeezed the trigger, the flint visibly sparked, which made both men smile. Then Nance's mood darkened, and he looked away. He said, "People talk about a man's heart breaking over a woman like it ain't no big deal, or like it's amusing or something."

"It is a big deal, isn't it Mr. Nance? Nothing can bring a man down faster than a broken heart."

"When it happens to you, Elijah, it's like getting kicked in the gut. And it don't get easier with the passage of time neither." Nance looked down at the pistols and said, "Tomorrow, I'm going to kill the man who stole thirteen years of my life. I've waited a long time, and it's going be sweet, I tell you. Guess it'll be like pulling out a splinter. How I will relish seeing *her* heart break, as mine did."

Laval said sympathetically, "Revenge is sweet, ain't it, Mr. Nance."

Nance cracked a malevolent smile. After a moment's silence, he said wistfully, "One of these pistols could be the one that kills me tomorrow, Eli."

"I'm proud to work for such a brave man, Mr. Nance," said Elijah. "You've worked hard for all you got. Yes, sir, you deserve all you got, and tomorrow you will get that splinter out of your paw. You will kill that Frog in the morning. Yes, sir, you will do fine tomorrow."

"Nothing is guaranteed, Elijah, I—" He turned and walked out of the room and never finished his sentence.

CHAPTER TWENTY-FOUR

MAY 16, 6 A.M.

JEAN-LUC BLINKED twice and squinted over at the bedroom door. He thought that he had heard a soft tapping, and he cocked his ear. He rolled over and looked for his wife and was surprised she was not beside him. He stumbled to the door and opened it. Standing before him was Belfort, fully dressed, who announced, "Breakfast is almost ready. Your wife and daughter are putting together a splendid meal."

"I will be right down," said Jean-Luc as he ran his fingers through his dark hair. After closing the door, he rubbed his eyes and then walked to the table beside the bed, took the pitcher and filled the basin. After splashing the cool water on his face, he noticed that his wife had laid out his clothes on the chair. Her thoughtfulness conveyed the depth of their regard and love. He stood before the mirror and reflected on the selfishness of the situation. Today lives would be ruined and certainly their trajectories would be altered irretrievably. "There is no time to dwell on the future," he thought. "I must concentrate fully on the task ahead." Jean-Luc dressed and walked downstairs.

As he entered the dining room, Molly said cheerfully, "Just in time." Around the table sat the paladins and his father. "We want you two at your best this morning, don't we?" After breakfast, we'll have a few more practices, then walk to the boat."

Surprised, Jean-Luc said, "You are not accompanying me."

"Oh, yes, I am—and so are the children."

"What?" Stunned, Jean-Luc glanced around the room to gauge the others' reactions. "I forbid it," he said sternly.

Sieur St. Alembert said in a strained voice, "The children know nothing and will remain at the convent until this unpleasantness is complete."

Little Peter looked up and asked, "What unpleasantness, Grandfather?"

"Never mind, Peter," said an embarrassed Rafael. The boy dutifully returned to his breakfast.

"I, I do not like this at all!" stammered Jean-Luc.

Molly said, "What is the alternative? Besides, you have a more important thing to worry about. Now, eat your breakfast. I think that afterwards, we should depart Montréal immediately."

Sieur St. Alembert wisely interjected, "Eat up, son. We need to be at our best."

A skeptical Jean-Luc took a forkful of eggs. Charnay, who liked Jean-Luc, became melancholy. Charnay had worked hard and undergone hardships to groom Jean-Luc for leadership in the American independence movement. Charnay, above all others save the man's wife, knew what impact Jean-Luc's death would have. If that fur-trapping baron were to succeed in gunning down Charnay's protégé Jean-Luc, Charnay himself would end up back in the Bastille. Charnay's memories of incarceration drove home the idea that all of his work on his king's behalf was imperiled.

Sitting quietly at the table, Charnay felt helpless and frustrated. Not feeling hungry, he neither smiled nor took part in the breakfast discussion. Automatically, he reached down and touched the pistol in his ankle holster. He thought back to the night before, when he had pulled Belfort aside to tell him to bring his own small pistol to the duel, and he wondered whether Belfort took his recommendation seriously.

After Molly shooed Peter into the kitchen, Belfort swallowed the last of his buttermilk. He looked about the dining room, ensuring that none of the children were present, and said, "Remember, keep your finger off the trigger, then *two* cocks of the flint, sight down the barrel, and *squeeze* the trigger."

Jean-Luc and Rafael nodded. Moments later, Nancy walked into the room with another plate heaped with ham and eggs. Jean-Luc glanced at his father. Rafael seemed relaxed. In a strange way, Jean-Luc was also. Jean-Luc put a piece of ham into his mouth, looked out the window, and thought about the paladins. Following several seconds of contemplation, he concluded that Belfort was simply incapable of empathy and that Charnay seemed distracted (but he had no idea why).

The kitchen door opened, and Molly entered with Peter. The boy bounded over to Jean-Luc and asked, "How are the eggs, Father? Momma let me turn them with the spatula. I was a huge help to her." Jean-Luc wanted to laugh but instead only patted his son's head.

Molly stood quietly beside Jean-Luc while he and the others finished breakfast. She stroked his hair and marveled at his calm demeanor. She easily could have grown angry over his masculine ethos of bravado and his exaggerated sense of honor. She, too, was strong-minded and wished to put the best face on this duel. She knew the best odds for success were to keep his spirits high to foster a relaxed and concentrated mind on his looming challenge.

After Jean-Luc finished his meal, it was time to start out. Molly quickly got the children into their coats and herded them out the door. Then, she and the children waited patiently for the four men to emerge. She forced a smile and was determined to keep the mood light. When the door finally opened, and the men came outside to a hazy gray sky that threatened rain, she quipped, "Isn't rain really liquid sunshine?"

Belfort piggy-backed on what Madame St. Alembert was doing. He said, "When I was a young boy, I would watch raindrops on my window and pretend that they were racing."

Molly's youngest, Rafe, looked up and said with a huge smile, "I do that, too."

Adults never quite know when children are listening, thought Charnay. His thoughts returned to the possible death of his protégé and his own resulting return to a squalid prison. Charnay had come from a culture where gentlemen settled their serious differences in a duel, and he was helpless to protect Jean-Luc. Charnay had to let Jean-Luc defend his own honor, and nothing could be allowed to interfere. Assessing Jean-Luc's mood, Charnay noted the resemblances between Jean-Luc and the elder St. Alembert. Both had the same slightly forward-leaning posture. Also, their expressions resolute, even under this terrible stress. Feeling that his own fate hung in the balance of this contest, Charnay didn't even realize his legs were carrying him toward the wharf. He reflected on his most fearful hour — the battlefield of Fontenoy — and remembered how he had tried to keep busy as he awaited the English Army's assault.

As the St. Alembert group approached the wharf, Jean-Luc's attitude changed and he automatically assumed his role as ship's captain.

When he spotted the skipper approaching, his second-in-command, Henry, waved enthusiastically from the gunnel.

Molly herded the children up the gangplank and straight to the captain's cabin. Moments later, the paladins entered and sat down by the window. Molly and the children watched the sailors, shopkeepers, and soldiers around the wharf. With the wind cooperating, Jean-Luc had the ship and the trailing sloop float away from the pier. When she heard her husband shout, "Make sail," she put her arms around her children's shoulders and smiled.

The sailors aloft allowed the ship's sails to gently billow as they slowly filled with wind. The keel redirected the wind's energy to the hull, propelling the vessel away from the wharf. Molly used to love the part of the trip when she watched her husband skillfully steer out to open water. But this short trip was different. Their ship was taking her husband toward the dueling site on Île des Soeurs.

Molly watched Rafael and Jean-Luc standing beside one another at the ship's wheel. Their posture reflected a psychological and ancestral unity. Each was defending Jean-Luc's honor within a system she condemned. Feeling helpless, Molly fell back on her maternal duties, to keep from bursting into tears. After assigning each child a chore, she looked out the window and decided that should Jean-Luc fall to Nance's pistol, her old shipmate from the *Pembroke* would never leave the island alive. She would see to that.

CHAPTER TWENTY-FIVE

MAY 16, 8:30 A.M.

RUNNING TO ANSWER the convent door, Sister Angelina shrieked with joy upon seeing Jean-Luc standing beside Molly. She rushed out and hugged her old childhood playmate.

After introducing the Frenchmen, Molly said, "Do you remember Jean-Luc's father?"

"Absolutely. He is very active in French Canadian affairs. Everyone knows Monsieur St. Alembert. How nice to see you again, sir."

"Thank you, Sister Angelina. We do appreciate your watching the children. We will not be long."

"I am happy to help out," said Sister Angelina. She turned to Jean-Luc and asked, "But why have you come to our little island?"

"Business," said Jean-Luc. He forced a smile and put his hand on Peter's shoulder and gently pushed the youngster forward. "We really must be going. But when we return, I will be in a better position to catch up on news."

Nancy, Peter, and little Rafe dutifully walked into the nun's cloister. Nancy and Peter sensed that something was wrong and looked back at their parents as Angelina slowly closed the door.

Oblivious to all around him, Rafe bounded into the nun's court-yard and pronounced, "I am hungry."

Disturbed by Jean-Luc' evasiveness, Sister Angelina looked back at Molly with concern. She then glanced at her old childhood friend, Jean-Luc. Her countenance turned cloudy for an instant, but then she turned to the children and said with fabricated cheerfulness, "I am sure we can find some food in the kitchen."

As the door closed, Belfort said, "How far is the walk, Sieur St. Alembert?"

"About fifteen minutes from here," said the elder, pointing toward the southeast.

"Lead on, monsieur," said Charnay. As the group started in the indicated direction, Charnay said softly, "Note the sun's location and make sure that you won't have it in your eyes." Jean-Luc and Rafael nodded grimly.

The five walked with long, purposeful strides. Molly glanced at her husband and his father. Both men seemed confident and ready. Doubts crept into Molly's mind. To keep from looking nervous, she checked the basket of medical supplies she toted under her arm.

In the distance, Molly could now see three men standing beside a large pond and a clearing. They were the now familiar presences of Rhis Nance, Ben Chartrand, and the assistant, Eli Laval. Seeing their adversaries, Molly's group walked just a tick faster.

Molly studied the three men and noted that Nance stood with his legs apart and his arms folded across his chest. His attire gave every appearance of a prosperous businessman. Under his green coat, he wore a white shirt trimmed in ruffles; his gray pants were tucked into splendidly polished riding boots. His expression exuded confidence and an air of invincibility. Molly thought, "Why shouldn't he be confident? For years, he has enjoyed an unbroken string of business successes and expansion, though none of it has brought him happiness." Once Jean-Luc came into view, Nance never stopped glaring at him.

The hulking woodsman was another story. He stood slumped,

with his chin almost touching his chest. Chartrand had ignored Nance's admonition to go easy on the liquor the evening before. Now he was paying the price with a hangover. Because of his disdain for the elder St. Alembert (and former French aristocrat), Chartrand felt little need to prepare for the deadly confrontation.

Molly turned her gaze upon Eli Laval, who was as nervous a long-tailed cat in a room full of rocking chairs. The small assistant stood close by his employer for both physical and psychological unity. Laval's eyes darted around, giving the impression that he had figured out how dire his situation was. Laval glanced at Chartrand and grimaced. Molly noted the psychological distance between the two subordinates. Adding Laval's behavioral clues together, Molly concluded her father-in-law was dueling a rat. She approached her father-in-law from behind and whispered, "I can see that the seconds are going to become involved. Be extra careful." Sieur St. Alembert nodded, and his posture noticeably stiffened.

Jean-Luc glanced at his father, and then at Molly, and wondered what she had said. He, Molly, and his father halted twenty feet from the opposing trio. Belfort and Charnay continued walking up to Nance, Chartrand, and Laval.

Belfort said, "Shall we step over here to examine the pistols and preparations? Perhaps a quick review of the procedures would help all concerned." As he held out his hand, he brushed it against Laval's overcoat.

Laval nervously glanced at Nance. Receiving a nod, he walked to the spot indicated by St. Alembert's second. Holding two wooden boxes precariously at chest level, Laval stood ramrod straight.

Belfort and Charnay walked up and slowly opened the lids of the pistol cases. Meticulously examining the pistols, shot, and powder horns, they sprinkled some gunpowder into their palms and slowly rubbed the grains between their fingers. They nodded to one another. Next, they poured a handful of musket balls into their palms and selected the four thought to be the best in the pouch. "Everything is in order," Belfort announced as he rolled the musket balls between his hands.

Laval noticed their precision and wondered who these men were. Laval asked, with his voice cracking timidly, "Would you assist me, gentlemen, in loading the pistols?" Belfort nodded.

Molly watched Charnay step away from his ally. Laval concluded that Charnay wanted to keep an eye on Nance and Chartrand. Molly then walked over to her husband and gently pulled him a few feet away. Molly stepped in close to ensure no one else heard their *tête-à-tête*, and whispered, "Remember how we practiced? Be deliberate." Jean-Luc forced a smile. "You must go through your progressions rapidly: cock for two clicks, sight, and squeeze."

Jean-Luc nodded and glanced back at Nance, who was glaring at him. Jean-Luc turned back, and nose to nose, said softly, "Molly, I—"

Placing her finger on his lips, Molly smiled and said, "I know, darling." She kissed him and then took a step back, smoothed his lapels, and whispered, "Make your shot count; do not rush it."

Molly studied her husband as he walked to the dueling ground. As instructed, he nonchalantly faced at an angle toward the sun. His father did the same. Molly now knew that Jean-Luc and his father would have the sun over their shoulders when they turned to fire.

The St. Alemberts had moved into position innocently enough. Not surprisingly, neither Nance nor Chartrand suspected anything. Nance walked over next. Exuding confidence, took his position with his back to Jean-Luc.

Chartrand had spent the last twenty minutes ruing his bacchanalian overdose and cursing the ensuing headache. He just wanted to kill his man and put this gentlemen's contest behind him. Though he felt like puking, the idea of losing to the white-haired father of his boss's enemy had never occurred to him. He stumbled as he approached Rafael but then quietly took his position facing away from his opponent.

After Charnay returned the flints so that they rested in their frizzens, Laval took the pistols in turn and returned them to their places in the wooden boxes.

Belfort broke the silence by announcing, "The challenged shall select pistols first."

Laval, accompanied by Charnay, walked over to Jean-Luc and Rafael. Jean-Luc quickly looked over the pistols and saw nothing to distinguish one from another. "Father, please go first."

Sieur St. Alembert nodded solemnly and gripped a pistol and held it upright against his shoulder. Jean-Luc followed his example. Next Nance angrily snatched a pistol. Finally, Chartrand took the final weapon.

Chartrand turned his head slightly and asked, "Old man, are you ready to die?"

Charnay said, with rising anger in his voice, "Silence! There is no talking until the duel is completed."

Chartrand angrily glared at Belfort but said nothing further. The four men stood in silence. Even nature appeared to be holding its breath, as the island's fauna fell silent.

Belfort said, "I shall count out ten steps. On the tenth step, you will halt, cock your weapon, turnabout to face one another. Await my signal. I shall raise, then drop my handkerchief. When you see the handkerchief fall, you may fire. Does anyone have a question?"

The four men grimly shook their heads. Molly kept shifting her attention between Laval, Nance, and Chartrand. Ignored by the participants and seconds, she slowly opened her sack and gripped the pistol stashed there. Her hand remained in the sack, her finger was off the trigger, and the flint wasn't cocked.

Belfort said, "Then let us begin, shall we? One." The four duelists took a step. With a mere moment of hesitation, Belfort continued, "Two... three—"

Molly felt her body shudder. She straightened her back to hide her anxiety, though no one was observing the bystander. She glanced at Laval, who now stood between Belfort and Charnay. He looked upset. His friend, Chartrand, also commanded Molly's attention; he appeared extremely agitated. In Molly's opinion, Chartrand was behaving suspiciously by glancing back at Rafael repeatedly.

When Belfort said, "Four," Chartrand startled the onlookers. He cocked his weapon, spun around, and hurriedly fired. Jean-Luc and Nance flinched.

Molly screamed, the birds in the treetops took flight, and the seconds, Charnay and Laval, drew their weapons. All eyes looked to Rafael.

"Father!" shouted Jean-Luc. He started to take a step toward his father.

Belfort said loudly and commandingly, "No one move!"

Chartrand looked astonished that the old man had not fallen to the ground mortally wounded. "Swive it! I missed," he blurted.

Molly watched in horror as Rafael's tunic turned crimson near his right shoulder. Then, her father-in-law dabbed at his earlobe, where Chartrand's musket ball had ripped through the skin. Sieur St. Alembert said in volume of rising anger, "It's only a *flesh wound.*"

Laval asked sadly, "Ben, what have you done?"

Belfort said, "We have witnessed a serious breach of etiquette. Sieur St. Alembert, as the offended party are you able to answer this dishonorable act? You have that option, sir, or you may request that your second respond in your behalf."

"I—I am capable. I will answer this cowardly act," angrily said the elder St. Alembert.

"Then you have five seconds to turn and shoot," said Belfort coolly.

"This is bullshit. I am not going to stand here and get shot," said Chartrand.

"What did you expect, Ben?" asked Nance in disgust. "I warned you repeatedly last night about overindulging. I knew that you did not understand dueling, but you just tried to shoot a man in the back. Even you know that's wrong."

Looking chastened, the nauseous Chartrand did not respond to his employer. "Get on with it, old man, you are too old to hit anything anyway," he said in his most disdainful voice. Sieur St. Alembert slowly turned to face the hulking woodsman, cocked his pistol (two distinct clicks), extended his arm, and squeezed the trigger.

The muzzle blast belched forth a musket ball aimed true. Chartrand spun half around and clutched his chest, staggered backwards one step, and collapsed. On the ground, he tried to say something, but the blood foaming in his throat made a hideous gurgling sound. Laval took a step toward his friend's body, but Charnay put his arm on his shoulder and stopped him.

Molly remained motionless. She had witnessed violence before, but now she wanted to rush to Rafael's side. Yet she held back. She looked down at her pistol, but still she did not draw it from the sack.

Laval said, "You murdering bastards. Ben was my friend."

Nance said, "Stand silent, Eli. I still have work to do."

Nance's proclamation of the obvious brought everyone's attention back to the business at hand. Belfort said, "Mr. Nance is correct."

Laval's hands shook, but he consciously tried to control his anxiety. He stared at Chartrand's body and wondered how Nance's plan had suddenly gone so horribly wrong.

Belfort startled him back into the present when he asked, "Shall we continue?"

Molly, a bit shaken herself, dedicated her attention to Nance, who gave her the impression that he was singularly focused on killing her husband. Should that come about, she intended to walk up to Nance and shoot him point blank.

Once again, Belfort abruptly ripped her from her considerations with his command, 'Five.' After Jean-Luc and Nance renewed the duel by stepping off, Molly guessed that the distance separating her husband from the muzzle of Nance's pistol was a mere twenty-five feet. Even at double that distance, the pistol would almost certainly deliver a mortal wound. In seconds, Molly understood she may become a widow; she cocked her flint back twice.

"Six."

"Seven."

"Eight."

"Nine."

Charnay had the identical plan, and his eyes darted back and forth between Laval, an armed second, and Nance, the jilted lover. He held his breath as the electrified atmosphere made the next few seconds seem like an hour. He reached inside his coat and placed his hand on his pistol.

Nance's mind, desiring a head shot to kill or disfigure St. Alembert, knew that he had chosen a smaller target than his opponent's torso, but he was confident and wasn't one to waver.

"Ten," said Belfort. Nance and Jean-Luc halted.

Jean-Luc's fingers repeatedly relaxed and tightened on the pistol's smooth wooden grip. Knowing that he tended to allow his trigger pull to bring the muzzle down and to the left, Jean-Luc decided to aim for Nance's left shoulder. Using his apprehension to his advantage, he had decided to end this threat to his family *forever.*

Molly did not draw her pistol just yet. Within seconds, Belfort would drop the handkerchief, and she did not wish to distract her husband from his task. Looking up from her pistol, Molly saw Laval move unexpectedly.

Belfort ensured that he had the attention of both duelists. Satisfied, he dropped the handkerchief. Nance and Jean-Luc spun around and aimed simultaneously. Nance squinted down his barrel and aligned his sights on St. Alembert's nose. Jean-Luc lowered his pistol and aimed for Nance's left shoulder.

Molly averted her eyes. Two shots rang out; Jean-Luc's trigger pull had been a split second behind Nance's.

Molly heard Laval curse, and she turned back to learn her husband's fate. Both Nance and Jean-Luc remained upright. She wondered whether they both missed. She took a step toward the duelists. Jean-Luc clutched the side of his head and slowly bent over. Molly gasped and blurted out, "Jean-Luc!"

Nance clutched his chest and dropped slowly to his knees. He looked at his crimson shirt and realized that his opponent's musket ball had found his heart; he realized that he had only moments to live. Slowly, he extended his arm toward Molly.

Ignoring Nance's supplication, Molly went straight to her husband. She asked, "Where are you hit, darling?"

Jean-Luc said, "In the earlobe." He winced and reached out for his wife's shoulder to steady himself.

Molly said, "Tilt your head to the side, and I will bandage your lobe."

"I do not feel well," said Jean-Luc.

Charnay approached and said, "You should lie down, my friend. You may be entering shock." Jean-Luc nodded and did as suggested.

As Jean-Luc lay on the ground, Molly applied a clean bandage to his ear. Always quick with the gallows humor, Jean-Luc said, "I would say that his trigger pull needs practice as well."

Molly glanced at Nance's body, and said, "Practice will not help him where he is going." She turned back and cupped her husband's cheek and pulled him to her. She said, near tears, "I almost lost you." For the first time in their marriage, Jean-Luc had no clever retort. Molly said lovingly, "Let's get back to the ship." The couple began to walk away.

Sieur St. Alembert looked at Charnay questioningly, with a tacit question of whether he should remain to help with the disposal of the bodies. The paladin shook his head and nodded toward Jean-Luc, walking unsteadily with Molly.

Laval ran to Nance, and knelt in front of him. Nance collapsed and slumped face-first into Laval's arms. Laval cried out in anguish, "You murdered them. You murdered my friends."

Belfort and Charnay glanced at one another with concerned expressions. An imperceptible nod between the paladins indicated that some dirty work was in order. They approached Chartrand's body. Belfort knelt and placed his pointer and middle finger on the woodsman's carotid artery. He shook his head slowly. He stood and approached Nance.

Laval said, "Don't touch him." Laval gently laid his employer's dead body on its side.

Holding his palms shoulder high to demonstrate a willingness to accommodate, Laval said in a soft voice, "We need to bury them, quickly!"

"Are you afraid of the redcoats? Of what they will do with murderers?"

From behind his partner, Charnay said, "Do not act senselessly. Did you three give no thought to this possible outcome?" Laval did not answer but glared at them both with hatred.

Charnay said, "This *affaire d'honneur* is ended. It ended honorably, and your unreasonable threats are unhelpful."

Sister Angelina heard rapping at her convent door. "Come with me, children. It is probably your father and mother." Nancy and Peter looked relieved, and little Rafe squealed in delight. The four hustled down the stairs to answer the door.

When Sister Angelina opened the door, Molly and Rafael stood there with Jean-Luc hanging back.

Molly forced a smile and asked, "How were the children? Have they made you crazy yet?"

"They were perfect angels. I heard distant gunshots. Was that your group?" asked Sister Angelina.

Rafael said, "It was. Two bears swam the river and came ashore. It was a little frightening. We fired to chase them back across the river. It succeeded."

"I am relieved to hear that. We do not need those creatures of God on our island. By the way, where are your two friends?"

Molly said, "They remained behind to ensure that the bears swam all the way across. We will pick them up with the ship soon."

Sister Angelina pursed her lips in thought but then looked past Molly at Jean-Luc. She thought it was odd that he was keeping his distance. Speaking past Molly and Jean-Luc's father, Sister Angelina asked, "Did your business go well, Jean-Luc?"

"Yes. Yes, it did, Angelina. Thank you, for asking," said Jean-Luc, politely.

Rafael said, "I appreciate your minding my grandchildren, but we must hurry home. You see, we are pressed for time. But the children will be staying with me for a while, and they will see you again at Mass."

"Oh, you are leaving, Jean-Luc? I hardly got to spend time with you and Molly. Could I have a good-bye hug?"

Sister Angelina hugged Molly quickly and waited for Jean-Luc to come over (which he did, but with obvious reluctance). Jean-Luc turned to keep his wound out of the nun's line of sight. They hugged briefly, and Angelina felt her friend's tenseness and uneven breathing.

She didn't know why, but her friend was upset about something. The embrace was brief and awkward.

"Well, all right." Turning to the elder St. Alembert, the nun said sweetly, "I'll see *you* at Mass then." She turned to address the children. "Until we meet again. May God be with you, children."

Molly's group turned and walked toward their ship. Sister Angelina, troubled by Jean-Luc's enigmatic behavior, stood in the convent doorway musing and watching the St. Alemberts. As the tree-lined path enveloped them, she turned to go inside for her late morning prayers. But out of the corner of her eye she noticed something on her left shoulder. She hurried over to the looking-glass in the foyer and saw a dark-red drop — and immediately deduced its origin.

Twenty minutes after the St. Alemberts had departed, Sister Angelina observed two men (the ones who were with Jean-Luc when the children were dropped off) walk past the convent toward the pier. 'What is going on?' she wondered.

CHAPTER TWENTY-SIX

MAY 16, NOON

WHEN THE ST. ALEMBERT party returned to Rafael's house, a flurry of activity commenced. Molly gathered her brood and said, "Children, collect your things. We shall walk to the ship as soon as we're packed. There is no time to waste."

The three children were familiar with that particular tone of voice and knew that their mother was serious. They ran upstairs. Jean-Luc slumped into the foyer chair. Rafael also sat down in the chair across from his son, as the gravity of what had transpired that morning sank in. Three men were dead. Three men who had tried to kill them, but still. Once the authorities learned of the deaths, they would begin looking for the killers.

Rafael asked, "Is there any chance that the bodies are going to surface in the future?"

Charnay shook his head and said, "You have nothing to worry about. We have taken care of the matter." He placed his hand on Rici's shoulder and said, "We have one slice of unfinished business to settle before we depart Canada."

Belfort nodded and started to open the front door.

Molly, revealing the stress she felt, put her hand on his forearm and asked, "Is this necessary?" Belfort did not respond. "We must get out of town *toute de suite*." Both paladins nodded. Molly added, "Don't be long. *Please!*"

Mindful that this lady was not to be trifled with when a loved one was threatened, Belfort and Charnay nodded and walked out. As the door closed behind them, Charnay said, "Let us get this unpleasantness over, shall we?"

Molly turned to Jean-Luc and said, "I will get our things together. We must leave Canada." She turned to her father-in-law and asked, "Papa, won't you please come with us to New York?"

Sieur St. Alembert said, "That is unnecessary and would draw unwanted attention. I will remain here. Perhaps I will come later."

Charnay and Belfort walked the short distance to the Rochebeau-court house and knocked. Madame Rochebeaucourt answered and said, "Oh, hello. You are Jean-Luc's friends—Monsieur Brown and Monsieur Smith, is it not? What can I do for you?"

Belfort asked, "Is your husband home? We would like a word with him."

Gabrielle replied, "I'm sorry, gentlemen, but my husband has not returned from his business trip."

An awkward silence ensued. Charnay fought the urge to look over her shoulder for the thieving husband. Gabrielle cocked her head as if to ask, "Is there anything else?" Charnay said, "We are sorry we missed him. Thank you, Madame Rochebeaucourt. *Adieu.*"

Belfort was stunned. After walking a short distance (and after Gabrielle closed her front door), he asked, "Geoff, the husband could be hiding in the house. Why did you give up so readily?"

"First of all, Rici, I believed her. Second, the amount is a pittance to King Louis and isn't worth our delaying our departure from Montréal." He slapped Belfort on the chest good-naturedly and said, "Besides, I am anxious to reach the islands in the South Atlantic."

Belfort sighed and said, "You are right, we have spent far too long in North America. And as much as I wish to bring justice to this thief, if another person went missing, it could complicate our departure."

Two hundred and fifty-five miles south of the great lake, Erie, Lone Eagle and Hopping Bird entered a council house. This dwelling housed not a family, but the Great Council of Miami Tribes. Sachems and their war chiefs had gathered from the Illinois, Indiana, and Ohio regions to discuss issues. This hour was set aside for the report on the spring hunt of the fifteen-year-olds.

Lone Eagle's sachem welcomed him and bade him and Hopping Bird to sit in the circle. The attendees knew them either personally or by reputation. His sachem said, "Tell this council what you saw in these boys."

Lone Eagle said, "Great Council, Hopping Bird and I led fifteen young Miamis into Wyandot territory on the annual Spring Hunt. Our purpose was to test their training, to teach, and to study their behaviors in enemy territory. Our path placed them in situations like those they will meet when they lead tribal hunts or war parties." He stopped to gather his thoughts. The council members focused on his every word, and the council house was eerily quiet. "This was a talented group, perhaps the finest group I have led into enemy territory. I will review events for the Great Council."

Lone Eagle took pains to put a positive spin on each boy and made sure to tell an anecdote about each that placed the young warrior in a positive light. He did not wish to impugn any fifteen-year-old or bring dishonor to any family's name. When he had finished reviewing the hunting party's stories, Lone Eagle knew that the time had come to relate his recommendations.

"Two of the group clearly stood out. As important as their hunting exploits, they held the respect of their fellow hunters. Chava, sometimes called "Fertile Land," of the Illinois Miamis was the most daring of all. He will make a strong war chief. Next is Miakoda of the Ohio Miamis. Also known as "Moon Power," he showed a good mixture of daring, prudence, and concern for the others. He will, one day, make a good sachem."

Now for the hard part. Lone Eagle glanced at Hopping Bird. Following Hopping Bird's imperceptible nod, it was his duty to report one negative event. He had to report it because the Wyandot tribe would want its pound of flesh. He cleared his throat (his first sign of nerves) and began. "The sachems must know of one meeting with a Wyandot. The Miami people should be vigilant. During one test, one of the boys was trying to steal an object from a lone Wyandot warrior. He was discovered." Lone Eagle's implication was apparent. The sachems turned to each other and murmured their disapproval. "The young hunter would have been killed by the Wyandot warrior, but I prevented that from happening."

Silence followed. Every sachem understood the implication. Some villager totally innocent of this event would be killed by the Wyandots to even the score.

An Illinois sachem asked simply, "Who of the hunters caused this?"

Lone Eagle said, "It is better not to burden the Great Council with some of the things that happened on the hunt. I intervened, killed the enemy warrior, and reviewed for the young warrior his mistake."

The sachem hosting the annual gathering rose and declared, "Sachems of the Miami, we are grateful to these two warriors who shared their knowledge with our young warriors. We must caution our villagers, particularly those living in the Ohio region, to take extra precautions against a Wyandot reprisal."

With that simple pronouncement, Lone Eagle and Hopping Bird's report concluded and they were dismissed.

◄ ─ ● ─ ►

Molly hustled her children along and reminded them several times not to dawdle. As she folded items and placed them into their trunk, she fretted that Jean-Luc's flesh-wound would attract unwanted attention. She stopped packing and hurried to the top of the stairs. Molly called down to her father-in-law, "Papa, do you have anything that could hide Jean-Luc's dressing?"

Rafael nodded and scurried into his bedroom. A few moments later, he emerged with the perfect solution: a leather hunting hat with a brim wide enough to cover the blood-soaked bandage.

There was a knock on the front door loud enough to be heard throughout the house. It startled Jean-Luc. Rafael emerged from his bedroom and said, "Rest easy, son, I will answer the door."

No sooner than Rafael had opened the door, but the paladins hustled inside. Molly scolded from the second floor landing, "We are nearly packed. You two need to get cracking."

Paladins are unaccustomed to such direction, but having spent several months in this woman's company, they nodded and went straight to their rooms. Everyone in the house knew better than to cross Molly at this moment. Both Belfort and Charnay threw their belongings into their valises.

As soon as everyone had assembled in the foyer, Molly scooted the children out the door and directed the waiting crew members to carry the groups' belongings. Rafael intended to accompany his visitors to their ship. Waiting for them at the gangplank were four crew members, who took the trunks and went ahead. As the St. Alembert party began the short walk to the pier, Molly made certain that the children kept pace with the sailors carrying the trunks. She walked behind her children and shepherded them.

Jean-Luc's group walked a few steps behind her. Charnay made certain that Jean-Luc remained between his father and himself, and Belfort walked to his left. As they approached the port authority, an unanticipated snag arose.

"I do not think it a good idea to get too close to anybody. My bandage—"

Rafael suggested, "Molly could pay the docking fees."

Molly nodded. Jean-Luc reached into his jacket and handed over the folded packet of papers for clearing port and his leather wallet. Molly took them without reacting. She turned and walked briskly to the Montréal Port Authority Office.

When she emerged minutes later, Molly smiled for the first time.

Her expression revealed her relief that her husband was leaving Canada alive. She walked briskly to her awaiting family.

Before she arrived, the counts de Charnay and de Belfort shook Rafael's hand. Charnay said, "Thank you for your gracious hospitality. France will not forget your service."

Molly and Jean-Luc came next. Molly said, "Papa, I do not know how to express my appreciation for your watching the children." She and Rafael hugged, and she kissed him on the cheek.

Rafael said to Molly, "Well, no limbs were lost nor eyes poked out. I suppose I did well."

Jean-Luc hugged his father tightly. When they parted at last, he said, "Father, Molly and the children and I all want you to move in with us."

"I will consider it, son. All I have known is New France." He patted Jean-Luc on the back on his cheek. Leaning in, Rafael whispered, "Your mother would be so proud of you."

Nancy rushed over, hugged Rafael tightly and said, "*Grand-père*, I shall miss you terribly." Not about to be left out, Peter and Little Rafe squeezed in and hugged Rafael. Watching from the side, Molly and Jean-Luc beamed. They knew, for a grandparent, that this was the grand finale.

Rafael said, "I shall miss you three." He then kissed each grandchild's forehead.

With the grandchildren not leaving, the elder St. Alembert said to the adults, "You should get under sail. That man's employees will report his absence to the authorities today."

When he heard his son give the command "Away aloft,' Rafael's mind drifted to yesteryear, when Jean-Luc was a little boy. Rafael knew that his son, with Molly by his side, would continue to prosper. Rafael felt his breast fill with pride, and as he watched the ship turn and sail toward the far-off ocean, he could not pull his gaze away. He continued to watch from the pier until the ship disappeared around the river bend.

Finis

THE MOLLY LAKE SERIES
continues in
The Devil's Belt

About the Author

SAMUEL ENDICOTT served in the United States Army as a combat engineer from 1975–1995. A Ranger and paratrooper, he is a graduate of the University of Mississippi, University of Southern California, Command and General Staff Officer Course, and the Naval War College. Samuel is the author of the *Molly Lake* Series, www.mollylakebooks.com. Born in Louisville, Kentucky in 1949, he now resides in Mt. Pleasant, SC with his wife, Elaine, and English Setter, Probie.